## Praise for ***Serenity's Secret***

Lisa Jones Baker's *Serenity's Secret* will delight readers of Amish fiction. Serenity and Stephen's romance is a heartfelt story of love, forgiveness, and second chances. This book has everything readers love—an authentic portrait of the Amish community, the power of grace and hope and, above all, faith in God's Word and His promises.

~ Amy Clipston, bestselling author of *The Heart's Shelter*

You'll fall in love with Serenity and Stephen. They seem like the perfect couple, but will Serenity's secrets keep them apart? The intrigue woven through their romance will keep you guessing until the end. A touching story that will bring you closer to the Lord.

~ Rachel J. Good, *USA Today* bestselling author of the Surprised by Love series

# Serenity's Secret

LISA JONES BAKER

Print ISBN 978-1-63609-958-3
Adobe Digital Edition (.epub) 978-1-63609-959-0



Cover Design: Kirk DouPonce, DogEared Design

Published by Barbour Publishing, Inc., 1810 Barbour Drive, Uhrichsville, Ohio 44683, www.barbourbooks.com

*Our mission is to inspire the world with the life-changing message of the Bible.*

Printed in the United States of America.

## Dedication

To John and Marcia Baker, my best friends in the world, and to my beloved Buddy in heaven.

## Acknowledgments

In this story, I heeded numerous resources, and any mistakes are the fault of my own.

To Officer Livingston and Dawn at the Douglas County Jail in Tuscola, Illinois. I'm fascinated by the legal process that ensues every day in jails throughout the U.S. I thank you and admire you for all that you do to keep us safe. You offered a trove of information, and it is my hope that I accurately conveyed that information. Thank you!

Tons of continued gratitude to *New York Times* bestselling author, the late Joan Wester Anderson, for believing in me and playing a significant role in launching my writing career many years ago. I'll never forget your kindness.

To Margaret: it is my great pleasure to know you.

To my long-time Amish reviewer who prefers to remain anonymous; thank you.

To Lisa Norato, confidante, true friend, and talented author. You continue to play a strong, supportive role in my writing career.

To bestselling author Amy Clipston and *U.S.A. Today* bestselling author Rachel J. Good for their wonderful endorsements.

To Dr. Gregory Krauss, MD and Dr. Robert Rosman, MD, my God-sent angels.

To my amazing editor Rebecca Germany, incredible Becky Fish, and everyone at Barbour who played a role in this publication; thank you!

To my esteemed literary agent, Tamela Hancock Murray at

the Steve Laube Agency; thanks for your relentless belief in me and my stories over many years.

To my family, my street team, and everyone who continues to read and promote my books, huge thanks!

To Stitch and Sew in Arthur, Illinois, for being a constant source of information.

Last but not least, I'm indebted to my sister extraordinaire Beth Zehr for assisting with numerous computer issues for over three decades at all times of the day and night; I love you so much.

# CHAPTER ONE

Only *Gott* knew her secret. For some reason, it played heavily on her mind today. Serenity Miller wasn't sure why. Perhaps it was because of the gusty wind that continuously picked up speed and its low, eerie whistle as it met the cracks in her tall, old barn in Arthur, Illinois.

Maybe it was due to the strong flashes of bright lightning that made loud crackling noises. Or the root of her uneasiness could have something to do with the unique smell of rain and damp air—nature's obvious signals that a May downpour would start any second.

Angel clomped his hooves and unleashed a loud, desperate-sounding whinny. "It's okay," she assured him.

She clenched her jaw. *Something's wrong. Storms never bother him.* A bright flash of lightning bolted through the small windows and quickly reminded her of her purpose. *Get to work. Obviously, there's not much time. Finish securing the barn and ensure that Angel has enough food, water, and fresh bedding to make it through the night. Close up the chicken coop. Get the clothes off the line and take them inside.*

Her neck tensed. While Serenity checked the thick tank hose, which brought in water from the backyard well, Angel's whinnies and clomping became louder and more desperate.

Serenity reached inside the opened gunny bag, gripped the

metal handle of her scoop, and retrieved a generous helping of oat mix. As sweat trickled down her chest, she emptied the grain into a plastic bucket and repeated her action three times until the bucket was nearly full.

Wasting no time, she stepped quickly to the stall's wooden feeder where her beloved standardbred hovered. With one swift motion, Serenity lifted her bucket and dumped its contents into the trough.

Satisfied that there was plenty of clean straw, she shifted her focus to the larger and deeper wooden trough. When she saw that it contained a sufficient amount of hay, she nodded in satisfaction. The fresh batch, baled just a few weeks ago, had come from the nearby alfalfa field. She breathed in the pleasant, light scent.

Her peripheral vision caught a large black rat scurrying across the cement floor and disappearing into a crack at the side wall. She frowned. *That issue will have to wait.*

The dim light suddenly darkened a notch, and Serenity reached for the portable, battery-powered lantern, which hung on a hook on the wall, and flipped on the switch.

A strong bolt of lightning illuminated the space on the floor around her, quickly reminding her of her purpose and the short time frame she most likely had to get things done. Oddly, again, her secret drifted back into her thoughts. Thunder crackled. Angel let out an ear-piercing neigh. The wind whistled loudly as it hit the old, large structure. A strong gust coming in through the open entrance stirred straw dust. She closed her eyes a moment to allow them to tear.

*I've got to finish up and get to my house.* She looked down at her scoop and returned it to the bag next to the wall.

Rain hitting the roof alerted her to stop what she was doing and make a dash down the long dirt path to her quaint country dwelling that was some distance away.

Putting her hands on her hips, she pressed her lips together in a determined line. *I didn't check the chickens. The clothes are still on the line.*

Again, thunder crackled. She could hear the chickens clucking in the nearby coop.

*I think everything's as secure as it can be.*

She offered a final glance at her standardbred and frowned. As she stepped away from the stall, she turned and spoke in a loud voice: "People think I named you inappropriately. It's no secret that men watch their hind sides when you're around. But I can only imagine what it was like being abused. That's why I rescued you. I know what you've managed to overcome. And to me, you're an angel."

The damp, heavy air forced beads of sweat down her cheeks as she rushed to the large sliding door. At the entrance, she put her finger on the lantern's on/off button. As she did so, a noise caught her attention.

Serenity stopped and listened for a repeat noise. Instinctively, she sensed that what she'd heard wasn't a typical barn sound from a rodent or a bird. Or even the occasional banging of the wind blowing loose siding against the structure.

She pressed her finger against her lips. *I thought I heard a human noise. It must be my imagination.*

She was fully aware of the dire need to get inside her house. But curiosity prompted her to leave the lantern on, turn around, and make her way toward what seemed to be the source of the noise.

*I'll bet it's the possum that hides under the building. If it is, I need to shoo it out of here before my horse tries to jump the gate and breaks a leg. The last thing I want is for Angel to injure himself.*

A strong gust of wind thrust tree branches against the tall structure. Wasting no time, she grabbed the rake from the wall with her free hand to shoo the animal. She headed to the far side of the building.

It was darker near the back because the few windows in this part of the barn were small. She slowed, stepping with great care through straight rows of straw bales, which extended nearly halfway to the ceiling.

The lantern's light helped only a little now amid the darkness between the bales. She stopped. Listened. She heard nothing. Then what sounded like balls began hitting the roof. *Hail. Looks like I'm stuck here.*

Suddenly, she heard a faint noise that seemed to come from the bales. A combination of uncertainty and nervousness prompted her to grip the lantern handle in her right hand so tightly that her knuckles froze in place. Her left hand gripped the rake.

She saw a small beam of light that wasn't from her lantern. As she stepped between two tall piles of straw, a set of strong hands came from behind, tearing away her rake and her lantern and pinning her arms to her sides, while a different set of hands yanked something over her face, covering her eyes, nose, and mouth.

The tight cloth muffled her screams. She could barely hear herself cry out for help. It was hard to breathe. Her heart pumped so fast and hard she thought it would jump right out of her chest. She shook uncontrollably.

In the background, Angel's loud protests of neighs and whinnies accelerated. Serenity barely heard a short conversation between two men. It didn't take long for her legs to give way. She fell to her knees. Her face met the concrete. Pieces of straw poked at her face. As a downpour of rain and hail hit the roof, she closed her eyes. *They're tying my feet.*

She couldn't think straight but silently prayed. Now she understood Angel's strange behavior. But it was too late. Because she was going to die.

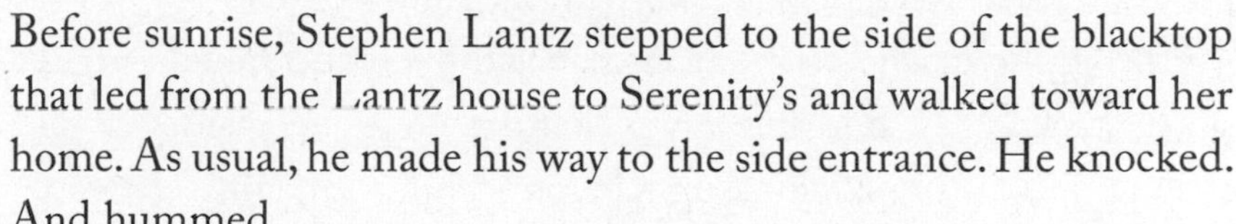

Before sunrise, Stephen Lantz stepped to the side of the blacktop that led from the Lantz house to Serenity's and walked toward her home. As usual, he made his way to the side entrance. He knocked. And hummed.

No answer. He knocked louder. Still nothing. He turned to face her shed and glimpsed Serenity's buggy through the large window.

He frowned. He turned the door handle, entered the porch, then opened the door to the kitchen. As he stood inside, he breathed in the pleasant scent of cinnamon. There was no smell of freshly brewed herbal tea. No indication that she'd eaten breakfast.

He respected her privacy. *But my instincts tell me something's wrong. I need to check her house. What if something happened to her?* He bit the inside of his cheek and then rushed from room to room, hollering her name.

*She's not inside. I'll check her barn.* He didn't bother closing the kitchen door as he dashed across the porch and out the screen door, which slammed shut behind him.

*She's probably assessing the storm damage.* Quick steps took him up the dirt path that led to her barn. He clenched his jaw.

His heart pumped harder and faster than usual. As he approached the back of Serenity's property, he pressed his lips in a tense, straight line and focused his efforts on finding the owner of the town's floral shop, the Pink Petal.

Branches from the large, old oak trees lay ravaged on the ground. Towels and bedding were wrapped around the clotheslines. A large white sheet was in disarray on a tree branch. A light green dress clung to a nearby bush. *Something has happened to her.* He cupped his mouth with his hands and hollered as loudly as he could: "Serenity!"

Automatically, he opened the shed door and hollered. No answer. He rushed to the barn.

His heart pumped harder. . . The large sliding door was open. He could hear loud, demanding whinnies and neighs.

When he reached the entrance, he stopped and said an urgent prayer to Gott to find her alive. Then he bounded inside the old structure and stopped, looking all around him. "Serenity!"

The misnamed Angel was going crazy with whinnies and neighs, trying desperately to move the latch on the bar that would allow him access to the building's main area.

Stephen rushed to the east wall. Then to the west. He cupped his hands to his mouth and shouted, "Serenity! Are you in here?"

He put his hands against his hips and stopped while he eyed the numerous stacked bales of straw and hay near the rear of the barn. Not sure what to expect, he continued shouting her name as he pushed himself between two rows of straw toward the back wall. As he did so, loose straw poked him. He used his elbows to push his way to the end of the row, which narrowed so substantially he could barely get through. At the back, he heard quiet moans of distress.

Behind the bales, he spotted Serenity face down on the floor.

Immediately, he knelt next to her and began to untie the face covering. She fought.

His voice shook when he attempted to reassure her. "It's okay, Serenity. It's me. It's Stephen! I'm going to roll you over so that you're face up. Here."

When she was on her back, he continued, "Now I'm untying you. You're going to be okay."

His pulse sprinted with an odd combination of relief and despair. When he undid her face covering, he glimpsed horror in her deep blue eyes.

But immediately she gave a sigh of relief. "Stephen! Thank goodness you're here!"

"I'll move you onto your side." After he did so, he undid the tight rope that bound her wrists. "Just give me a minute, and I'll have you out of this."

Several tense moments passed while he tried to undo the knot. Then he reached into his trousers pocket and pulled out his work knife. "Hold still. I'll cut the twine."

She stayed very still while he worked. The moment the rope was severed, she moved her hands in front of her. He couldn't help but note that her skin was white and clammy. He quickly ordered her to move her fingers and took her right hand to massage it. "We've got to get your circulation back and running." He pinched her wrist. "Can you feel that?"

"It's a little numb. But there's feeling."

"*Gut*. Now rub your hands together. Like this. Don't stop." While she did that, he used his knife to cut the twine around her ankles.

He removed her black shoes. Her socks. He rubbed her feet. "Is there feeling in your toes?"

"A little."

He pressed harder and massaged her feet and ankles.

"The sensation's coming back."

As he continued relentlessly rubbing her cold feet, he asked, "Are you okay?" Before she could answer, he went on. "I mean, aside from being gagged and tied."

She nodded while alternately extending her fingers and making fists. Emotion edged her voice. "I thought they were going to kill me." A grateful breath escaped her before she looked into his eyes. "Oh, Stephen! I'm so glad you're here!" She leaned forward to hug him. His heart melted. When she released her arms from around his shoulders, she coughed. Then she adjusted her hips on the concrete floor.

"Here." He stood and supported her. "I'll help you up."

When she was on her feet, he wrapped his arms around her and kept them there to support her. And to reassure her. And himself. "Keep wiggling those toes. Keep moving those feet. I won't let you fall." He tried to maintain an encouraging tone as he asked, "You think you can stand by yourself?"

"I'm not sure. My right leg tingles."

He helped her toward the barn's entrance, although they were quite a distance away.

All the while, he kept an arm around her, and she leaned against him. "Just take slow steps. Hopefully, your circulation is returning. The tingling is a sign that it will."

With his assistance, she stepped forward. He held on to her tightly for fear that she would fall. . .and because he never wanted to let her go.

A short silence ensued before she spoke in a hushed voice.

"My head aches. The men who tied me up weren't gentle."

With great concern, he motioned her to the nearest lone bale of straw and helped her to sit down. Then he quickly moved to the floor and vigorously massaged each foot, one at a time. While he worked, he glanced up at her.

"While I work on your circulation, you want to tell me what happened? Then I'll call the police."

As they looked at each other, a knot stuck in his throat while the enormity of the situation sank in. He took in her disheveled appearance. Her *kapp* had come off.

Long thick strands of beautiful, wavy blond hair seemed to be everywhere. On her shoulders. On her back. Her creamy, soft-looking cheeks were dirty and bore scratches. Her eyes didn't show their usual calm-looking, reassuring blue depths. Instead they reminded him of a relentless, turbulent storm.

The only thing important to him was making sure she was okay.

She met his gaze, and her lips parted, but no words came out.

She bent her chin to study her bruised wrists. His heart ached.

They sat in silence as he continued encouraging circulation in her feet. Color was returning. She wiggled her toes. A strange but wonderful feeling swept up Stephen's arms and landed in his shoulders. Despite the ugliness of what had happened, something beautiful filled him until he was so warm, he thought he'd catch fire.

A dire need to know what had happened tugged at him with such force, he ached. Yet he didn't utter a word. Because deep down inside, he was afraid to hear the truth. *But it has to be addressed.*

She rubbed her temples and closed her eyes. When she finally opened them, her voice was soft and shaky. "Stephen, I'll tell you about last night." After a slight hesitation, she shook her head in disbelief. "But you won't believe it. I still don't."

"I will believe you. And we'll tell the authorities so they can catch whoever did this and lock them up."

Again, she coughed. She whispered in a hoarse voice. "I'm so thirsty."

He got up, went to the nearby shelf, and returned with a bottle of water that he handed to her to drink.

*Of course, she's dehydrated.*

He sat next to her and laid a firm hand on her back. "Whoa. Slow down. I don't want you to choke." She coughed. Then she nodded in agreement. He tried to stay calm while plucking straw from her clothing. *Dear Gott, please instruct me to do Your will to help her and to catch whoever did this. Please guide us both and the police too.*

She set the partial bottle of liquid between them. His brows narrowed with great concern while sunlight began to float in through the windows.

He rubbed the back of his neck before returning his attention to Serenity. "You're shaking."

He wanted to hold her again. But if he did, it would be for him.

So instead he ran his hands down her right arm, then left, putting pressure to warm her.

"Stephen, I'm very lucky to be alive." Her voice cracked as she went on. "Here's what I remember."

A cricket chirped at his feet while he listened. She spoke slowly and thoughtfully, describing the awful scenario.

His heart pumped to an angry beat. *Please, Gott. Forgive me.*

He cupped his chin with his hand while she explained about the noise she'd heard, and how thinking back, she believed it was possibly a man's cough.

She told Stephen about two men talking while one forced the cloth around her eyes and mouth and the other yanked her arms behind her back until she thought she'd pass out. He'd bound her wrists together with the very same twine that held together numerous straw bales. Stephen noticed there was plenty of excess twine loose on the floor and figured that was what the men had used.

His heart ached while she explained that she had realized Angel's unusual behavior was sparked by the intruders Serenity had instinctively believed would kill her. She'd prayed to live. And finally, when she'd heard Stephen hollering her name, she had been confident that he would look until he found her and that she would not die in the barn.

Sometime during the night, she'd stopped trying to scream because her attempts had made it too difficult to breathe. Then she'd lost consciousness. Upon reviving, she'd tried numerous tactics to move, and thankfully, because the twine had some give, she'd managed to move her hands and feet enough so they wouldn't go completely numb.

She sat up a little straighter. "I just remembered something else."

"What?"

"One man spoke in a raspy, throaty voice. I can say with full certainty that I've never encountered him before." She narrowed her brows. "It was unpleasant sounding." She shrugged.

They looked at each other with what seemed to be a mutual blend of despair and joy—and some other unidentifiable emotion morphed itself into the equation. Something unique and unfamiliar. Unexplainable.

Finally, a laugh escaped her. "Stephen Lantz, you don't believe me, do you?" Before he could answer, she went on. "If you don't, I can't blame you." She breathed in and lifted her palms to face the ceiling. "I realize how incredible it all seems. Now, I'm not sure I didn't just dream it."

Reality kicked in, and Stephen straightened. He knew what needed to be done next. His voice was firm, and he made a conscious effort to convey understanding and sympathy. During the year or so he'd known this kind, beautiful woman, he'd never dreamed that something of this nature could or would ever happen to her. Right here, in one of Illinois' safest areas.

He touched her right hand. "Is the numbness gone?"

She nodded.

"Do you need to go to the hospital?"

She offered a certain shake of her head. "No. I thank Gott I'm okay. He kept me safe and led you to me."

Salty moisture sprang from Stephen's eyes, and he blinked at the sting.

He forced himself to hold his emotion back. *Be strong for her.* "He sure did." Stephen couldn't stop the way his arms automatically wrapped around her waist. Her warm touch consoled him. But there would be no comfort until they'd caught who'd done this. He pulled away and placed a finger under her chin, gently lifting it a bit so they looked directly into each other's eyes.

"Now it's time to involve the police."

# CHAPTER TWO

That evening, Serenity sat at her oak table with her parents and Stephen. The battery-powered wall clock made an even ticking sound. Serenity took in the beautiful floral arrangement that hung neatly on the wall in front of her. The refreshing scent of dried eucalyptus complemented the delicious aromas of the courses her *mamm* had made for this evening's dinner.

When Serenity's stomach growled, she realized that she hadn't eaten all day. While Mamm made trips back and forth to the kitchen, Serenity's *daed* talked with Stephen about the storm damage and how it would affect this year's crops. Their topic of conversation conveyed a sort of peacefulness and normalcy. Serenity's shoulders relaxed.

She could hear Mamm open and close drawers as Serenity admired the large wooden salad bowl Trini Sutter had gifted her before getting married and changing her name to Lantz. The owner of the Quilt Room was one of Serenity's besties.

The sheet of aluminum foil that covered a large round plate couldn't contain the mouthwatering smell of her mother's freshly baked yeast rolls. To Serenity's right was a chicken-and-dumpling casserole. On her left was an oval dish of sweet corn from Mamm's freezer.

This wasn't just any meal though. To Serenity, this particular dinner signified a special message of love from her mamm. The first indicator was the yeast rolls. It was common knowledge within their small Amish community that Clara Miller didn't like to make them. That for some reason, her dough usually didn't rise the way it was supposed to. Yet this evening, Serenity had glimpsed a beautiful plate of rolls just before Mamm had covered it.

Mamm's soft voice floated in from the kitchen as what sounded like a piece of silverware met the floor with a light noise. "I can't remember if I put butter on the table."

Serenity called, "It's right in front of me." She moved the small knife closer to the golden block on the beautiful crystal that had been handed down from three generations of Millers.

Her eyes traveled from the hooks on the walls to the left of the porch door, to the small kitchen window that overlooked the dirt path leading to the barn, to the homemade blue curtains that were pulled back quaintly, to the unusually cluttered granite countertop.

Serenity couldn't stop her lips from curving in amusement. She was like her mother in many ways. For instance, they both loved to work in the barn. But Serenity kept her counters clear except when Mamm descended to fix a meal. Mamm always managed to clutter the cleanest of countertops. To be fair, Serenity lived alone. And Mamm had a slew of children and grandchildren who loved to visit the "*dawdy*" house.

Mamm cooked because she had to, but when it was planting time, she was in heaven. It was widely known throughout the area that no weeds could be found in her garden. And fall was her favorite season, partly because of how much she enjoyed spreading mulch around the blue spruce trees that lined both sides of their long drive. She'd always stressed to Serenity that the best mental therapy was working outdoors. Serenity agreed.

The gentle conversation between the men migrated to a new ceiling fan that her daed had recently installed in their buggy shed.

Mamm's voice was coated with equal parts humor and seriousness when she jumped in on the conversation. "Joe, you know you don't like doing that kind of stuff. And there's folks around here who'll do it for you."

Serenity vividly recalled some of her daed's former projects and the helpful neighbors who'd ended up redoing them. The man across from her was a great furniture craftsman. But as far as things that needed to be hooked up or assembled? Serenity pressed her lips together to stop a grin.

The big, burly man across from her had the kindest soft brown eyes she'd ever seen. And when Serenity studied her daed's gentle expression, all she could see were honesty, love, and dependability.

Mamm took quick steps to the table with a clear glass pitcher of freshly squeezed lemonade. Sliced lemons floated at the top. Serenity could smell their tart scent. Without wasting time, she stood and leaned forward to clear a spot large enough for the pitcher. As she did so and the container met the coaster, Mamm's hand touched hers. A familiar sense of comfort swept up Serenity's arm, and she released a comfortable sigh.

By appearances, this seemed to be a normal dinner. After all, the conversation was focused on crops. Weather. Mamm busied herself making sure everything was on the table. And chicken and dumplings were served routinely in their family.

But Serenity could sense tension underneath the seemingly calm voices. The thin skin under Mamm's eyes was a bit swollen And worry lines had etched themselves around Daed's jawline.

Stephen too showed signs of great concern by his overly attentive actions toward Serenity. Of course he was always kind and thoughtful, but she didn't think it was her imagination that he constantly looked at her to check if everything was okay.

Serenity couldn't stymie her memories of everything that had played out since she'd begun preparing her barn for yesterday's storm. Although the awful chain of events had ended well, it would be difficult to move her recollections out of her mind and into her imaginary "past" box. *But I will.*

As usual, Serenity's daed stood and helped his wife to her chair, laid a hand on her shoulder as she sat, and gently assisted her in moving closer to the table until she looked up at him with a smile and nodded. After Daed was seated, her parents turned to each other and smiled with loving affection. He squeezed his wife's hand before adjusting his own seat and turning his attention to the food in front of them.

*Things seem back to normal*, Serenity thought as she observed her parents following habits developed during decades of marriage. *But they're not.* A heavy sense of emotional loss and insecurity overcame Serenity. She wasn't sure why. After all, everything was okay now. And she was incredibly thankful to be here in her home with the three people closest to her.

*This isn't like me. I'm used to focusing on the positive. It's the only way to stay healthy. And happy. Stress is not welcome in my world. I've got to put what happened in the past, where it belongs. Life is short, and nothing will steal my joy.*

She breathed in, straightened her shoulders, and forced a half smile. As she did so, a light, warm breeze came in through the window screens, and the battery-powered fan made a low whirring sound.

The aroma of Mamm's homemade yeast rolls and her chicken and dumplings created a heavenly atmosphere that prompted Serenity's hands to relax. Automatically, she glanced down at the bruises. Then she looked over at her parents with loving affection.

Because of the numerous serving dishes and place settings,

she couldn't see much of the beautiful dark-stained oak table that had been crafted by her daed for her move into this comfortable home that she'd purchased from an elderly couple who'd gone to Lancaster. But she knew the gorgeous wood grain by heart, as well as the depth of the two coats of polish he'd given it. Daed had made her furniture, cabinets, and shelves, including her bed frame and large work desk in the corner of her bedroom.

Serenity's daed cleared his throat and asked everyone to bow their heads for the prayer. At the end, he paused before adding in a soft, emotional voice, "And thank You, Gott, for protecting our *dochder*."

The statement tugged at Serenity's heartstrings.

The food dishes were passed around the table, and Stephen spoke while he carefully used plastic tongs to pluck a warm roll and slowly place it on his plate. "Tonight we have much to be grateful for."

Serenity reached to take the bread plate from him while he glanced at her. When he placed his fork between his fingers, he shook his head in despair. "I have to keep asking myself if what happened to Serenity really did take place." He breathed in and straightened his shoulders. "It's hard to believe, especially in our safe community." His eyes reflected surprise. "It hasn't really sunk in."

Serenity's daed used two hot pads to hand the cream-colored casserole of chicken and dumplings to his wife, and the conversation picked up speed as they talked about the terrifying events that had taken place in Serenity's barn. As much as she didn't enjoy reliving the experience, she realized that it was the obvious topic of conversation.

Despite Serenity having already recounted the sequence of events in her barn, her parents continued to crave more details. As she watched them and listened to them, she noted that their words came out faster than normal. Their facial expressions and the way they sat up a little too straight led Serenity to think that perhaps, like Stephen, they hadn't truly absorbed or accepted reality. Finally, Stephen spoke in a more reassuring tone. As he did, Serenity's father poured a refill of lemonade and returned the half-empty pitcher to its spot.

"I'm sure glad the cops caught those bank robbers that were hiding out in your barn." He heaved a sigh before swallowing a drink. "If they hadn't, we wouldn't be enjoying this relaxed conversation."

Serenity lifted a doubtful brow while she cut her chicken into small pieces. *This dinner talk is edged with concern and uncertainty. There's absolutely nothing relaxed about it.*

Ice clinked against Mamm's glass as she sipped lemonade. After she swallowed, she shrugged. "But why? Why did they have to. . ."

She put her hand over her mouth while her husband rubbed her shoulder. "It's okay. I think the problem is that Serenity took them by surprise." He lifted his palms to the ceiling. "No one would harm our Serenity." After a tense pause, he added, "At least now we don't have to worry about them coming back."

The emotional catch in Mamm's voice touched Serenity's heart.

"When I think about what could have happened. . ." She bent her head.

"Gott watched over our girl, Clara." Daed was quick to reassure and comfort his wife. "Don't think about everything that could have happened. We can't live like that. Just know that she's okay." He pulled a handkerchief from his pocket and tucked it in the palm of Mamm's hand.

She dabbed at her eyes, nodded, and appeared to compose herself. As Serenity took in her mamm's gray hairs tucked under her kapp, she noticed new worry creases on her otherwise flawless skin. Mamm had a slight, delicate build that could be deceiving. Serenity had watched her carry fifty-pound bags of mulch and place them around her prized blue spruce trees.

This evening the usual glow of her hazel eyes was replaced with a misty brown hue. The color reminded Serenity of how the vegetable leaves looked in the fall right before she tore out her garden plants.

If Serenity had the option, she'd wipe away what had happened. But she couldn't. All she could do was trust in Gott's guidance to get her and her family through this bitter aftermath. They had to move on. And they would.

Several moments later, Mamm looked at Stephen. "I want to make sure I'm clear about this. How can the police be positive that the men in the barn are the same men who robbed the local bank?"

Serenity offered the serious question careful thought. She was fully aware of her mother's current fragility, and Serenity needed to reassure not only Mamm but also the entire family that they were fortunate the guilty men were behind bars.

Daed spoke in a thoughtful tone as he regarded Stephen. "From what I'm hearing, after the bank was robbed, a tip was called into the police. Because of that storm, the thieves couldn't get far. Because of this and the fact that things of this nature just don't happen in Arthur, they have no doubt that the men who harmed Serenity are behind bars. At least until a judge determines what happens next."

After a slight hesitation, Serenity lifted her chin to reassure her mamm, who appeared unconvinced. "As a precautionary measure, they dusted for fingerprints. The barn door handles. The shovels. The shelves. Even the gate that keeps Angel in her stall."

That statement sparked a deep chuckle from Daed and Stephen. "I don't think we have to worry about your horse letting the men get close to him."

The corners of Serenity's lips curved in amusement. "When the results come back, we'll hopefully know for sure that they're a match to one or both men."

For long moments, the only noises at the table were the clinking of silverware against porcelain plates and an occasional ice cube meeting the side of a glass.

Serenity suddenly realized the immense amount of work that her mother had obviously given this dinner. Serenity smiled a little as she addressed her. "Your rolls taste like heaven."

The compliment prompted Serenity's mamm to sit up a little straighter. Her eyes sparkled in delight.

Serenity's heart melted. She loved her parents so much. Despite having no *kinder* of her own, she was able to comprehend Mamm and Daed's grave concern for her. Serenity wasn't her parents' only child, but it had been obvious for some time that she garnered most of their attention. She guessed that it was because her long bout with the Epstein-Barr virus had taken its toll on all of them. She imagined the huge relief that everyone must have experienced when her health had finally improved.

As the conversation shifted back to this year's crops, Serenity thought about the special diet she'd required and the extra care her mother had taken to ensure Serenity would eventually recover.

But Stephen's late *aendi*, Margaret Lantz, had routinely said, "Something gut always comes out of something bad." Serenity couldn't deny that the hardship had strengthened her in many ways.

What she'd gone through had made her the patient, understanding person she'd become. As she'd spent time in bed, she'd read numerous books that had taught her about natural remedies and herbs that helped a person to maintain good health and fight diseases.

And during one of her hospitalizations, she'd fallen in love with plants. Curiosity had prompted her to learn as much as she could about the fragrant, beautiful blooms that she credited for her inspiration to recover. The floral gifts had led her to deep appreciation of the art of arranging flowers to inspire others. She recalled the moment that she'd known her dream was to own a floral shop.

The conversation returned to the incident in her barn when Daed lowered his gruff voice and met Stephen's gaze. "Son, I want you to know how very grateful we are"—he motioned to his wife—"that you rescued our dochder."

Serenity noted how her friend's cheeks took on a light shade of pink. She smiled because she knew Stephen well. He never tried to garner credit for anything. He was humble, through and through.

She echoed the appreciation. "Stephen, I can't even begin to express my gratefulness to you." Her voice overflowed with emotion. "I'll never, ever forget my relief and happiness when I heard you shouting my name."

Tears slipped down Mamm's cheeks. Serenity watched as she closed her eyes. When she opened them, her irises glistened. They reminded Serenity of morning dew on the vegetable leaves.

Clara dropped her fork on her plate. All heads turned at the light sound of metal meeting porcelain. She breathed in before directing her attention to Stephen. "You're our angel, Stephen." Again, she teared up. "I can't imagine our baby tied up and gagged. I still can't understand why this happened." She started to cry.

"It's okay," Daed whispered while caressing her shoulder. "This is one of those obstacles that our last preacher talked about. There's nothing we can do to change what happened. But Gott took care of her, and that's what we should focus on."

Stephen shook his head in disbelief. "Things rarely scare me, but"—he breathed in and appeared to force composure—"you can't believe the things that went through my head when you weren't in your house."

Serenity's mamm cut in. "It's amazing that you found her. I mean, she was in the very back of the barn. You must've looked hard."

"Well, after I checked the house, I glimpsed her buggy in the shed."

Approval filled Daed's eyes as he quickly dished a second helping of dumplings onto his plate. Inside, Serenity smiled. Her daed's large stature and wide shoulders could wrongly offer the appearance of a gruff man. But looks could be quite deceiving. Inside, he was a teddy bear. Serenity would never forget how he'd read her scripture each day she'd been bedridden. Afterward he'd held her hand and prayed for her to get well.

This evening, he displayed a brave front. But she was sure, without a doubt, that what had transpired had shaken him. And her mother. Serenity could tell by the way they'd asked the same questions over and over, as if searching for different answers.

Of course whenever Daed was uneasy, his upper lip quivered. And right now, his upper lip was doing just that. When he'd entered her home, she'd noticed the moisture on his deep brown eyes. His hands were shaking when he'd reached for the sweet corn.

Mamm was acting out of character too. Clara's eyes seemed more alert than usual, and her tendency to run her sentences together this evening told Serenity that she was shaken. Of course, her mother was naturally talkative, the antithesis of her daed.

When Stephen glanced at Serenity, he lowered his voice. "I never dreamed I'd find you behind all of those bales and bales of straw." He cleared his throat. When he continued, his voice cracked. "And when I finally saw you, face down and tied up. . ."

To Serenity's surprise, he looked down at his plate, unable to finish his sentence. Instead he choked up. Serenity's heart ached while she watched him breathe in. *He really, truly cares for me.*

The last thing she wanted was to worry anyone. This time, however, things had played out in a way that had most of her friends and family on edge.

Mamm stepped in with a tone that obviously attempted to shift the conversation to a more upbeat pitch. "Everyone has been asking what happened and why on earth two men were hiding in *your* barn."

Serenity, her daed, and Stephen stopped eating and looked at her with concern.

Her daed narrowed his eyes and cleared his throat. "That's what bothers me the most."

"Why?" Serenity lifted a brow.

He shrugged before turning to his wife. Then he met Serenity's curious expression. "I understand why they'd hide. The downpour took everyone by surprise. But here's what stumps me: your barn would have been so out of the way for them to get to. Let's reason this out. There are tons of barns around here that are more easily accessible than yours. If they'd walked the long distance through the woods to hide, that surely wouldn't have been easy."

Stephen shook his head. "My sentiment exactly. At the same time, maybe that's why they chose your barn. Despite the effort it obviously took to get there, it was a great place to hide *because* of its hard-to-reach location." After a sigh, he added, "That is, if you hadn't been inside."

Daed pressed his lips together in a straight, thoughtful line. "There are a lot of unanswered questions. But the police surely know what they're talking about."

The corners of Stephen's lips lifted into a wide smile. "You've got that right. I guess this teaches us that we can never take our safe community for granted. But at the end of the day?" He shook his head. "I'm grateful that the robbers were caught."

"Amen," Mamm added.

A growl edged Daed's voice. "I'd like to have a word with those men."

"Me too," Stephen agreed.

Serenity released a sigh of relief while taking in Stephen's concern. His disturbed tone melted her heart. Like her daed, the youngest Lantz brother was protective of her. And he was kind. She loved those two things about him the most. She smiled a little when their eyes met in what seemed to be a mutual understanding.

"We might never have all our answers, but the main thing was that Gott was right there in my barn with me yesterday. Remember what the preacher said?"

Three sets of eyes searched hers. "That sometimes things happen, and we have no idea why. But Gott does. He's omniscient. He knows our entire life story, including the ending. And we're to trust His plan." She reached for her glass and took a drink. Serenity lifted her chin. "Gott sent me warning signals." She offered a sad shake of her head. "Through Angel." She offered a conciliatory shrug. "If only I'd listened."

Mamm narrowed her brows. "What on earth are you talking about?"

Serenity sat back and crossed her legs at the ankles. She told them of her horse's extreme behavior.

Mamm gave an impatient sigh. "Honey, you know that I respect your love for animals."

Serenity nodded.

Her mother's brows narrowed a bit. "But sometimes you tend to humanize your Angel." She added, "Remember, Angel is only a horse."

Serenity didn't respond. She'd learned years ago that a person either appreciated an animal's special gifts or they didn't. And she'd never been able to convince anyone, especially her own mother, that they were much more complex than most people understood. The bond between her and her horse was strong enough to overcome anything. It didn't matter if Angel had four legs. Love was love.

Still, Serenity went on to explain Angel's behavior and added that his obvious distress should have immediately warned her that the weather wasn't the crux of his problem.

"That's right." Stephen looked at her mother before focusing on Daed. "During the past year, I've gotten to know Angel." He winked at Serenity. "I know I often joke about the irony of the horse's name, but to my knowledge, storms have never bothered him."

Stephen appeared to get that Angel had tried to warn her. The obvious understanding in his voice made Serenity feel gut.

Daed chuckled. Under his breath, he muttered, "Don't ask me what I did to make that horse have a grudge against me. Despite my numerous attempts to befriend him, he has never liked me. But I'll give him credit this time. Even though he's just a horse, it sounds like he tried to tell you something." He smiled at Serenity.

She returned the warm gesture. It pleased her that her daed finally was giving Angel some credit.

Mamm's eyes widened. "Joe, I'll never forget when he bit your backside."

"He did?" Stephen placed his silverware on his empty plate.

Mamm nodded. "That bruise was a big one. And you had trouble walking for a while."

"*Jah.*"

Stephen harrumphed. "He's tried to bite me too."

Clara's lips curved before she leaned forward. "Serenity, horses don't think like we do, but if I didn't know better"—she shrugged—"I'd think your Angel had a crush on you." She raised her voice a notch and threw up her hands. "He's jealous of men."

Serenity didn't comment. There was no need to defend her beloved Angel. From experience, she was all too aware that her words would fall on deaf ears. She'd tried to convince her parents many times that animals possessed human qualities. But she wouldn't try again. Her parents were gut, hardworking people. There was nothing she could do to change their minds about animals. In particular, about Angel.

Daed paused. "You know that I don't wish bad things to happen, but I can't help but wonder how the scenario would've turned out if your Angel had managed to escape that stall while those criminals were in your barn."

Stephen laughed. "A bite on each of those two hind ends with those big teeth would teach them a lesson!"

The men laughed. Clara joined in.

Serenity knew that any being with a heartbeat was one of Gott's valued creatures. She cleared the knot from her throat and tried one last time to champion her horse. "Don't ever forget that the book of Revelation mentions horses in heaven. If that's the case, and it is, then obviously they're important to Gott. And whatever you believe, the bottom line is that Angel came through for me. It was my fault for not taking time to figure out what was wrong. I was in such a rush to get to the house before the winds and rain got too strong."

Mamm lifted an inquisitive brow. "Next time, maybe a serious conversation should be in order when Angel acts up." Her eyes drifted to the dark bruises on Serenity's wrists. "It's Gott's blessing to all of us that you're here eating dinner with us," she said, her voice shaking.

Serenity nodded. "I'm giving Gott extra love and thanks in my prayers for letting me live through it. I am blessed. My faith is strong, and my prayer now is to get my life back as I knew it. I want to work in my barn without that nightmare hovering in my thoughts." She lifted her shoulders in a helpless shrug.

Serenity's mamm jumped in. "Honey, thankfully, those men will never be able to hurt you again."

Serenity bit her lip. "There's no guarantee they'll stay in jail.

The judge could release them on bail. But even if he does, I'm not worried. The only reason they walked all that way through the woods to get to my barn was to hide out. Everyone knows that the Amish don't have anything worth stealing."

Mamm was quick to disagree. "That's not true, honey. You have your grandma's dinnerware."

Daed's tone took on a lighthearted pitch as he nudged his wife's shoulder with affection. "That's what they call sentimental value, Clara." He cleared his throat and scooted back his chair. After he stretched his legs, he crossed his hands over his chest. "I doubt that would bring much money at an auction."

Mamm's eyes widened with newfound interest. "Speaking of auctions. . . Serenity?"

Serenity lifted her chin a notch to meet her mother's curious expression. "Jah?"

"I see that you've put that beautiful wooden horse on your new shelf." She nodded toward the walnut piece that Serenity's daed had smoothed, polished, and added to her living room just the week before. "Didn't you buy it at a garage sale?"

Serenity sat up a little straighter.

"Jah. And I'm so glad I found it."

All eyes were on her. She offered a half smile. "It provides inspiration."

Mamm nodded while folding the foil in a neat square and placing it on the empty roll dish. "I remember all those books you read on positive thinking while you were down with that virus."

"Uh-huh. I've told you how little things that inspire can play a large role in a person's outlook on life. And when I look at that hand-carved horse. . ."

She glanced back at the piece of art before turning to Stephen. She lifted her palms and returned them to her lap. "It makes me smile. Just like my flower arrangements."

Serenity continued her train of thought. "Besides, it reminds me of Angel."

Daed appeared to study the horse before offering his attention to Serenity. Doubt edged his voice. "I don't see any resemblance."

Stephen agreed. "Me neither."

Serenity defended her theory. "I do. If you look closely at the eyes, they hint that he's keeping a secret, although you can't see their mystery from here. And sometimes when I peer into Angel's large eyes, I wish I were privy to his thoughts."

"I'll tell you what that ornery horse is thinking, and it's who he'll bite next." Daed chuckled. Mamm and Stephen laughed along with him.

But Serenity's mind was still on her garage-sale buy. "It's something that's not worth much money, but to me, it's important."

Serenity turned toward the living room to get another glimpse at her unique find. Clara's voice held a more serious tone. "Stephen, remember when your aendi Margaret used to say that the eyes were the lens to the soul?"

He pressed his lips together thoughtfully. "Now that you mention it, jah."

Daed offered a quick nod. "She sure did." He turned to Stephen. "Your aendi—she was insightful."

Stephen smiled. "Thank you for that." He dipped his head and glanced back at the shelf before turning to Serenity. "As far as your source of inspiration"—he nodded—"I understand why you were inclined to buy it."

"You do?"

"Jah. In fact Aendi Margaret had a liking for things that piqued her interest. She didn't have many extras. But for some reason, I have no doubt that she would have appreciated your garage-sale find." He glanced at the horse.

After a slight hesitation, his eyebrows lifted in surprise, and he focused on Serenity. "I've just learned something new about you. You've never shown this horse to me, and I had no idea you collected such things."

Serenity smiled. "I don't. It's just a unique find that intrigued me." She shrugged. "A few months ago, Trini, Abby, and I went to a sale just out of town. Abby was hoping to find fabric and yarn. Sometimes she lucks out. Usually I just browse. I guess you could say that part of me enjoys imagining the stories behind the items for sale." When no one responded, she continued. "In a way, I like to think that things end up in the hands of someone who appreciates them."

Stephen regarded her with curious intensity. "You're an interesting person, Serenity."

He cupped his hand to his chin and added, "As often as we've talked, how did I miss your interest in garage sales?"

Serenity grinned. "I don't know." She offered a quick, dismissive shrug. "Maybe I never mentioned it."

"Garage sales!" Mamm chimed in. "Leave it to you, Serenity, to associate inspiration with someone else's items."

Serenity felt the need to convince her mamm that there was an innate value in her passion. "When you think about it, everything on the sale shelves has a history. Of course, it's doubtful that I'll ever know the story behind my intriguing horse. But don't you wonder how something so unique ended up being for sale?" Serenity softened her voice. "Of course in this case, that particular garage sale came from unfortunate circumstances."

When the others looked at her to continue, she went on. "Apparently, the man whose things were sold was in the last stages of Alzheimer's, and his family got rid of his home in a rush, as well as his belongings, when they were forced to admit him to a full-time care facility."

The corners of Mamm's lips dropped a couple of notches. "That's awful."

Serenity nodded.

Stephen commented with obvious disapproval, "I'm not in the shoes of those family members, so I won't judge their decision to do what they did. But"—he lifted his palms in a helpless gesture as he eyed the other three—"don't you think it's awfully sad when we send our loved ones to a home to spend what's supposed to be their golden years? I understand staying a few weeks for physical therapy and things like that, but to live out the rest of your life in a strange place with people who don't even know you?"

Mamm's expression saddened as she nodded. "Jah, it is devastating. As far as physical therapy, plenty of us stay here in our local care home after hospital procedures. But when you suffer from a disease that attacks the mind. . ." She looked away as if deciding how to finish her statement, then firmed her voice and glanced at Stephen. "You're right. We're not in their shoes. So I'll give his family the benefit of the doubt. There may not have been other options."

"Hopefully his family will be there each day to make sure he's getting gut care," Daed said, his tone thoughtful. "It's one thing to be terminally ill, but Alzheimer's is like a broken buggy wheel. I don't know anyone who has it, but I've heard things that would break your heart."

He lifted his glass to his lips before smiling warmly at Serenity. "Now I'm even more interested in the origin of this horse." He chuckled.

Serenity turned again to glimpse her find. "That horse knows something. That's why I can't stop looking at it." A long silence ensued before she lifted a curious brow. "The sleuth in me wants to know what the secret is."

# CHAPTER THREE

Trini readied the back of the Quilt Room for that very special afternoon of the week when she and her two besties, Serenity Miller and Abigail Shrock, shared their deepest, darkest secrets while quilting.

As Trini organized numerous spools of thread and piles of fabric, she smiled while she thought of her new husband, Jacob Lantz. *He's the love of my life. And I nearly lost him.*

The quilt on the wooden frame was to be for the queen-sized bed that Serenity's daed was constructing from oak. It would be a Christmas present for Trini and Jacob. Thanks to Abby, Jacob knew about it. Trini's dark-haired friend who owned Abby's Alterations had accidentally spilled that confidential piece of information. *It's okay. Keeping secrets isn't always easy. I know that all too well.*

While she considered Jacob and the batch of sponge cakes she'd made him for tonight's dessert, she began to hum "Jacob's Ladder." In some ways, she believed the old hymn held a connection to them. For instance, the song bore her husband's first name. And as far as the ladder? A laugh escaped Trini as she recalled falling off her own ladder when Jacob had surprised her in her peach orchard. She looked down at her wrist at the light scar that lingered from the stitches after her ulna and radius were repaired.

Automatically, the horrible incident that had recently happened to Serenity prompted the corners of Trini's lips to drop. Trini stopped her work, heaved a distressed sigh, and pressed her palms to her hips as she thought about the tragedy that had shocked their tight-knit community.

As a ray of sun beamed in through the window, it lightened a spool of navy thread to sky blue. Trini barely noticed the stock in front of her as she contemplated what she'd heard about the crime in Serenity's barn. *Yes, it was a criminal act.* In their Amish community, despite them not using cell phones, word had spread like wildfire. Even though the thugs who'd apparently hidden in Serenity's barn were supposedly behind bars, people in this neck of the woods were unsettled. Their actions showed their uneasiness. For instance, Trini's Mamm now refused to go to her own barn unaccompanied. And one of the church ladies had asked the bishop's permission to install a security system. To Trini's knowledge, there had been no response. A widowed grandma in their church was having solar lights installed around her property.

*I'm fortunate to have Jacob. To think that I nearly lost him because of my lists. And the crazy dream that took me away from my friends and family.* She shuddered.

The bell above the entrance sounded. As Trini stepped out to the main shop area, Serenity and Abigail bounded in with excitement. She greeted them with a big hug as Abby immediately expressed a vigorous plan to further her budding relationship with Gabriel Lantz.

The topic of discussion was not new to the Quilt Room. Not at all. As the three women stepped to the back area of the shop, Trini couldn't stop a cautious vibe from lifting her brow.

Abby was relentless with her quests. She always had been. But never had Trini seen her so determined to accomplish anything as to carry out her plan to marry Gabriel. Before the Lantz brothers had moved to Arthur about a year ago, Abby had already sewn ten baby bibs for the kinder she'd planned to bear with the eldest Lantz brother. This had happened before the two had even met.

And so far, to Trini's chagrin, none of Abby's plans to interest Gabriel had come close to materializing. Still, it was obvious that Abby's quest to become Mrs. Gabriel Lantz was far from over.

Back in the quilting area, Trini and Abby claimed their usual seats around the frame while Serenity poured hot water over her herbal tea bag. She joined them, holding her mug while stepping carefully to her chair. The calming scent of Trini's cinnamon-scented candles floated through the small area. While Trini threaded her needle, the shop phone rang.

"Please excuse me while I get this."

She proceeded toward the sound and answered. On the other end, a woman inquired about the date of completion for her Christmas quilt. Trini thumbed through her work calendar and gave her a date. After she hung up, she made her way back to where her friends had begun stitching and cutting.

What had happened to Serenity filled her thoughts. It was the elephant in the room. Trini had heard many different stories about the incident in her friend's barn, but she couldn't wait to hear what had happened straight from the owner of the Pink Petal. She breathed in and straightened her shoulders, glancing at Abby before her gaze landed on Serenity. "We've got lots to talk about today!"

Abby was the first to respond. Her expression was a blend of uneasiness and curiosity as she glanced at Serenity. "First of all, I'm relieved that you're okay. But please tell us exactly what happened. Is it true that you tried to fight off your attackers with a shovel?"

Serenity held her scissors in front of her and laughed. "No!" After a slight hesitation, she went on with a smile. "It sounds like I need to spill the awful details."

Understanding accompanied Abby's voice. "I'm sorry. I'll bet you're tired of talking about it."

Serenity paused. Then she shrugged. "At first, it pained me to relive it. But now I realize that sharing it is gut therapy for me. Going through the sequence of events helps to stymie the tremendous agony that it caused.

Automatically, Trini glanced at Abby, who was the antithesis of Serenity. While Serenity was a "no drama" kind of woman, Abby could rarely contain her yearning for details about anything, especially information that involved the three Lantz brothers: Gabriel, Stephen, and Jacob. Right now, however, she appeared ready to listen.

Serenity cut around a plastic form. She worked while she talked. In a calm voice, she went through the timeline that had begun with her preparing her barn for the storm and ended with Stephen finding her the next morning.

After a long silence, Abby threw her hands in the air. "But why? Why did they attack you? And how can you stay so calm about this? Weren't you scared? For heaven's sake, you couldn't even scream for help!"

Trini lowered her gaze to her lap and pretended a sudden interest in her white apron while she tried to stop the corners of her lips from curving in amusement. Now it was up to Serenity to ease Abby's obvious irritation.

Trini looked up long enough to glimpse the two friends as Abby stood and laid her material on her chair. Curious as to how Serenity could satisfy Abby's inquisitiveness, Trini quietly got up and made her way to the window, where a bird pecked against the wood trim. She listened as Serenity tried to convince Abby that it wasn't healthy to get so worked up. That what had happened to her could not be undone, as she wished it could. But that laying out the steps that had ended in Stephen finding her was the best way to eventually move on.

Abby persisted. Irritation edged her voice, and she paced to the water holder and back until she finally stood in front of Serenity, lifting her palms in a helpless gesture. She looked down at her. Abby's expression was part frustration and part devastation. "I'm sorry, Serenity. I'm so upset this happened. I wish I could make this awful thing go away. It kills me that someone tied you up and gagged you. What if. . ."

Tears slipped down Abby's cheek.

Serenity stood and laid a calming hand on Abby's shoulders. "Abby, it's okay."

Abby offered a conciliatory nod before closing her eyes a moment, and when she opened them, she wiped her cheeks with the back of her hand and lifted her chin in defense. "I live alone too. And even though the guys who did this are supposedly behind bars, how can we be sure?"

Trini returned to her chair, but inside, her stomach tied in knots. She totally understood Abby's erratic behavior. The main issue, Trini believed, was that Abby could not accept that their friend had been treated so cruelly. Nor could Trini.

Serenity faced Abby, who began to hyperventilate. "Take a deep breath, Abby."

Abby did as she was told.

Serenity rubbed Abby's shoulders and spoke in a soft, reassuring voice. "There you go. Good job. How 'bout I make you an herbal tea?" She quickly added, "It will help you calm down."

Abby shook her head and tried a half smile. "I apologize." She glanced at Trini. "I didn't mean to get so emotional. It's just that talking about it somehow made it harder to comprehend."

Serenity nodded. "I understand. In fact, I try not to get worked up. But it's not easy." After a long, drawn-out breath, she softened her voice. "To be honest, it has shaken my soul." She released a sigh. Then she stepped to her chair and moved it next to Abby's. The legs made a light squeak as they traversed the wood floor. She sat down. Trini moved her chair closer to her friends'. She faced her two besties.

For long moments, the three women held hands. Trini's heart melted. It was such a sweet gesture. Abby should have been comforting Serenity, but instead it was Serenity who tried to console Abby.

Serenity finally offered, "We need to pray. It's the only way to truly heal from what happened. The Lord will take away our fear."

They closed their eyes. Trini detected a slight shake of Serenity's voice. "Dear Gott, please put your protective shield around us. And please forgive the men responsible for this." After a slight hesitation, her words came out in a whisper. "I pray that they will find You. Amen."

The women released their strong handholds. Serenity looked at Trini before her attention migrated to Abby. Determination accompanied her statement. "This will be okay. We've got to live our lives. No one can rob us of that. And there's no way I can stay away from the barn. My horse lives inside."

Trini steadied her pitch, trying to exude hope. "Serenity, we're your dearest friends."

At the same time, the three women wrapped their arms around each other in a tight hug. Suddenly the dismal mood changed to joy. Abby smiled. Her eyes were a little red. "I love you two."

Trini and Serenity said in unison, "We love you too."

Serenity straightened her shoulders and proceeded to the corner where she resumed her work. "I suppose there's still time to get something accomplished."

Trini replied. "I suppose so. But at the end of the day, we've comforted each other. So even if we don't work any on the quilt, we've still accomplished a huge feat." She glanced at Serenity, who was tying a knot in her thread.

Serenity stood to pull her chair closer to the quilt and remained standing as Trini broached some questions. "Serenity?"

"Jah?"

"While we're on the subject, I just want to make sure I understand this correctly."

Two sets of eyes focused on Trini.

"The police are convinced that the two guys in your barn are in jail, right? The bank robbers?"

Before Serenity could answer, Abby jumped into the conversation. "Did they actually confess?"

Serenity shrugged. "That, I don't know. But soon the results from the fingerprints will be back."

Trini considered the response before turning her attention to the florist with a curious intensity. "So. . .does that mean we're not 100 percent sure. . . ?"

Serenity reached for her tea mug and took a sip before addressing Trini's question. "Are you asking me if I think there's a chance that the cops are wrong?"

In silence Trini and Abby nodded simultaneously.

Serenity shook her head. "That's what my parents wanted to know. As for the authorities, I trust their instincts. After all, things of this nature never happen around here. I mean, what are the chances that two crimes happened on the same day?" She laughed. "In and close to Arthur, Illinois?" After a short silence, she shrugged. "That's not possible."

Trini focused on Serenity's experience and tried to figure out something that hadn't already been thought of. "Serenity, did you recognize their voices?"

"No. Like the police suspect, they were bank thieves. But I had never heard those voices before." Trini caught the sudden twinkle in Serenity's eyes. "Trust me. If I had, I would definitely have recognized them. At least, the one voice," she corrected.

Trini narrowed her brows and leaned forward while she sat and slid her sturdy black shoes under her chair. Her peripheral vision caught Abby, who'd also put down her quilt work. "Why do you say that?"

Serenity tucked a stray hair back neatly under her head covering. "The one guy—"

"Jah?" Trini and Abby spoke at the same time.

"His voice was raspy. Like he was hoarse."

Abby met Trini's curious expression. She pressed her lips together thoughtfully in a straight line before directing her focus to Serenity. "Do we know someone like that?" She glanced over at Trini. "Maybe someone who's come to our shops? Someone we've overheard in the grocery store?"

Trini snapped her fingers and jumped a little. "Samantha Lapp's husband! His voice sounds raspy."

Serenity laughed. Trini took in the flush in her friend's cheeks and her creamy complexion. The blueness of her eyes reminded Trini of a cloudless sky on a summer's day. It matched the beautiful shade of yarn she'd once used to knit one of her niece's Christmas slippers.

By now the barely noticeable stress lines around Serenity's mouth had almost disappeared. Her smile didn't look forced.

Serenity's eyes sparkled. "Trini, Eli Lapp would never attack me in my barn! He has a limp. Besides"—she threw up her hands before placing them on her thighs and running her fingers over a crease on her apron—"he's a gut man. He helps distribute hams every Christmas to people who can't afford them."

Trini sighed. "You're right. I'm trying too hard for answers."

A fly buzzed in front of Abby's face, and she swatted it away.

Then she made her way to the purified water jug, where she held a paper cup underneath the spigot and pushed the button. As her cup filled, she observed: "We're on to something, though. If we could find the man with that throaty voice, and you recognized it—"

She took a drink before rejoining the other two, but she didn't sit back down. "That's the sure way and the only way to know who attacked you, Serenity."

The three ladies stayed quiet while a bird pecked at the window trim. When it stopped, it was so quiet they could have heard a pin drop. The unique, light scent of herbal tea began to overpower the candles' cinnamon scent.

Trini was the first to respond. "You're right, Abby. I mean, I'm sure there's more than one man in this world with a raspy voice, but if Serenity recognized it. . ."

"I could certainly rest easier if I knew for certain that the guys who attacked me in my barn are now in jail." Serenity's voice was barely more than a whisper.

They quilted in silence. But Trini's mind traveled a mile a minute. She looked at the clock and sighed. She stood and returned her chair to its original spot. Abby and Serenity did the same. Then they cleaned up and organized their things, which they left on their chairs.

As they stepped to the store's main area, Abby's voice hinted at sudden, unexpected happiness. "Serenity, you know how you're always reminding us to look at the positive and to leave the negative behind?"

Serenity's expression conveyed uncertainty as she slowly nodded.

Abby dropped her empty cup into the nearby garbage container and offered the owner of the floral shop a sheepish grin. "Correct me if I'm wrong, but something definitely gut came out of this!"

Trini chastised her friend with a quick nudge of her shoulder.

But the gesture didn't deter Abby. Suddenly, her demeanor glowed. "I'm serious."

Trini edged her voice with obvious disbelief. "And exactly what is that?"

Serenity eyed their dark-haired friend. "Please. Enlighten me."

At the cash register, Abby gracefully plucked a lemon drop from the crystal bowl of candies that Trini kept for her clientele. After she unwrapped it, she crinkled the plastic. With a confident lift of her chin, Abby held the candy in front of her mouth. "Ladies, I can't believe that neither of you has realized the blessing that came out of this mess." The pitch of Abby's voice filled with excitement and rose so high Trini feared the windows would break. She didn't respond. Neither did Serenity. She just stepped toward the front door, stopped, and turned around to face Trini and Abby.

"Look at the big picture here, my friends," Abby explained. "Serenity and handsome Stephen Lantz. We knew all along that we'd face obstacles while trying to reach our dreams. But. . ."

Trini eyed Serenity.

"Isn't it obvious that this terrible thing will bond Stephen and Serenity together forever?"

The sudden expression in Serenity's eyes turned to a strong combination of horror and disbelief.

Abby tapped the toe of her sturdy black shoe as she crossed her arms over her chest and addressed Trini. "Remember when you fell from that ladder? That was the start of your relationship with Jacob."

Trini couldn't find her voice.

Abby's words rushed together. "Now Serenity's dream of marrying Stephen will come true!"

She glanced at Serenity, who appeared to be frozen in place.

"The trust between you and Stephen and your obvious love for each other will lead to a proposal, Serenity. I'm sure of it."

Serenity's lips parted in surprise.

A knot stuck in Trini's throat, and she tried to clear it.

"First, we've got to ensure that the men who attacked our Serenity are behind bars. It's the only way that Stephen and Serenity will truly be able to move on with their relationship."

Serenity glanced at Trini, then Abby, before reaching for their hands and squeezing their fingers. "There's one thing I didn't mention."

Two sets of eyes peered into Serenity's.

Trini asked, "What is it?"

"The police have asked me to try and identify the man's voice by listening to the bank robbers in a lineup." A short silence passed before Serenity added in an uncertain voice. "At the jail."

# CHAPTER FOUR

*Abby has lost her mind.* The following morning, Serenity pushed her wheelbarrow, loaded with a bag of oats, to Angel's feeding trough. She reached into her apron pocket, retrieved her scissors, and slit open the top of the bag. As she did so, Angel clomped his hooves and released a loud whinny.

"We need to work on patience," she pretended to scold the standardbred. She reached for the metal scoop next to the grain, scooped a generous helping, and emptied the oat mix into the feed box at the front of the stall. Wasting no time, Angel indulged.

Serenity returned the scoop to its wall hook and stepped to check Angel's water trough. She adjusted the placement of the end of the tube where the liquid emptied into the large container.

A sunbeam floated in through one of the side windows, and she blinked at the sudden light. Serenity put her hands on her hips and considered the serious talk that she, Trini, and Abby had shared just yesterday at the Quilt Room.

Her thoughts went automatically to her upcoming visit to the jail. As she contemplated identifying the man's throaty voice and knowing for certain that the men who'd attacked her were behind bars, she sighed with relief. Then her thoughts drifted back to Abby's crazy theory about Stephen, and Serenity shook her head.

*Abby's imagination has traveled to a whole new level. It's wilder than I ever imagined. In her mind, Trini's fall from her ladder last year was how Gott brought Jacob and her together. Now she has this ridiculous idea that what happened in my barn will lead to a happily-ever-after between Stephen and me.*

Quick steps took Serenity out of the barn to the chicken house, where she retrieved the basket she'd left. She ducked to avoid hitting her head on the low ceiling of the small building. Inside the coop, chickens clucked and flapped their wings. Dust made a foggy haze.

Serenity closed her eyes. When she eventually lifted her lids, she squatted to gather eggs. One by one, she placed them in her basket. *This is my least favorite job. But it doesn't take long.*

As her basket filled, Serenity stood and accidentally hit her head on the rough boarded ceiling. Chickens startled and flew from their perches. The abrupt motion caused even more dust. Again, she closed her eyes for several seconds. When she opened them, she looked around to make sure she had collected every egg.

Serenity pressed her lips together. She spotted one last egg and took it between her fingers with great care not to break it.

Slow, cautious steps took her back outside. She half closed the door behind her and smiled a little as she took in the beautiful sunrise. Jade-colored oak leaves moved a little with the light, warm breeze that caressed her face.

She headed toward the house, stopped, closed her eyes, and said a silent prayer of thanks for a new day and another opportunity to make people happy with her flower arrangements. She opened her eyes and smiled gratefully at the deep green grass that looked like a rich carpet. Flowers on both sides of the dirt trail burst with beautiful, bright colors. Her favorite part of the yard was the simple wooden fence she'd painted white.

She moved two eggs away from the sides of the basket. Satisfied that none would fall out, she took careful steps to her home. As she walked, she thought of the recent tragedy. Then Stephen stepped into her mind. Her heart warmed. Abby's theory about the growing bond between her and Stephen held merit. In Serenity's heart, she truly loved him. *How could I not? But I must remember that our relationship cannot go any further. Abby means well, but she's not privy to my secret.*

She forced Stephen from her mind and focused on her yard's beauty. That her parents and siblings were still alive.

*Some people take every moment for granted. But I appreciate each second that I'm on this earth. Because time here is short. And we don't know the day or time Gott will call us to heaven.*

Inside her house, she placed her basket next to the kitchen sink and turned the faucet to warm. She tested the water with her finger and washed her hands. When she was satisfied with the temperature, she wet a white rag, wrung it, and began wiping each egg individually until all were clean. Taking great care not to break the shells, she transferred each one to her refrigerator.

She looked down at her dirty apron and stepped to the bathroom to clean up for work. While she tidied herself, she swallowed an emotional knot. *I miss my parents. But I just saw them.* She pressed her lips together in a thoughtful line and reasoned that she was thinking about Mamm and Daed more than usual because of her close call with death. She could have suffocated on the barn floor; or if Stephen hadn't sought her out, she could have died from lack of water before anyone found her.

Slowly she shook her head. *Anything could've happened. Gott protected me. I'm still alive. And fortunately, the men who harmed me are behind bars. At least, that's what I believe. Soon I'll know for sure.*

For some strange reason, the incident in Serenity's barn sparked painful memories of her four-year episode with Epstein-Barr. She'd never forget her daed praying with her at her bedside. He'd asked their Creator to work His miraculous hand on Serenity.

Daed had never conveyed any signs of doubt or resignation. When he'd prayed, he'd asked their Lord and Savior for Serenity's recovery with assurance. His prayers had always left her with a sense of awe. And when he'd left her room, she'd routinely fallen asleep with a welcome sense of joy and confidence that she'd recover. And miraculously, eventually she had.

*My daed is my hero. I don't know where he garners his strength. Stephen is my hero too. When he untied my hands and feet and removed the rag from my face, I looked into his deep brown eyes. And he stared into mine.*

The emotional recollection prompted an excited shiver up her spine. It landed at the base of her neck, and she parted her lips. *I've got to dissuade Stephen from getting closer to me. But how do I do it?*

Stephen yearned to make Serenity his wife. *Today I'm going to tell her.*

Behind his home, he stopped to adjust the binoculars around his neck before entering the woods that separated the Lantz property from Serenity's house. As he started on the dirt path that took a slight incline, he slowed to avoid tripping on a large tree root that stuck up out of the ground.

On the other side, he paused and squinted at the sound coming from a group of trees. *It's a redheaded woodpecker. I know it.* He pulled his binoculars to his eyes and adjusted the lenses until the beautiful bird was in clear view.

As he took in the feathered creature, his thoughts migrated from Jacob and Trini's new six-bedroom, two-story home on the opposite side of Margaret's home to his recent uplifting phone conversation with Mamm. . .to the weather prediction that today was supposed to be in the eighties. . .to the moment he'd found Serenity tied up in the barn. The last memory prompted him to squeeze his eyes closed in agony. As he did so, he held the strap around his neck and gently allowed his binoculars to drop to his chest.

A pheasant rustling among some leaves and sticks forced him to think of the delicious Amish dishes that Mamm had promised when he and his brothers returned to Lancaster for Christmas. But inevitably, the horrifying scene of Serenity in her barn eventually trumped that happy thought as well as the morning's Gott-given beauty. He cringed. The tragedy prompted an eerie shiver to trickle slowly and eerily up his spine until the uncomfortable sensation made its home at the base of his neck. He rolled his shoulders to rid the uneasy feeling.

What sounded like footsteps crunching on fallen leaves caused him to turn in the direction of the light noise.

From behind a long pine branch, Serenity suddenly appeared. He lifted his hand in a friendly gesture.

She returned his wave while pushing aside a branch to join him. "What a beautiful day!"

He walked toward her and extended his hand to help her over a large stump and prevent her from falling. *Of course, she's quite used to making her way through these woods. And never once have I seen her fall.*

As they stood face-to-face, he smiled. "*Gut mariye.* I've been thinking about you."

She pulled her water bottle from her apron, took a drink, and placed the plastic container back in her belt pocket "You've been on my mind too, Stephen."

He softened his voice for emphasis. "All gut thoughts, I hope."

She lifted her chin. "Nothing but."

Her clean, natural beauty and the genuine kindness in her eyes left him speechless for a moment. He finally got some words out.

"How's the floral business?"

They headed up the slow incline that would eventually lead to the clearing that revealed a vast panorama. When some brush crowded the trail, he motioned her in front of him. As soon as the path presented enough room, he stepped up to her side.

"Busy." She blinked when a bright ray of sun came through an open area between the trees. She stepped around a dip in the trail, and he did too. "I've been getting a large number of bookings lately. I mean, that's not a total surprise. This time of year means numerous weddings, birthday parties, anniversaries, and graduations. For the first time, I've hired someone to help me through the end of August."

"You're a good businesswoman, Ms. Miller."

"Why thank you, Mr. Lantz." She smiled. "I'm awaiting a special order."

"Oh?"

"Um-hmm. It's for a large supply of calla lilies." She glanced at him with a smile. "They're exquisite. Unique. I can't wait to work with them.

"I'm trying to recall if I've ever seen one."

"They're breathtaking!"

He was so taken in by the obvious enthusiasm in her voice and the way she gestured while she spoke, he almost missed an unusual-looking bird that had landed on an oak limb. He pulled his binoculars to his eyes. As he adjusted the lenses, curiosity edged Serenity's voice.

"What is it, Stephen?"

He confirmed his initial thought. "A brown-headed cowbird. I haven't seen many. They like forests and shrubs."

From his peripheral vision, he glimpsed Serenity squinting.

"Here. See for yourself."

He lifted the binoculars and strap over his head and handed them to her. Then he helped her to put the lenses over her eyes, hoping the bird wouldn't fly away before she'd seen it.

He watched as she focused. *Her hands are as delicate as the flowers she arranges. She seems to appreciate everything that has life. She's a very special person.*

As she moved the binoculars a bit, she claimed with enthusiasm, "Its color blends in nicely with the bark."

She continued to study the bird. Stephen glimpsed it without the lens. The feathered creature was very still.

But his thoughts were on the woman next to him and her obvious interest in the bird. *I think she appreciates nature as much as I do. And I love her remarkably soft heart for living creatures.*

The joyous lift in her voice pulled him from his reverie. "I've never seen one of these."

"They're common here in Illinois. As you can see, the little creature isn't flashy in color. But listen."

She stood very still as she pulled the binoculars from her face and gently lifted them over her head. Without making a sound, she returned them to Stephen. As she did, a faint *glug-glug-glee* could be heard coming from the cowbird.

They listened. Serenity stepped forward. "It's a peculiar sound."

"Jah." Stephen followed her after placing his lenses around his neck.

As twigs and leaves crunched under their shoes, Serenity glanced back at him. "Stephen, you know what I find so interesting about birds?"

He stepped over some vines to join her. "What?"

"They're like the sunset. They're unique with different colors and sounds. But every bird in the universe, like each beautiful sunset hue that paints the sky, plays a role in this world. I think people need to focus more on birds. I mean, they all survive with very few needs, and they're obviously happy enough to sing!"

He chuckled. She joined in the laughter. Then she moved an evergreen branch to the side to pass. "Don't you agree?"

He nodded while cautioning her about the coming dip in the earth. They stepped around it then continued on. "I do. And you know something else?"

"What?"

The sun's light brightened several notches, and Stephen blinked. "I'm sure Gott appreciates when people are so in tune to His unique creations. What He designed is truly special. His gifts are everywhere, but people who notice them are special."

At the same time, they put their hands on their hips and looked at the Lantz crops in the distance. "Your beans look gut."

"*Denki.*"

*Tell her how you feel. There won't be a better time.* Stephen's hands shook. His lungs worked extra hard to pump air. But if he planned to marry this wonderful woman, he first needed to tell her that he truly and unconditionally loved her.

In the distance, he could see his late aendi's home. A surge of warmth filled his heart until he thought it would burst. As he took in Margaret's pasture, he remembered something she'd once told him. "*You'll never accomplish your dream if you don't take the first step to make it happen.*" He stuck his hands in his pockets and looped his thumbs over the openings.

*Okay, Aendi Margaret. I'll heed your advice.*

He turned to Serenity. She smiled up at him.

"Serenity, I think you know how I feel about you."

Above them, the sun slipped underneath a cloud. For a moment, he hesitated, deciding what to say next.

He met her gaze. As he did so, the sun fully reappeared, and the light on her irises created the most beautiful shade of blue. The fast beat of his pulse slowed to a more comfortable speed.

"Serenity, looking at the farm makes me wonder what we'll see down the road."

"What do you mean?"

He rocked on the toes of his boots. His voice softened. "I yearn for little ones playing chase in the Lantz yard." He breathed in. "I want to extend my heritage." His voice became merely a whisper. "Our heritage."

A tense silence followed. He could see her lips make a straight line. Suddenly, he knew he'd said something wrong. The corners of her mouth dropped a notch.

Long seconds passed before she spoke. Her half smile looked forced. "Stephen, I'm sure you'll make an excellent father." She cleared her throat. "Speaking about fathers, did I tell you I've booked over twenty weddings in the next eight weeks?"

His breath caught in his throat. She'd deliberately nixed what he'd been about to tell her.

A combination of disappointment and surprise fought inside him until he didn't know what else to say. He nodded approval. "Wow. That'll keep you busy. Gut thing you have an assistant."

"Uh-huh."

Unsure of what to say and disappointed at Serenity's reaction to his attempt to reveal his dream to her, he turned and stepped onto the trail. "Are you ready to head back?"

She nodded.

As they returned to the woods, he breathed in the pleasant scent of pines. He held back a large branch and motioned for her to walk in front of him.

"Thank you, Stephen."

After they stepped away from another dip in the trail, they

rejoined each other, side by side. His arm brushed hers. But this time he wondered if the surge of warmth and emotion he felt was shared. Something had happened at the mention of children and passing on their heritage. *Does she not want kinder?*

*Talk to her. She'll listen.* His voice cracked with emotion. "Serenity, I know that what happened in your barn is over and that the people responsible are behind bars. But. . ."

She looked at him, drawing her brows together in curiosity before quickly returning her focus to the path. When he didn't go on, she probed, "Stephen?"

"I don't want to put a cloud on this glorious morning or this beautiful scenery and fresh air. I guess what I'm trying to tell you is that, Serenity—"

A knot blocked his throat. His shoulders tensed a notch. He breathed in and tried to maintain his calm demeanor. *Say it. Speak your mind. It's the only way she'll truly know how you feel.*

When he stopped, she did too. They turned to face each other. For long moments, he took in her serene expression. The cleanness of her skin and the beauty of her lips. He swallowed. Her natural beauty emanated from inside her. From her heart.

Her eyes were the most beautiful shade of blue he'd ever seen. The hue reminded him of the sky on a summer day when there were no clouds to dilute the deep color.

But something was happening. Cream-colored flecks danced in what appeared to be an uncertain beat. They pulled the breath from his lungs. They compelled him to lift his chin a notch. The silence that loomed between them seemed to adopt its own language. And it spoke in a tone that was a serious blend of mutual respect and great uncertainty. He wished he was privy to her thoughts.

As a wonderful sensation filled him, he smiled a little. He bent closer to her. The only other sounds were the chirping of songbirds and what sounded like an animal scurrying over the landscape of twigs and leaves.

He was so close to her, he could smell the fresh scent of her kapp. Or it may have been her hair. He wasn't sure. But it didn't matter.

"What I'm trying to say is that never would I have imagined something of that nature happening in our area of the country."

To his disappointment, she started up the path again. He followed. But unfinished business lay between them. It would have been easier to have the discussion while he'd had her full attention.

As evergreen branches caressed the bare part of his arms where he'd rolled up the sleeves, determination kicked in. *I have to tell her.* "Knowing that you were put in that position..." He stopped to hold back a large oak branch, allowing her to pass. She offered a quick *thanks*. After that, he followed before letting go of the foliage. "It really bothers me."

"Stephen, what happened troubles me too," Serenity replied in a gentle voice. "Even though it's a relief that the men supposedly responsible are behind bars. . ." She stopped to glance back while offering a helpless shrug. Then the path widened, and he took advantage of the opportunity to walk next to her again. Because she seemed focused on the path's irregularities, and due to the choir of birds seemingly determined to outsing each other, her words were sometimes hard to catch.

She looked up at him just as he glanced down at her. They slowed, making their way up a slight incline that led to another clearing. At the top, they both stopped and caught their breath.

She hugged her hands to her hips and sighed while taking in the beautiful picture surrounding them. The trees mainly consisted of oaks and evergreens, but there were other varieties too. It was the combination of the different species that transformed the scene around them into a view that claimed Stephen's breath.

He watched Serenity's serious expression as she seemed to contemplate her words. "I think what bothers me most is that the guilty men have stolen our sense of security."

Before he could respond, she pulled her water from the belt around her waist. As she twisted off the lid, she faced him again, her eyes full of regret. "Their actions not only affected me. Now everyone around has this awful intrusion on their minds. You know, Stephen, being comfortable in my home and on my property is something I always took for granted. Now two men have robbed me of that privilege." She drank and remained holding the bottle while she shook her head and met his eyes. "It's just not fair."

"If we truly plan to return to normalcy, we need to be certain this won't happen again."

Serenity faced him and told him of the recommendation from the police to try to identify the throaty voice in a lineup.

"His face was close to the back of my head. I wanted to cringe as I listened to him. If I heard his voice again, I would recognize it. There's only one way to be sure, though. And that's to hear it for myself."

Stephen glimpsed a beautiful bird in the distance that perched on a tall oak branch. But he didn't bother with his binoculars. He was too preoccupied with what Serenity had just told him.

Finally, he shrugged. "I understand why a visit to the jail could be of value," he began, his voice edged with concern. He shook his head. "But to be honest, the mere thought of you confronting your attackers sends a chill up my spine."

While he contemplated her plan and its possible repercussions, he frowned. A leaf floated gracefully down from a tall branch. When it landed on the ground, the surrounding beauty reinforced that Gott would protect Serenity. He'd pulled her through a serious illness years ago. And He would get her through this.

"Stephen?" She smiled a little as she looked at him. "If the men are behind bars, they can't harm me."

A sudden smile tugged up the corners of his lips "Of course, you're right. Forgive me for my strong protective nature."

She swatted a mosquito away. Her eyes sparkled. "There's nothing to forgive. In fact, your protectiveness is one of your most admirable traits, Stephen."

His heart warmed. Coming from such a wonderful woman, the compliment made his day. While they stood in silence and listened to the rustling leaves, Stephen's mind was on the eventual visit his friend would make to alleged criminals.

When he spoke, his voice sounded a bit out of place amid the woodsy sounds. But unfortunately, the jail visit was a topic that needed to be addressed.

"I don't like the thought of you so close to two dangerous men. I know that they're locked up. Still, I don't want them near you."

He clutched his palms together. "At the same time, if indeed you recognize the voice of the throaty-sounding man, we can all rest assured that this won't happen again. At least not while they're behind bars. And hopefully, the police will do the visit in a way that prevents them from seeing you."

"Whatever the case, it's something that needs to be done." She extended her arms in front of her, palms up, and closed her eyes in what appeared to be a great sense of relief. "It's my responsibility to put this widespread fear to rest." As she dropped her hands to her sides, she turned to look up at Stephen. Regret filled her eyes. "What happened isn't my fault, but at the same time, I need to end the worry." As large clouds scudded across the sky, she added, "And I'm sure that the entire community will be more comfortable knowing that the barn men aren't on the loose."

As a woodpecker sounded from behind them, she spoke in a soft voice. "I feel sorry for people who rob others and do bad things."

Stephen looked at her for an explanation.

"Stephen, do you ever truly appreciate how fortunate we are to have been raised to believe in Gott and live in His Word?"

Her eyes glistened with moisture. "Not everyone believes in the cross and that we are blessed with wonderful eternal life because of it."

A honeybee buzzing around her ear broke the spell that had captivated him. Immediately, he pulled her away from the flying insect. "Stephen?"

"Jah?"

"I forgive the robbers."

For a moment, he absorbed what she'd just said and wondered if he'd heard correctly. Finally, he acknowledged that she was right. "Serenity Miller, I'm amazed at what you just said." He lowered his pitch to a more serious tone. "But not surprised."

"You agree?"

After a slight delay, he nodded. "Absolutely."

As they studied each other, he yearned to be her husband. He longed for her love. But instinctively, he was sure that this wasn't the right time to broach his feelings for her, because something was holding her back.

Jacob loved being a hands-on farmer. Most neighboring farmers paid people to weed their beans, but Jacob and his brothers chose to do their own field. He extended his sickle to snap a butter print weed while he and Stephen "walked beans" behind their home. As the plant fell to the ground, his gaze drifted over several rows between him and his younger *bruder*. For a moment, he glanced at Stephen's serious demeanor.

Jacob snapped another butter print and proceeded between the rows. The plant immediately dropped to the ground. But Jacob's focus was on Stephen. His unusually serious expression prompted Jacob to frown.

Jacob thought of how life had changed since the awful incident in the town florist's barn. Stephen hadn't said much about it to Jacob, but he didn't need to.

Since that day, changes in the youngest Lantz had become obvious. And Jacob wasn't sure he could do anything about the new Stephen. He'd taken note of the sudden lack of conversation between them. He missed Stephen's wide smile and the sparkle in his eyes.

After Jacob and Trini had married, he and other church members had torn down the small home she'd been living in and built a new house. They were still getting settled in and were planning a large family.

During construction, Trini and Jacob had lived with his two bruders in the house their late *aendi* Margaret had left them in her will. But the four of them together had been far from a hardship. Trini had quickly become a close sister to Gabe and Stephen, and it had bonded him closer to his brothers than he'd imagined possible.

A lot had happened since Jacob, Gabe, and Stephen had transitioned from Lancaster to Arthur. And during the past year, as they'd acclimated to Central Illinois, Jacob hadn't missed the obvious budding relationship between Stephen and the owner of the Pink Petal.

A bee buzzed close to Jacob, and he shooed away the insect with his hat. In front of them, the bright sun made the soybeans appear a shade lighter than their natural deep green. It was obvious where the field had been weeded.

When the three Lantzes had first moved into the house, Serenity and Abby had brought gifts. Jacob smiled a little as he recalled the pleasant visit when they'd first met the two young women. *It seems like yesterday.* The women were already in the house with Stephen when Jacob had joined them. Abby had gifted them a special quilt. And Serenity had baked sponge cakes for him, Stephen, and Gabe. Those treats had been nothing less than mouthwatering.

Since first meeting Serenity, Stephen had become a different man. The light in his brown eyes had brightened. He'd walked with more energy. And he'd laughed more.

Now things were different. The corners of Jacob's lips dropped a notch as he recalled how, since the day not too long ago when Jacob's younger brother had found Serenity tied up in her barn, that radiant light had disappeared from Stephen's eyes. His strides had become less energetic, and most evident of all, Stephen's already naturally protective nature had become more intense.

In fact, Stephen's new, serious demeanor had sparked a noticeable wave of concern on Jacob and Gabe's part. Stephen's reaction had altered his easygoing personality. Numerous red flags indicated that Stephen had been extremely affected by what had happened. But the brightest one was that Stephen had declined Jacob's recent fishing invitation. That was when Jacob had realized that he and his kid brother needed to talk.

At the end of the field, they turned, counted six rows on each side of them, and continued back to the opposite side. When Stephen glanced at him, Jacob tried a half smile, hoping to encourage Stephen to share his thoughts. But all Stephen offered was chitchat.

"The beans look great. I mean, where we've weeded," he said.

Jacob drew his brows together. "It'll be a gut harvest. They're already waist high." After a moment, he peered at his brother.

"Steve?"

Stephen didn't look at him. Instead he extended his sickle to snap a tall milkweed. After the large plant broke and fell to the ground, Jacob acknowledged a much greater need to engage in a serious conversation with his little brother. This morning, Stephen hadn't finished his coffee.

Jacob used his calmest tone to spark conversation. "Just want you to know I'm here if you ever need to talk."

After a slight hesitation, Stephen's tone conveyed some interest. "What makes you think there's something on my mind?"

Jacob breathed in before stepping over a row of crops to reach a large thistle. He snapped it before moving closer to Stephen to cut a cornstalk.

When they were only a row a part, Stephen looked at Jacob and said, "My worries are mine and mine alone. You can't fix them." An odd combination of doubt and reassurance edged Stephen's voice.

"No. I can't. But it might help you to run your concerns by me. You know what you say here stays here."

"Aw, Jake, I know what you're trying to do. You want to help." They took a few steps. "And I appreciate your concern. I surely do." Stephen lowered his voice. "Aendi Margaret always warned us that there would be obstacles in life. But what happened to Serenity a few days ago..." Stephen stopped and took a breath. Jacob stopped too. Stephen looked down at the ground before glancing at Jacob and shaking his head. "To be honest, it really made me think hard about things."

Jacob sighed with relief. Even though a long silence passed, at least the conversation had started. Now he just had to get his bruder to keep talking.

They reached the ditch where they had left their water jugs, and Jacob bent to retrieve his. Stephen got his own. The ice was nearly melted, but the cool water prompted Jacob to close his eyes in relief while the liquid eased his dry throat.

The only sound, besides the ice clinking lightly against the containers, was a tractor engine in the distance.

Stephen stood still, taking in their crops and nodding approval. "We've done a lot," he remarked, motioning to the clean rows.

While Jacob took another swig, the hot sun slipped behind a large marshmallow-like cloud, and a breeze caressed the back of his neck. He glanced down the road at his and Trini's new home.

"It's looking mighty good, Jake," Stephen said with sudden enthusiasm.

Jacob grinned. His gaze lingered on the spot where his wife, Trini, had lived before they'd married. "At first I was hesitant to tear down the one-story house, but Trini didn't have any qualms about it." After a slight pause, he added, "Everything's finally coming together. In a few months, we'll finish the interior. Hopefully by then we'll be expecting."

Stephen chuckled. "I like the way you said that."

Jacob's heart nearly melted when he thought of filling the bedrooms with kinder.

"Let me ask you something," Stephen said, his voice heavy with doubt.

"Go ahead," Jake replied encouragingly, locking his gaze with Stephen's.

They put down their jugs and returned to the field. Despite standing several rows apart, Jacob caught the hopeful expression on Stephen's face.

"I'm really happy for you, Jake. But"—Stephen let out a low whistle—"for a few months last year, I didn't know if you'd ever become Trini's hubby."

Jacob chuckled. "I know." Jacob thought back on his longtime dream to marry the owner of the Quilt Room and the secret plan she'd harbored that had nearly nixed his aspirations. "Our marriage is a blessing from Gott. I admit that when she moved to Rhode Island to live with her brother"—he paused to wipe away a bead of sweat that was making his nose itch—"I lost faith."

"You? Lost faith?" Stephen sounded surprised.

Jacob nodded as he snapped two butter prints together. The light green leaves disappeared. "I'm ashamed to admit that, by the way."

Jacob had a bird's-eye view of his late aendi's beloved wishing well. Stephen's voice pulled Jacob back to reality. "You sure went through a rough patch."

"But at the end of the day, she came home to marry me." Jacob lowered his pitch. "Stephen, life's not easy. But you know what?"

"What?"

"After Daed left us, Aendi Margaret used to stress that easy things don't make us strong and draw us closer to Gott. Difficult times do. And strength comes from how we deal with the challenges. I agree."

"I really miss her. And when I look at this beautiful property and her house. . .it makes me tear up. She worked so hard."

"And left it all to us."

"Jake, I'm really torn up over what happened to Serenity. I'm thankful that she's safe. That I found her before she became dehydrated or worse. But the more I think about what happened, the more it upsets me." His voice cracked with emotion. "Jake, they could've taken her life." After a slight hesitation, he went on. "What bothers me more than anything is that I was close by, and I did nothing to stop it from happening."

Jacob finally had a better understanding of what was eating at his brother. He tried his best logic. "What could you have done?"

"Before the storm hit, I'd thought about checking on her. But it came so quickly and unexpectedly. Now I wish I'd gone with my first instinct. If I'd been in that barn, I could've fought them off."

Jacob didn't respond. He considered Stephen's words. Stephen was a big, strong guy. Still, there was no way to be sure that he would have saved Serenity.

He tried to be realistic about the incident without bringing his brother down. "Stephen, from what I hear, the bank robbers were armed. And there were two of them. In my opinion, things could have ended worse than they did had you been in the building with her." His voice cracked with sudden emotion. "You wouldn't have won against two men and a gun."

A long, thoughtful silence passed before Stephen glanced at Jacob and smiled a little. "You're right. But Jake?"

"Jah?"

"When I think of them yanking her delicate arms and pulling that dirty cloth over her beautiful face. . ." He paused. "It makes me crazy."

Jacob nodded. "I understand. But accept what happened and be grateful that your Serenity is alive and well."

"My Serenity?"

Jacob chuckled. "Jah. And don't try to tell me otherwise."

Stephen chuckled. "Okay, you know me too well. But something else troubles me."

Jacob lifted a curious brow while snapping a group of weeds. "What?"

Jacob listened as his brother poured out his love for Serenity, how he'd expressed it, and how she'd changed the subject as soon as he'd brought up continuing his heritage.

Several moments passed while Jacob absorbed his brother's serious, heartfelt confession. While they walked, he realized that Stephen was going through much more than he'd suspected. As he considered Stephen's concerns, Jacob couldn't help but be surprised. All Amish women yearned for kinder.

"So? What do you think?" Stephen's voice prompted him to turn.

After pondering the question, Jake tried to encourage Stephen. "Maybe you put a little too much on her, Steve. I get where you're coming from. But think about what you told her. She's obviously not recovered from what happened. She's a strong woman, but maybe you should have given her more time to regroup before you talked about having a family. It might be too much to have on her plate right now."

Stephen blew out a deep breath before he darted Jake a half smile. "As usual, you're right."

Jacob warmed inside. "I'm sure Serenity must reciprocate your feelings. I've witnessed how she looks at you when you help her from the buggy."

Strong curiosity edged Stephen's voice. "How does she look at me, Jake?"

Jacob thought a moment. "Well it kind of reminds me of how Trini looks at me."

"Are you sure you're not just trying to make me feel gut?"

"You know me better than that. Now I'm gonna shoot straight, Stephen."

Stephen chuckled. "You always do."

"I know from experience that timing plays an important role in relationships. When Trini moved out of state, I thought it was over for us. But it wasn't. And I'm sure things aren't over between you and Serenity. But Steve—"

"Jah?"

"Give her time to absorb what happened. She has to heal, and you can help her. Then, when she's ready to move on, you can talk to her again about your plans."

The two stopped and regarded each other with what Jacob was sure was mutual respect and understanding. "Then we can plan another Amish wedding."

# CHAPTER FIVE

In the back seat of a neighbor's SUV, Serenity glanced at Trini as they proceeded east on Route 36 to the Douglas County Jail in Tuscola. She knew the road by heart. Angel had pulled her buggy on this route more times than she could count. But today she barely saw the homes on either side of the road.

Her thoughts were stuck on the men in her barn: Why had they attacked her? Were they really the same men who'd robbed the bank? If they weren't, what could she do? And would she soon recognize the throaty-sounding voice?

While the engine purred, she considered her two conversations with the nice woman who had helped her to arrange this opportunity to identify one of her attackers. She'd asked Serenity if she was sure she wanted to do this and had suggested that maybe she should give herself a little more time. But Serenity had replied, "This has to be done. And there's no good time to do it."

This wasn't merely an impromptu visit. From what Serenity had been told, it had taken quite a bit of planning. For one thing, visiting hours were limited. Second, she would see a lineup with cops as some of the men, but they would not be able to view her or talk to her. Of course she wouldn't be able to identify them by their looks because she hadn't seen them. But they would be asked to state their names, and it was then that she would hear their voices. In Serenity's mind, there was no doubt that a short time from now, she would be certain that at least one man who'd attacked her was—or wasn't—in the Douglas County Jail. Third, the lineup would be done in a secure area. It was a small facility where such lineups happened, and who would be involved was decided on a case-by-case basis. Now that Serenity was privy to today's protocol, everything she'd learned made sense.

She looked down at her hands. They shook. So did her arms. She interlaced her fingers and closed her eyes to pray in silence. *Gott, please help me do this. I pray that the men who harmed me are truly behind bars. Please let me recognize the throaty voice so I can be at peace and know that I can't be harmed again. That my community will be safe from harm.*

She opened her eyes and breathed in slowly, straightening on the leather cushion and crossing her legs at the knees. Next to her, as if reading her thoughts, Trini spoke in a soft, reassuring tone and laid a hand gently on Serenity's arm. "It's okay. I'm with you. We will get through this."

"Abby can't wait to find out what happened. I wish that she wasn't under the weather today, but I'm also kind of glad she's not with us." Serenity lowered her voice. "It's in her best interest because she's so emotional."

Trini nodded. "Agreed."

When Trini squeezed her hand, Serenity smiled in relief. Trini slowly withdrew her fingers and inched toward her. Today Serenity hoped for answers. At the same time, she was fully aware that she might not get them. She whispered, "I just want closure." After a slight hesitation, she went on. "But what if I don't get it?"

For long moments, Trini pressed her lips in a straight line. When she finally spoke, she did so in a motherly tone that Serenity knew all too well. It was the way Trini talked whenever she tried to console or convince. And Serenity was sure that right now Trini was trying to accomplish both.

"There are no guarantees. In life there never are. But we'll try to get the truth. At least today we'll know whether or not the men in jail harmed you. That's our first step. We'll go from there." She released a long sigh before smiling.

Serenity nodded.

Trini leaned closer. "Serenity, we'll do what we can. But realize that so much of this is out of our control. Remember that."

"Jah. But I can't help but wonder what closure would feel like. Not only for me." As the turn signal clicked and the vehicle slowed, she lifted her chin a notch. "But for everyone so that people won't be fearful." She sighed before lifting her palms in a helpless gesture. "I never knew how gut we had it in our little town."

The driver's voice cut their conversation short. "Ladies, we're almost there."

Both Serenity and Trini leaned to look out their windows.

"I'll drop you off in front, then park. And no hurry. Good luck."

The car's engine continued to purr as the vehicle stopped in front of a redbrick building. Two aisles of parking spaces held only three vehicles. As the driver turned the radio dial, Serenity squared her shoulders. *I'll put on a brave front. Maybe if I act confident, I'll feel it.*

She got out and closed her door. Then Trini's door slammed shut. She walked in front of the vehicle to join Serenity on the other side. Together they proceeded to the entrance. To their left was a memorial dedication to a fallen officer.

Serenity opened one of the glass doors and motioned for Trini to step inside first. Serenity followed her. They stopped as the door closed behind them and looked around. To the right were two restrooms. Between them was an ATM. In front, two workers behind separate glass partitions busied themselves.

Serenity glimpsed the woman who appeared to do paperwork on the other side of the first window. Trini lifted her chin and squared her shoulders. "We're doing the right thing," she said.

Serenity was quick to catch the hopeful lift in her voice.

She nodded. "Jah."

Before either stepped forward, Trini's tone took on a more assured and relaxed pitch. "It's kind of a relief to finally be here."

Serenity breathed in and squeezed Trini's hand. "I love you."

"I love you too."

After they glanced at each other with what seemed to be a mutual hope for answers, Serenity approached the nearest window. On the opposite side, a woman stepped forward and opened the small partition. "Can I help you?"

Serenity explained the reason for her visit.

The woman nodded. "Of course. Officer Dunn is expecting you." After checking Serenity's identification, the woman motioned to the row of seats between her and the entrance. "Please. Have a seat, and he'll be with you in a moment."

"Thank you."

Serenity sat down. Beside her, Trini made herself comfortable. The door on their left opened, and a fit-looking uniformed male introduced himself.

His gaze was sympathetic as he looked down at Trini, then Serenity. "I'm real sorry for what happened to you, Ms. Miller."

"Thank you," Serenity replied. Then she lifted her chin with newfound confidence. "I hope I'll recognize the voice of one of my attackers."

"We hope so too. Here's what will happen. First, I'll take you into a secured area to what we call the deputy room. Over there, all you have to do is sit. I'll be with you as they bring in the first lineup."

"The first?" Serenity interrupted. "Oh. You mean there are two?"

He nodded. "Yes. We're keeping the two men apart. In fact, they're in different wings of the jail."

"So each of them will be in a separate lineup?"

He nodded. "The other men are officers dressed in street clothes."

Serenity bit her lip nervously. She'd had to summon all her courage to do this even once. She was dismayed to find out she'd have to do it twice.

Seeming to sense her discomfort, the officer briefly laid a hand on Serenity's shoulder and said, "Rest assured, your safety is our highest priority. The men won't be able to see you. You'll watch and listen to them on a video screen."

Serenity nodded. That didn't sound so bad. She glanced at Trini. "Would you mind if my friend comes back with me?"

"We think it's best if you do this alone. It won't take long." He motioned to Trini. "Please. If you don't mind waiting. . ."

Trini shook her head. "Of course not."

He looked directly at Serenity. "Both men have agreed to do this without a public defender present. And in Illinois, there's no bail, so they'll have to wait for a judge before we'll know what will happen next. Probably today or tomorrow. At that time, the judge will determine whether the guys will be held or if they'll be released from custody with a notice to appear in court."

Serenity's breath stuck in her throat. "I didn't realize that they could be released so soon."

The officer lifted his palms to the ceiling and smiled a little. "It's all in the judge's hands."

He proceeded to the entrance, where he stopped to press in a code. After a click, he opened the door and held it for Serenity. As she followed him, her pulse sprinted. She breathed in to compose herself. To stay calm.

Inside the room, she tried to slow the rapid rising and falling of her chest as the officer motioned to a simple wooden chair. She sat down and rested her hands on her lap. He looked at her and nodded. She took in the video screen in the front of the room and watched as four men appeared and stood in a line.

She listened as a different officer spoke. "Number one. Please step forward." The man was asked to state his name. He did so. Serenity didn't recognize the voice. The officer went on in the same fashion. "Number two. Please step forward." He stated his name. So did number three. And number four.

Serenity's heart pumped harder when the men walked off the screen in single file. A short time lapsed before a second lineup appeared. She clenched her palms in her lap. She sat still and very straight. Her lungs tried to pump air while the same procedure took place. She didn't recognize the voices of number one, number two, or number three. She breathed in and listened to the officer's low voice. "Will number four please step forward?"

She pressed her lips together. And listened. The man spoke. And Serenity had her answer.

This wasn't over. Stephen considered his recent conversation with Jacob and smiled a little. Despite the uncertainties, he was sure of one thing: he wanted Serenity as his wife. Although he agreed with Jake that there was too much on her plate right now to broach the subject of marriage or anything close, Stephen was certain that something he'd said had changed her demeanor. It was up to him to make things right.

His focus was on Serenity's visit to the jail and what she'd found out. He breathed in and finished his coffee. He recalled what she'd told him about the calla lily and smiled. Then his thoughts returned to the dilemma. Word had traveled fast that the town florist and the area's famous quilter had headed to the Douglas County Jail in Tuscola. But what had happened? There was only one way to learn about yesterday. And that was to ask Serenity.

He stepped outside his late aendi's home. Today he would take the shortcut to Serenity's house. He made his way to the front yard and proceeded to the blacktop. As he glanced at the rising sun, he believed that many surprises would be revealed before the sun reached its noon position and that they would change the course of numerous lives.

*It's funny, but the sun is like the kitchen timer Mamm used when baking. In a sense, the sun schedules everything a person does in a single morning. Really, in a single day.*

As he glanced at the mixture of light orange and blue sky, an appreciative breath escaped him. He pressed his hands on his hips and continued taking in Gott's wonder. From a very young age, Stephen's belief in Gott's existence had been reinforced by the miraculous beauty of sunrises and sunsets. Each time he'd taken in these miracles, something inside him expelled a certain energy that he was sure could come only from his Creator.

In the far distance, he glimpsed an SUV passing a green tractor on the narrow blacktop. He also viewed a horse being hitched to a black buggy at a neighbor's place. At another home, an Amazon Prime delivery truck made a stop, and the driver walked to the door with a box.

Quick steps took him toward Serenity's home, where he made his way to the side door and knocked. As he waited, fear reared its ugly head as he recalled the day she hadn't answered.

The door opened. When he saw her, he sighed with relief.

"Stephen, gut mariye." She motioned him to her table. "Would you care for a cup of herbal tea?"

He breathed in the interesting scent and shook his head. "No. But thanks for the offer."

As always, there was a joyful lift in her voice. But he sensed that something was wrong. He sat down on an oak chair at the table. "Please. Don't let me interrupt you."

"You never interrupt me, Stephen."

Her voice lacked its usual enthusiasm. *I thought she'd jump right in and tell me about her visit to the Tuscola jail. Maybe she doesn't want to talk about it. I need to ask her. I have to know if she's still in danger.*

He cleared his throat. "Serenity, I thought about you all day yesterday," he said softly, trying to keep his tone casual. "I hope you were able to identify the voice that belonged to one of the men."

She didn't respond. For some reason, she obviously didn't want to discuss the jail visit.

Finally, he firmed his voice. "I've prayed that the men who attacked you are behind bars."

She breathed in and sat opposite him. After setting her mug on a coaster, she lifted her chin and looked directly into his eyes. "Stephen, the men in jail didn't tie me up."

Stephen's heart sank. His words stumbled out of his mouth. "They didn't?"

She gave a quick shake of her head. "No. Yesterday I listened to everyone in two different lineups. During the drive to Tuscola, I prayed hard for confirmation. Something to put me at peace once and for all. More than anything, I longed for this thing to be behind me."

She threw up her hands. "Not just for me but for the entire community." She stopped. And the corners of her lips dropped.

As they looked at each other in silence, he noted the desperation in her eyes. She was afraid, but she was attempting to present a brave facade.

She took a drink and returned her mug to the coaster. When she met his curious gaze, he glimpsed defeat in her expression. "Stephen, I would have recognized that throaty voice." She pressed her lips together doubtfully before offering a small shrug of her shoulders. "The men in the lineups didn't attack me."

Stephen stiffened, absorbing the significance of her explanation. His shoulders froze in place. So did his jaw. And he wasn't sure what to say. *I need to be careful with my words. I can't tell her everything will be okay, because it might not. At the same time, I can't stress how serious the situation is. I can't induce more worry than she already has.*

To his relief, she began to tell him everything that had happened from the ride to jail to the moment the last man in the second lineup had said his name.

A long silence followed as the sound of the battery-powered wall clock ticked to an even beat. She looked at him with the most innocent, hopeful, yet desperate expression he'd ever seen. "Stephen, I've never been in such a dire situation. There's so much at stake here. For one, I don't want the whole town to worry. Secondly, I don't want you to feel you have to watch over me every second of the day."

She shook her head. "This isn't over. I've got to find them and make sure they're in a place where they can't hurt me—or anyone else—again." After a lengthy, thoughtful pause, she lowered the pitch of her voice. "But I've been wracking my brain for how to start looking for them. And I have no idea where to begin."

*I've got to protect her. But she asks a legitimate question. How do we find the men if the only identifiable trait is the voice?* Stephen prayed that the fingerprints would render a match.

Then he had an answer. He tried a calm tone to help her relax a little. "You can't find these men on your own, Serenity."

When she glanced at him and opened her mouth, he stopped her by raising his hand. "We need to talk to the police. This time at least we know that the men who harmed you are on the loose.

Thank goodness for the authorities. They're the professionals, and they have access to leads that we don't. There must be a backup plan to find them."

"I have no idea what they were doing in my barn. And there's nothing of great monetary value inside my house or in my barn. So. . . If they weren't hiding after the robbery, why did they come here? And will they come back?"

Stephen wondered the same thing. "I don't know," he said simply. "But they might."

Serenity laid her palms flat on the table and leaned forward. "You're right. We need to have a more serious talk with the police."

It was bonding time with her two besties. That evening as Trini and Abby chitchatted, Serenity's thoughts floated back to the morning's conversation with Stephen and the meeting afterward with the authorities.

In Serenity's kitchen, the aroma of fresh garden vegetables filled the small area where the three cooked and canned. Constant, light clicking sounds made a soft, uneven beat as they broke off the green beans' blossom ends and snapped them in half.

Serenity's heart felt lighter than it had since her attack. Two things could cheer her despite any problem—her besties and fresh veggies. But her relationship with Stephen kept breaking into her thoughts. Not because she didn't like him but because she liked him too much.

As she scooped a pile of bean ends and emptied them into her garbage, she tried to tell herself that everything was and would be okay.

*Stephen is very concerned about me. His interest in my safety reminds me of when Daed worries about Mamm.* The corners of Serenity's lips tugged upward. *Daed is always checking to make sure she's okay. And it's really sweet. But Stephen's interest in me makes me uncomfortable. I like him—I do. Very much. But he's not privy to everything about me, and he never will be. Still, I need him.*

She pulled another bag of green beans from her porch and transported the vegetables to the countertop. Her friends were in deep conversation about Gabriel, of course, while Serenity filled a bowl with tap water.

Soon the loud, uneven popping of lids sealing on the tomato jars began to override the light snapping sound of the beans. The faster the pops and snaps came, the more Abby talked about her frustration with Gabriel. Serenity listened with interest as Trini tried to explain to Abby that men in their church didn't seem to go for overzealous women. Abby was unique and special, and part of her uniqueness was her determined personality. But sometimes in life, you had to read others, and Gabriel seemingly preferred more low-key people.

Serenity silently agreed. Now if only Trini could make Abby understand. The lively conversation prompted Serenity's lips to curve into an amused grin. It was a welcome diversion. *It's nice to have something on my mind other than men attacking me and not having a clue how to find them.*

Serenity continued washing the beans in front of her before transferring them to dry paper towels. She'd get back to them after she started another pot of tomatoes. She placed a paper towel over the green veggies to absorb the excess water. Then she moved to another area of her countertop to fill a large bowl with tomatoes.

She stepped back to the sink to clean them. Then she placed them on a wooden cutting board before dumping the clean tomatoes into a pot of hot water on the stove. From experience, she knew they needed to boil only a few minutes. While she waited, she readied a bowl of ice water. The cubes popped as they broke free from the tray.

Abby told them how Gabriel Lantz had approached her after church and had initiated a conversation about the welcome quilt she'd gifted the brothers. "He said that it looked gut on one of the living-room walls," she gushed with enthusiasm.

"I knew it!" Trini squealed in response. "I noticed a spark in Gabriel's eyes while you and Gabe were talking. In my opinion, you shouldn't give up."

As they went back and forth on why or why not the oldest Lantz brother would eventually court and then marry Abby, Serenity pulled a small strainer from a hook on the wall and began to retrieve each tomato, one by one, and transfer them to her bowl of ice water, where they would cool before she removed their skins.

The more she considered Stephen's role as her vigilant protector, the more an odd combination of deep appreciation and fear fought inside her. He'd already confessed his feelings to her and his vision of a future together.

As she began removing the skins from the tomatoes and transferring the peeled vegetables to another bowl, she frowned. *It's not Stephen's fault. Nor is it mine. What happened in my barn last week has greatly impacted his need to take care of me and protect me. Of course I'm grateful. After all, the man rescued me. If not for Stephen finding me, I could have been tied up in my barn for a long, long time.*

*Stephen seems much more sensitive than other single men in our church. Maybe that's because his daed left him and his family when Stephen was a mere toddler. I'm sure that awful incident plays a huge role in what he does and how he perceives things. He has a sensitive side. A nurturing side. It's probably why he was once a volunteer fireman. He yearns to protect everyone because he wasn't able to protect his mother and his brothers when his daed left his family. There seems to be a fire within him to nurture and rescue.*

She smiled a little. Because he was wonderful. And his attributes were exceptional traits, really. It's just that there was no way she could ever marry. She frowned.

"Caught you!" Abby's excited voice startled her before sparking laughter between the three. Serenity wasn't sure why she laughed too.

She turned toward Abby, put a firm hand on her hip, and lifted her chin defensively. "And just what did you catch me doing?"

Abby's tone lowered a notch and became more serious. "You were thinking about Stephen and how he saved your life." Abby lifted a challenging brow. "Am I right?"

Trini chimed in while she snapped two green beans at once. "Serenity, it's okay. In fact, it's like those stories the Englisch read to their kids about the handsome prince who rides through town on his horse and saves a damsel in distress."

Serenity couldn't stop her jaw from dropping. "It is?"

Two sets of curious eyes landed on Serenity until she finally shrugged and joined in the laughter. A long silence followed while the three women continued their tasks. In the background, the soft, light whirring of the large battery-powered fan made for a peaceful ambiance. Serenity wasn't sure why she was so happy and at ease.

As a cricket chirped, Serenity continued with the tomatoes to the right of the sink. Trini broke the silence. "Serenity, I'm surprised that you're not talking more about Stephen. Word has it that you two are practically courting."

"Has he asked to court you?" Abby's voice was edged with curiosity.

Serenity wiped her hands with a dry towel and pressed her palms against her apron while she responded with a long, drawn-out no.

Trini's expression conveyed doubt while Abby's face wore pure disappointment. Abby spoke in a low, firm tone. "Serenity, Stephen's a wonderful man. Any parent in our church would be happy to have him as a son-in-law." She paused to scoop a handful of stemmed beans and transfer them to a large bowl of water.

"Earth to Serenity!" Abby's voice pulled Serenity back to reality. "You haven't heard a word we've said, have you?"

Serenity sighed and met Abby's gaze before her eyes drifted to Trini's concerned expression.

"I'm sorry."

Trini used a sympathetic combination of compassion and concern while she stepped to Serenity and extended a hand to her arm. "Here. Please sit down. You've been through a lot, and I think the three of us need to have another serious conversation.

*There's a lot on my mind—that's for sure. Only it's not what they think it is.* But maybe a conversation with her two besties would help her.

Trini pulled out a chair, motioned to the seat, and waited for Serenity to sit. On the other side of the table, Trini and Abby made themselves comfortable. As an uncertain silence loomed between them, Serenity forced herself to regain the positivity she routinely practiced. She sat up a little straighter, squared her shoulders, and forced a smile.

Abby played with a faux daisy in the table arrangement. After she placed her hands in her lap, she offered her attention. "Serenity, I feel your pain. Really, I do. Trini told me all about the jail visit, and I'm disappointed that you couldn't identify the voice." She lowered her voice to a more confidential tone. Serenity wasn't sure why. No one was in the room except the three of them. Abby lifted her palms in a helpless gesture and shook her head. "I wish I knew what to do."

Trini leaned forward and rested her elbows on the table. Her expression was a fierce combination of doubt and determination as she fidgeted with her fingers. "Serenity, since we went to Tuscola, I've given this situation quite a bit of thought, and the only way to be at ease again is if your attackers are caught." After a slight hesitation, she repeated the gesture Abby had made with her hands. "How do we find out who they are?"

Abby scooted her chair closer to the table. The legs moving across the wood floor made a light squeaking noise. "We've got to do something. Right away. But what?"

While Serenity agreed with everything both friends had said, she didn't know how to respond. She'd thought plenty about the dire situation. And despite her efforts, she'd come up with nothing to solve it. "Maybe if we put our heads together, we can figure out how to find these men. At the very least, I wish I knew what they were up to in my barn. I mean, the police's theory about them hiding on my property after robbing the bank doesn't hold water now."

Trini's words came out quickly. "There has to be a way to find them. They're a threat to all of us, and there's no way to predict if or when they'll strike again."

Serenity smiled a little. "I love both of you." She pointed to her chest and then to each of them. "And my heart breaks because I know how much you want to help. But"—she lifted her palms in a helpless gesture before releasing a defeated breath—"I've lost plenty of sleep over what happened. And to be honest, I'm no longer worried."

Trini and Abby turned toward each other to share a surprised glance before they faced Serenity. She took in their expressions of shock and distress.

Trini rested her arms on the oak tabletop. "Serenity, one of the reasons I've always looked up to you is because of your calmness. You're the most at-ease person I've ever met."

She wasn't sure what to say. Trini was partially correct. Serenity was at peace with most everything. Still, the secret that weighed so heavily on her shoulders would remain just that, even though she longed to share it with these two women.

Frustration filled Abby's voice as she asked, "Don't the police have any leads?"

Trini snapped her fingers before chiming in. "What about fingerprints?"

The corners of Serenity's lips dropped a notch in disappointment. "Unfortunately, the barn guys covered their tracks." She sighed. "The only full prints were mine and Stephen's. Some partial prints couldn't be identified."

Abby's tone turned defensive. "They must have left fingerprints."

Serenity shook her head. "Not if they wore gloves. Or if the prints were wiped down."

Trini parted her lips in awe. "Seriously?"

Serenity nodded. "I know. Stephen and I just found that out today." She added, "We went to the police again."

Trini frowned. "That's bad news if we don't have a plan of action." After looking down at the table, she lifted her chin and glanced at Abby before locking gazes with Serenity. "Because it means that our attackers were apparently smart enough to get away with what they did."

Serenity tried to keep the subject upbeat. It was the only way to move on. "The good news is that I can recognize his voice." She added softly, "If I hear it again."

"Did he ever say your name?" Trini pressed.

Serenity paused to consider the question. "I'm not sure. . . Remember, my mind was focused on escaping." After a slight pause, she shrugged. "Now that I've talked with the police again, I know they don't have anything to go on. They still have no idea why I was attacked or why the men were in my barn."

Trini narrowed her brows. "It's weird. Because your home wasn't broken into. At least it didn't appear to have been."

"And there's definitely nothing of value to steal in my barn." Smiling, she added in an affectionate voice, "Unless you want Angel."

Abby's lips curved in amusement. "And I doubt anyone wants a horse that bites."

All three laughed. Trini looked at Abby before she turned to Serenity.

"You know what I think?" Serenity asked as two pairs of eyes stared at her. "I believe some things only Gott knows. Maybe the police will get a viable lead, but until then, we've got to move on with our lives. Right now, there's absolutely no way to find out the identity of the guys. That is, unless someone knows and they aren't talking."

Abby grinned. "Serenity, thank goodness that you have an angel looking after you."

Trini was quick to agree. Her gaze met Serenity's while Abby whispered, "And I'm not talking about your horse. I'm talking about Stephen Lantz."

# CHAPTER SIX

There was no better place on earth to think. It was Stephen's first fishing trip since having moved to Central Illinois. Jacob had planted the idea when he'd invited him. After declining, Stephen had decided that fishing might be the very activity that could help him sort things out.

As he rowed his boat out to the deep part of the lake behind the woods that separated his late aendi's home and Serenity's house, he breathed in the fresh air and smiled with satisfaction. Above, the full sun hit his face. The deep blue of the sky surrounding the large orange ball was almost as beautiful as Serenity's eyes.

But it was Gott's artwork. He'd made it. And no one in the world could match it. As the beat of his heart picked up to a healthy speed, Stephen pressed his lips together in a thoughtful line. A woodsy scent reached his boat. He even smelled a touch of pine. To the side of him, a fish jumped and made a light splash when it landed.

Ever since he was a kid, once he'd accepted that he no longer had a father, fishing had been Stephen's outlet for maintaining a peaceful mental attitude. And now he needed it to help him garner a fresh view on everything. Two main issues nagged at him. The first was that the men in jail weren't the two who'd attacked Serenity, and right now, the police had nothing to go on. The second was that he wished he was privy to Serenity's thoughts. Since he'd brought up marrying her, he was certain he'd hit a pothole. Something told him that Serenity was not planning her future with him. His heart sank a notch.

He quickly regrouped. *I'm out here to think. And I need a positive, open mind.* As he continued to move the small boat out to deeper water, he recalled something his late aendi used to tell him and his brothers: some problems in life couldn't be fixed, but some could.

A breeze caressed his face. He wished Jacob were with him. But Trini had needed his help for something having to do with her shop. Stephen's lips curled into a smile. Something about being out on the water alone and the positive outlook it sparked prompted him to accept what had happened to his family many years ago.

*I'll never forget trying to console my mamm. Even after Daed had been gone for several years, I still caught her crying in bed at night. And the ache I feel for her pain has stayed with me all of this time. After years and years of prayers, at least I've learned to accept that while I was always there for my dear mother, I was a child, so there wasn't much I could do. But even though I'm a man now, the moment I saw Serenity tied and gagged, that very same helplessness rushed back into my heart. Only the pain I endure is worse than ever since I could have stopped what happened to the woman I love and yearn to marry. . .if only I had been there.*

Water droplets from an oar splashed him in the face, reminding him of a passage in chapter 16 of the book of John he had learned by heart: "*I have said these things to you, that in me you may have peace. In the world you will have tribulation. But take heart; I have overcome the world.*"

He smiled a little and said a silent prayer of gratitude for all he had. Then he stopped rowing where the water was the darkest. He'd always had good instincts on where to fish. And he knew to look for algae or any kind of plants because fish needed to eat.

He baited his hook and, with one swift motion, cast his line into the lake. He'd heard that there was a good crop of walleye. *My aendi is no longer here to cook it. Mamm's too far away. Maybe Serenity will fry it in a special recipe of herbs, and we can share a dinner. That will give me an excuse to be with her.*

He propped his pole inside the boat and baited another hook. After he threw the second line on the opposite side of his rowboat, he sighed with satisfaction. It felt gut to fish. There was just something about it that benefited the soul. And right now, that's what he very much needed.

But there was more on his mind than the evil at Serenity's barn. Before Serenity, he'd never been romantically interested in a woman, but something about her was very different than any other women in their church. Or in his Lancaster group. She was unique in every way. He admired how she appreciated all kinds of plants. Even weeds.

Her great respect for nature and her positive outlook on life claimed his full admiration. But there was more to his fascination than that.

When he was with her, he yearned to protect her and take care of her. The weird thing was that she took care of him too. She might not even be aware of it, but her oftentimes unique opinion of things and the warm way she offered it provided Stephen with newfound energy. The desire to be a better person.

At the same time, he was aware that if she was afraid to have a relationship with him or if she just didn't want one, he needed to find out why so he could try to change her mind. Before he approached her again with his longing for a forever relationship, it was important to get a woman's perspective. That definitely ruled out his brothers. Besides, they were busy with other things.

Aendi Margaret could help him—that is, if she were here. *But she's not.* Whomever he discussed his dilemma with must be someone who would maintain his confidentiality. As something on the end of his fishing line started to pull, he stood. But as he did so, he couldn't stop trying to think of the right person to confide in. Who could it be?

Later that day, Serenity arranged her stack of magazines in a neat pile. Customers enjoyed flipping through the various issues while they waited for their arrangements.

On top was the *Good Samaritan*, a well-known, well-respected Christian magazine. Most of her Amish friends subscribed to this particular Christian periodical for its advice column. Routinely, Serenity took in and thought about the numerous questions that were addressed to a woman named Charlotte. Because the responses were scripture based, Serenity had used this column for years to help deal with her own issues. In fact, she knew some of the questions and answers by heart.

She took one last glimpse at the recent issue before stepping to the door, turning off the lights, and closing up the Pink Petal. As the lock clicked into place, she glanced down the street to see if Abby's Alterations and the Quilt Room were still open.

After confirming that the blinds inside both of her friends' shops were closed, she stopped to look both ways before crossing the street. As she made her way to her Angel and buggy, a voice made her turn.

To her surprise, it was Stephen. He offered a friendly wave and stepped quickly to meet her. "Stephen, it's gut to see you."

"Likewise, Serenity. Uh, I was wondering if you would mind frying the pike I caught today. There's enough for two, and I thought it would be nice to have dinner with you."

Her breath caught in her throat before she responded, but not just because the fish dinner sounded enticing. This afternoon, as he stood across the road from where she worked, Stephen looked taller and more muscular than usual. His brown eyes sparkled with a sweet blend of hope and excitement. She looked up to him, and for some reason, today she sensed a sweet vulnerability about him. His expression was nothing less than endearing.

"Of course! At your house or mine?" she asked with genuine enthusiasm.

"If it's okay, could we fix them at your place?"

Serenity paused to greet Angel with an affectionate pat on the side of his face. "Hey, you ready to take me home?"

A neigh and a lift of his long nose were the answers.

Serenity turned to Stephen. "Would you like a ride to my place?"

He waved a hand in dismissal. "No, but thanks for the offer. I was in town to do errands. If it's okay, I'll be at your house in about forty minutes, after I drop off my groceries."

"I'll look forward to it."

Something was wrong. After their dinner, Stephen stood with his hands deep in his trouser pockets and looked out at the acres and acres of farmland that had been left to him and his brothers by their loving aendi Margaret. Dinner with Serenity had been nice. But he'd been quick to note how she'd been careful to talk about general things. He frowned.

The healthy crop of soybeans that loomed in front of him seemed to go on forever. Strangely, this evening's breeze meeting his face seemed more like a message from heaven, assuring him that things would be all right. To keep his faith that Serenity was okay, that whoever had harmed her would eventually be caught, and that things would once again normalize.

He stretched his arms and returned his hands to his pockets. *Is Gott sending me a message?* He looked up at the sky and pondered the question that tugged at him. As crickets chirped and cicadas made their usual sounds, he narrowed his brows. *It sure feels like it.*

As his gaze lingered on the healthy crop and the large oaks in their yard that his aendi had loved, he glimpsed a milkweed between the rows in front of him. It stuck out like a sore thumb among the clean rows. The weed lifted his spirits, and an amused smile tugged at the corners of his lips until he couldn't stop a chuckle that escaped him.

*I'm focusing too long on something so irrelevant in life, but that's okay. It's a nice distraction.*

Walking beans was a simple job. There was no perfect science behind it. It wasn't difficult to miss a weed here and there. For one thing, sunlight on the leaves could easily make weeds invisible. Depending on how the sun landed on the beans, it could be difficult to differentiate the weeds from the actual crops. No matter how good an eye a farmer had, there was no way to catch every single weed. When he and Jake had walked the beans, this particular weed had been in Jake's row.

*I can't wait to tease Jacob next time I see him. I'm happy that he's married, but at the same time, I miss him. Especially drinking* kaffi *with him every morning.*

He looked again at the weed in Jake's row and chuckled. A second later, however, the corners of his lips dropped into an uncertain frown as an eerie chill swept up Stephen's spine and landed behind his neck. He shook his shoulders to try to rid himself of the uncomfortable sensation.

*Why am I suddenly feeling so uncertain? I'm sure it has to do with what happened to Serenity and how awful it was. The incident revived my appreciation for life. At the same time, it made me realize that in many ways, we've been living in a relatively safe bubble in this part of the country. In some parts of the world, things like this happen every single day. Incidents much worse, even.*

He closed his eyes a moment, breathed in, and looked out again. He lifted his chin a notch in forced determination as he swatted away a mosquito. As he recalled last Sunday's sermon, he parted his lips in awe.

The words of that meaningful message were just what he needed right now. They reminded him that his Gott was the same Gott of Daniel. The Gott of Moses and Joshua. The Gott of Noah. The Gott of David. These men had lived through trials much more severe and dangerous than finding the men who'd attacked Serenity. Yet their courage and tenacity and faith had made them biblical heroes. "*Be strong and courageous.*" Stephen remembered the words from Joshua 1:9 that the bishop had quoted. "*The LORD your God is with you wherever you go.*"

"*Talk to Gott,*" the bishop had encouraged them. "*He's the best problem solver.*" Recalling Scripture and the words of the sermon revived Stephen's spirit.

He blinked when tears stung his eyes. *No matter what happens in this world, my Creator is in charge. And He is my protector. No matter how hard I try, I can't save Serenity from what has already happened. But I can protect her in the future. I can play a role in finding the men who harmed her and make sure they are behind bars, where they belong.*

During Aendi Margaret's lifetime, whenever he'd gone to her with issues that had bothered him, she'd consoled him with her unique Gott-given logic. As she had done so, she'd reminded him of how very special he was in the eyes of Gott.

At that moment, he stiffened. He suddenly realized the root of the uncomfortable stirring inside him. Nervous tension made him rock on the toes of his boots. He stared at the beans as all the various hues of green morphed into a solid shade.

*It isn't just that Serenity was harmed. I miss my aendi. Serenity's tragedy reignited my insecurities from when I lost my daed.* During those times, Aendi Margaret had consoled him. Of course Mamm would have helped him through his grief, but instinctively, he'd known not to mention his agony to her because he hadn't wanted her to feel responsible in any way for what had happened. The last thing he'd wanted was to make Mamm feel worse than she already did.

Stephen blew out a long breath and pressed his lips together in a firm line. *I miss my aendi. Terribly. Since she died more than a year ago, I've never really had time to grieve for her.* And when Serenity's horrible attack occurred, his feelings of helplessness had returned with a vengeance. Only this time, the person who would know better than anyone what to say to him was gone.

*How can I heal from what happened to Serenity when I haven't yet recovered from suddenly and unexpectedly losing my aendi? Gott listens to my prayers. I know He does. But it might take a while to get through this because I've never fully recovered from what Daed did to Mamm and our family either. More than anything, I long to talk to my aendi. To hear her voice.*

When the *clomp-clomp* of a horse's hooves pulled him from his reverie, he turned and waved at Gabe. His brother returned the friendly gesture from his open buggy.

As Gabe's standardbred approached the back of the barn, Stephen knew there was definitely more gut in his life than bad. And in time, he'd deal with his issues. But he had an idea. He turned and started making his way toward the front porch.

*Aendi Margaret isn't here. But her room upstairs where she loved to spend time is. And since the three of us moved into the house, her room has remained untouched. We agreed that there was no rush to go through what had been her private space.*

But as Stephen took in the garden, he came to a decision. *Maybe it's time for me to step inside her room. It might offer me the solace I seek.* He was sure his aendi hadn't owned much, but there was a chance that Stephen would find something to ease his agony and uncertainty.

*I need a different perspective on things. Something to offer me a sense of peace. Will I find it in her room?*

The following morning, the sun was just appearing on the horizon when Serenity and Stephen met on the trail between their homes. Serenity took in the soft rustling of birds and other creatures moving in the trees and on the ground. The July temperature was a bit cooler than usual. To warm herself, Serenity had fastened the top snap of the heavy navy sweater that Abby had knit for her for last year's birthday. As she touched the soft fabric, she smiled a little at the thought of Abby making this just for her.

As they hiked in companionable silence, Serenity pressed her lips together thoughtfully while she stole glances at Stephen. She was quick to note that his jaw was set and the corners of his lips were a bit turned down. This morning, Stephen was unusually quiet. Since they'd said hello ten or so minutes ago, Serenity sensed that their typical friendly relationship was a bit strained. *What is wrong with him? Should I ask? What if I'm the reason for his change in behavior?*

The last thing she wanted was to waste one minute of this beautiful morning, so she decided to broach the subject. "Stephen?" she said in a soft voice.

"Jah?"

"I can tell that something's on your mind. You wanna talk about it?" Before he could respond, she went on. "I'm a gut listener. At the very least, I could be your sounding board."

He stopped a moment, turned to her, and cracked an appreciative smile. "I'm sorry, Serenity. You know me too well. But you're right. And unfortunately, my dilemma can't be fixed."

She lifted an encouraging brow. "Why don't you tell me about it?" She winked as she stepped forward. He stepped next to her.

"Oh, okay. I mean, I want you to know that I'm not complaining." Before she could reply, he went on. "Mamm and Aendi Margaret always told me to look at what I have and not what I don't have."

"That's gut advice." After a slight hesitation, she glanced at him with curiosity. "But what don't you have?"

She continued with a combination of encouragement and joy. "You've got a lot to be thankful for, Stephen. In fact, more than most people, I think." As he looked down at her to continue, she explained. "You have a wonderful family, the beautiful country home and Gott-given field behind it. You're healthy. You have food on your table." She lowered her voice to what was barely more than a whisper. "Most of all, your Creator looks over you and will protect you." She expelled a breath before she finished her train of thought. "Stephen, don't you see?"

A slight hesitation passed. "You've got everything in this world that's important."

He smiled. When his eyes misted, her heart strings tugged at her. The sheen in his eyes reminded her of morning dew on pumpkin blossoms. *His problem runs deep.*

He paused before whispering. "Gott gave me you. And I thank Him for that."

She swallowed. She wasn't sure what to say, so she didn't respond. Her shoulders stiffened. She lowered her gaze to the ground while she absorbed his sweet observation. Something inside her stirred with uneasiness until she forced a deep breath. She'd learned breathing techniques from a nurse when she'd been stricken with the Epstein-Barr virus.

"Serenity?"

She looked up and took in his serious expression.

"Gott certainly made you special."

As they studied each other, Serenity remained careful not to offer encouragement for a serious relationship between them. A few moments later, Stephen's hopeful expression changed to one of disappointment. There was a new uncertainty in his eyes too. It was as if he knew something but was afraid to tell her.

"Stephen, what on earth could be so bad that you'd let it steal even a minute of your happiness?"

They stopped while Stephen held back a large branch that obstructed the path. Serenity walked past, and he followed. But while she considered the beauty surrounding her, along with the pine-scented air and the thick foliage, Gott's blessings overrode everything else to her. And she would never view life differently.

They proceeded forward. To their right, a squirrel stood on its hind legs. To their left, they saw a bird's nest. Serenity couldn't help but weigh her relationship with Stephen, what he seemingly yearned for, and why she chose to remain platonic.

*A friend. That's what he is to me. He can never be more than that. Stephen has expressed his longing for a future with me. And why wouldn't he? He's a healthy Amish male. He's of courting age. Marrying age, even. I must be very careful to never lead him to believe our relationship can go to that level.*

"Serenity," he began, his voice low and serious. "I've always tried to protect the women in my life. Mamm, Aendi Margaret. . ." He moved to the side to avoid a dip in the trail. Serenity did the same. They rejoined each other side by side.

Serenity narrowed her brows. "Did your aendi need protection?"

He chuckled. "Probably not. But in my mind, it was my job to check on her and make sure she was okay." He shrugged. Then, to Serenity's relief, optimism edged the pitch of his voice. "Serenity, I let you down."

She started to retort, but he turned to her and stopped her with his hand. "Hear me out. They say that hindsight is twenty-twenty, and I fully agree. I'd planned to check on you before the storm hit. Then I got delayed, and I didn't make it over."

They slowed their steps where the path became uneven. Then they resumed their original quick pace. "Stephen, I truly appreciate your protective nature," she said with a smile. She caught her breath while she stepped over a large tree root that stuck up in the middle of the trail. "But dwelling on what happened is stealing precious time from your life." She gave a firm shake of her head before glancing at him. "You've got to move on. I have."

She noticed the sudden lines of doubt around his mouth. "Really?"

She forced a firm nod as she searched her mind for the right words. Obviously, Stephen was troubled, and the last thing she wanted was to make his concern worse.

"Jah. But I'm wondering if your worry really stems from something else."

"Aendi Margaret has been on my mind more than usual," he finally said. His voice cracked with emotion. "Serenity, ever since she died, I've been so busy with the farm and the legal paperwork and other stuff that comes with being her beneficiary, I haven't had time to grieve."

A long, thoughtful silence ensued. She didn't speak for fear of breaking his train of thought. Stephen didn't talk much about his concerns, and she wanted to ensure that she didn't stop him from opening up.

He shook his head while avoiding another dip. "Her death is finally hitting me." He sighed. "And it's a hard blow."

Compassion overwhelmed Serenity. His gentle tone caused her heart to flutter. She couldn't help it. *Stephen is such a loving and sensitive man.* Then she realized that he was awaiting her response.

"I respect your insight, Serenity. I'd appreciate any help you can offer."

She lifted her hands before dropping her arms to her sides. "I'm somewhat short on advice in matters like this, but just off the top of my head, I'd guess that what happened to me might've brought on hidden emotions on your part from losing your dear aendi." She softened her voice with sympathy. "Does that make sense?"

He didn't say anything. In silence they continued up their path until they reached a clearing. The sudden light made Serenity blink. She shaded her eyes with her hand until she adjusted to the brightness.

Then she sat on a flat stone. Stephen claimed the tree stump next to her. Serenity was grateful that, for once, she had time for a moment like this. Thanks to her new assistant, Serenity didn't need to rush to work. Besides, right now making sure her friend was okay took priority over everything else.

Stephen turned to face her enough so she could read his hopeful expression. *Maybe my insight helped a little. I hope so.*

Before he spoke, she glimpsed the creamy flecks in his irises. She didn't look away. The flecks seemed to add to his eyes' heavenly autumn brown shade that she could only identify as breathtaking.

The sun hit his face. When it did, she acknowledged again how very handsome he was. Of course, she had already been fully aware of that. But the way the light landed on his face catapulted him to a new level of gut-looking.

*Don't go there. It's wrong to look at someone's physical beauty. What counts is the heart. And that Gott's in it.*

Deliberately, she looked away. Because what she'd just experienced was wrong. It wasn't just the way she flushed in reaction to Stephen's manly attributes. What was truly out of line was the way her heart and the pulse in her wrist had reached a dangerously fast speed.

"Serenity, it's okay," he whispered with tenderness. "What you're feeling. . .I'm feeling it too. I connected with you the first moment we met."

She looked down at the ground to pretend an interest in a wildflower. She picked it and played with the small purple bloom. *I cannot go there. Change the subject.* Then an idea came to her.

"I think there's a way to work through the grief of losing your aendi."

After a brief moment of obvious disappointment, he lifted his chin a notch. "You do?"

She smiled at him, relieved that they were off the romantic path that had begun.

"I knew your aendi well. And everyone's aware of her love of nature." Serenity lifted a brow. "But I'm sure a lot of folks aren't privy to her strong love of beautiful flowers—in particular, gerbera daisies and purples irises. Many times she had vases full of them."

"Really?"

Serenity offered a nod. "Jah. She often said to me, when I helped her plant bulbs, that it was a miracle how you could put something in the ground one time and enjoy watching the bloom appear every year."

A pensive look filled his expression as he seemed to absorb what she'd just said. Then his lips lifted at the corners. "That's how she would look at it." After a few thoughtful moments, he went on. "I loved how my aendi viewed the simplest of things. It was always uplifting to hear her talk. I really miss that." He gazed off into the distance and smiled, almost as if he could see his aendi there, holding a bouquet of flowers. Then he peered back at Serenity. "What were you about to suggest?"

Serenity clenched her hands together before extending her arms in front of her. After she unlocked her fingers, she pressed her palms on the ground and sat up straighter. "I'd like to help you create a memorial for your aendi."

"A memorial?"

"Jah! Right by your front steps." An image formed in Serenity's mind. She waved a hand in front of her. "I can practically see it. I'll plant bulbs. In the fall, of course. And maybe Trini and Abby can contribute other perennials. And we'll have to have gerbera daisies." She straightened her shoulders as sudden enthusiasm swept through her. She snapped her fingers as she remembered something. "Abby bought a ceramic angel at a garage sale. I'm sure she would love to include it!"

When he didn't respond, she was sure she had to convince him to do the memorial. "Oh, Stephen, your aendi would love that! And we could make that area a place of reflection and beauty. I could find a small bench at an auction or garage sale. Margaret loved benches."

"She did?"

Serenity offered an excited nod. "Actually, a few months before she died, she'd mentioned getting one." Serenity lifted her shoulders in a dismissive shrug. "But she went to heaven before that happened."

He sighed. Then he smiled a little. "Already I'm feeling better."

"Really?"

"Jah. And I think this is a great idea for my aendi. But it will also help me. When can we start?"

No one had a clue that he'd attacked the Amish lady. Or why. At least, that's what he hoped. Little did they know that the floral shop owner had what he wanted. He scowled. Patience wasn't one of his virtues. When he and his buddy had attacked the woman, they'd really messed up his original plan. Their intent had been to go through her house.

Then the unexpected storm had hit, and they'd sought protection in her barn because the hail and the wind had made it impossible to make it the long distance to her home. Some distance away, he'd parked his vehicle, and they'd traversed the path through the woods that led to Ms. Miller's property. At the time, it had seemed the obvious route, since entering from the front would have made them clearly visible. He didn't know her personally, but he'd asked questions the times he'd been in her town, and eventually he'd formed a plan to retrieve what was rightfully his.

That afternoon last week, during the downpour, he and his buddy had taken shelter in the old barn at the end of the trail between the Pink Petal owner's house and where some brothers lived on a neighboring farm. Thanks to a talkative Amish lady at one of the local furniture stores, he'd gathered enough information to accomplish his agenda.

He grinned. Most Amish women he'd met didn't say a whole lot. But this one. . . He chuckled before running his hand over his unshaved chin. *She was a real live chatterbox.*

His thoughts drifted back to the infamous day when he'd taken his friend to help retrieve his wooden horse. Once in the barn, the hail had started. The sound had reminded him of extra loud Ping-Pong balls hitting a green table, back and forth.

The horse who lived there had made it crystal clear they weren't welcome. The animal had protested with the loudest whinnies and neighs he'd ever heard. It had even tried to move the bar of its stall with its nose. Thankfully, it hadn't succeeded.

Afraid of the animal's wild behavior and its obvious determination to boot him and his buddy out of the barn, they had found a spot to hide behind bales of straw until the weather would allow them to proceed to the house some distance away.

But the Miller woman—her name was Serenity, if he'd heard correctly—must have been in another area of the large structure because after they'd hidden, they'd heard her talking to the horse.

Maybe the storm had caught her off guard too. Whatever the case, fate hadn't been on his side that day. Everything had been okay until his buddy had coughed. The Miller woman must've heard the noise because from where they'd hidden, he had glimpsed her coming toward them.

If he could have, he would have turned around the moment the sky had darkened. His attempt to take back his prize had been all for nothing. But next time, his plan wouldn't fail. Fortunately, the Amish didn't use electronics, so there would be no video camera or security system to be concerned about.

Next time, he'd go alone. After all, his setback was because of the storm and his buddy. He nervously and excitedly drummed his fingers against the end table next to his recliner as he thought of his future.

He tensed while he considered the worst that could happen. He lit a cigarette and took a puff. As he blew out the smoke, he coughed. *The most challenging part of my agenda will be the moment I make it into Ms. Miller's home. And as far as the floral shop owner?*

He took another puff. Then he relaxed in his leather chair. He tapped on his cigarette, let the ashes fall into the ashtray next to him, and dreamed of how good his life would soon be.

He coughed again. Then he pushed his new wire-framed glasses up on his nose. He'd lost his old pair somewhere between Serenity's barn and the woods.

His gaze drifted to the nearby calendar. He reached for it. He retrieved an ink pen and circled a date.

Then he coughed and took another puff. His next trip to the Miller home would end in success. A big Amish gathering was planned for that particular afternoon, so hopefully, she wouldn't be there. But if she was, her house was far enough away from neighbors that no one would hear her cry for help.

He pressed his lips together and eyed his gun cabinet in the corner.

She was too pretty to harm. Of course, he didn't want to hurt or kill her. But he'd learned to put himself before anyone else. He sat up straight, leaned forward, tapped the toe of his shoe against the carpet, and focused on his calendar—on his next and final attempt to get back the wooden horse his grandpa had made for him. It wasn't actually the piece that he wanted. Rather, it was what was inside.

# CHAPTER SEVEN

The Pink Petal smelled so gut. Serenity breathed in the fresh, sweet sachet that was a delicious mixture of everything from red tulips and soft white carnations to the sensational aroma of gardenias. She had always loved the scent of gardenias from the time they'd been delivered to her hospital room during her youth.

When she'd been a patient with the virus, an Englisch friend had sent her the most beautiful floral bouquet of gardenias that Serenity had ever set eyes on. From that poignant moment, gardenias had become her favorite flower.

As she'd lain in bed, she'd breathed in the glorious floral aroma and had decided that she'd one day own a floral shop and bring smiles to people's faces.

Serenity slowly plucked a single gardenia from its holder and pressed the white flower to her face. As she breathed in the heavenly sweet scent, she closed her eyes a moment, vividly recalling that very memorable day when she'd received the bouquet in a beautiful cobalt-blue vase.

As she carefully returned the single stem to its place in her shop's refrigerated area, she closed the door behind her and moved to one of her worktables. She glanced at her notes while her assistant worked in the back room.

Typically, she did as much as possible from memory. But because of tomorrow's unusually large number of wedding arrangements, there was no way to get around writing things down. As she worked on a hand bouquet, her mind traveled to the Englisch bride-to-be. To the shipment of Calla lilies that would be here at any moment.

She couldn't suppress an appreciative grin. As she arranged, she thought of Stephen. There was a lot to ponder. Since he'd found her tied up in her barn, he'd changed.

She plucked a carnation from her bouquet in progress and moved it next to a yellow daisy. Whenever she arranged, she considered all sorts of things. Right now her mind was clear enough to realize that she hadn't dealt with something Stephen had said during their conversation the day before.

*He hinted that there was a connection between us. That we had a relationship. He didn't say it in so many words, but he alluded to it. He'd said it with his eyes. They spoke their own language, and when they penetrated mine, I realized two things.*

*What went on in my barn has definitely stepped up our relationship. Stephen's protective. He has been since his daed left them. And now he's my protector. Just like a husband would look out for his wife.* But the moment she'd pictured herself with him in a house with lots of kinder, a silent alarm had gone off. She'd remembered that she wasn't available for him or for anyone.

The phone ringing pulled her from her thoughts. She answered the questions she was asked, and then she hung up.

As the phone next to the cash register clicked into place, Serenity looked around the four walls of her shop. She knew by heart where everything was, the items' cost, and even how much stock was in the small room in back that faced the Quilt Room.

To the left of the refrigerated area, different shapes and sizes of potted plants with elegant flowery coverings layered the shelves.

The larger and heavier pots sat on ground level, and the top shelves housed the lighter ones. They were ready for sale.

To the right loomed all types of cards for inclusion with the plants and flowers. There were get-well, sympathy, wedding, birthday, anniversary, and graduation cards.

For space management, Serenity used every available spot. Handmade wreaths decorated the walls. An Amish lady she'd known for years had put together hanging plants with handmade bows and brown cord that added a more personal touch to the shop.

Her favorite worktable, opposite the cash register, offered a nice view of the small area behind her store where she grew fresh flowers in the spring, summer, and fall.

The bell above the entrance chimed. Serenity turned to glimpse Trini entering with quick steps and a friendly wave. "I came to check and see how you're doing."

Trini joined Serenity, and her eyes traveled to the area that Serenity prepared for delivery. She pointed. "Are all of these for the wedding?"

Serenity followed Trini's gaze. "Some. As far as the arrangements, I'll finish up early tomorrow." She smiled at her friend. "I want every flower to look like it's just been picked." Then she added in an excited tone, "I hope everything will be perfect for this couple."

Trini laid an affectionate hand on Serenity's shoulder. "And that's exactly why your business thrives."

An appreciative sigh escaped Serenity. "I was just about to take a break." She hugged her hands to her hips. "How about a sip of herbal tea?" Before Trini could respond, Serenity added with a lifted brow, "It's full of antioxidants."

Trini followed her to the back of the shop, where Serenity's assistant waved and told her she was stepping out for a moment. Trini spoke with an edge of amusement. "I'll pass on the herbs, but

I could use a glass of water."

After pouring both beverages, Serenity led Trini to two chairs between a huge fern and an extra-large peace lily. As Trini sipped her drink, she moved closer to the edge of her seat to avoid the greenery that touched the rim of her plastic glass. They laughed simultaneously. Serenity held her mug in front of her, savoring the delicious taste of homemade tea. "Sorry about the lack of space. Tomorrow most of these plants will be cleared out."

Trini grinned. "No apology necessary. In fact, I really like it back here."

"You do?"

"Uh-huh. I find it invigorating."

After a slight pause, Trini arched a curious brow. "Speaking of invigorating, how's Stephen?"

Serenity's lips curved up. "Do you find Stephen Lantz invigorating?"

Trini laughed. "Jah. I mean of course." She lowered her chin to look directly at Serenity. "How could he not be? The man saved your life!"

True. Every time she tried to remove Stephen from her mind, his name somehow reentered her head.

"It's funny. In many ways, your relationship with Stephen reminds me of my relationship with Jacob," said Trini.

Serenity sat up a little straighter. Her shoulders stiffened and she rested the mug of tea on her thigh. "Trini, you know I love you, and I have no doubt that you have my best interests at heart, but I must remind you that I am absolutely *not* in a relationship with Stephen."

Trini drew in a breath and held up a hand in defense. "I'm sorry."

Serenity softened her pitch. "It's okay. But he and I are just friends." She leaned back to move a potted fern so that its fronds were out of her personal space.

Serenity cleared her throat. "Why would you think my friendship with Stephen was anything close to what you have with Jacob?"

Trini grinned.

Serenity's heart warmed. Because any time she brought up the middle Lantz brother to her quilt friend, the expression on Trini's face reminded Serenity of what an entire tulip field must look like if every bulb bore beautiful, soft petals at the same time.

A thoughtful expression crossed Trini's face, and the brown hue of her eyes deepened as she pressed her lips together. When she adjusted her hips in her seat, she inched toward Serenity. "When I fell off my ladder and broke my wrist, Jacob was there for me every day while I recovered. . .and after. He was my hero. Just like Stephen is to you." She shook her head and lowered her voice to what was barely more than a whisper. "Despite you two being just friends, that man took what happened in your barn personally."

Serenity contemplated asking her friend just how she knew that Stephen took her own tragic experience personally. But it didn't matter. Serenity was fully aware that Trini's theory was true. *I've got to fix that. But how?*

Serenity deliberately changed the subject. The last thing she wanted right now was a lengthy conversation about Stephen. About love and happily ever after. Trini was newly married, and she seemed to be looking at everything through rose-colored glasses these days.

Serenity forced a smile and brought up the memorial idea. A small, beautiful memory garden next to the porch swing that Stephen's aendi had loved so very much. Excitement edged Trini's voice as she expressed all sorts of ideas.

The subject slowed Serenity's pulse to a more comfortable pace. Breathing in, she finished her tea before bending to place the mug on the floor next to her chair. "Did you know that this jungle of greenery absorbs the toxins in the air?"

The amused look in Trini's eyes made Serenity lean forward. "You don't believe me, do you?"

Trini looked away a moment before returning her attention to Serenity. "I believe you, Serenity. And you never cease to amaze me."

"I don't know how people can cut down healthy old trees or live in a home with no plants. There's just something about Gott-given greenery that makes me feel. . .safe. And healthy." She and Trini turned so that they looked directly at each other.

The pitch of Trini's voice took a sympathetic dip. "Serenity, I know that our new home isn't finished inside, but I'll remind you that you're always welcome to stay with Jacob and me." After a slight pause, she lowered her voice another notch. "You always put on a brave face, but I've known you for years, and underneath that assured facade"—she hesitated as if deciding on the right words—"you must be concerned for your safety."

Serenity crossed her legs at the ankles. As the long jade-green extension of the fern touched her shoulder, she agreed with her friend. "Trini, just between the two of us. . ." She sighed. "I'm uneasy. But what I'm truly concerned about might surprise you."

"Try me."

Serenity bit her lip while considering how best to describe what was on her mind. "What happened to me isn't what bothers me most."

"No?"

Serenity shook her head. "No. It's that someone could do something so horrific to me. To anyone." After a lengthy silence, her voice cracked with emotion. "Trini, we live in a safe community where most everyone loves Gott and attends church."

Trini nodded. "True."

"Whoever harmed me didn't really hurt me physically. Not permanently, anyway. But they still need forgiveness."

Trini's eyes widened in surprise. She swallowed. Serenity

shrugged. "I'm not afraid of these people, Trini. What I fear most is what could await them in the end." She whispered, "Eternity isn't a laughing matter. It's serious business. And I want everyone to go to heaven."

Trini's eyes sparkled with moisture. With one careful, steady motion, she bent to set her glass by her chair leg. A tear slipped down her cheek as she reached over to Serenity and embraced her.

As Serenity shared the hug, she sighed—this time with relief. Life had thrown her some battles, but right now, in the security of her best friend's presence and love, she instinctively knew that everything would be okay. Including her friendship with Stephen.

Stephen's thoughts were on his beloved aendi as he helped Serenity clear the ground cover from the area next to the front porch. Using his hoe, he loosened the dirt while Serenity loaded weeds into the wheelbarrow.

Her voice bounced with enthusiasm while she scooped another pile of weeds into her hands, deposited them in the wheelbarrow, and lifted the wooden handles to move the unwanted plants to the dump pile. "I wonder if Margaret can see what we're doing." She glanced at Stephen. He stopped and leaned against the wooden part of his hoe while he contemplated Serenity's statement.

He smiled a little. "I hope she can. I often wonder if the souls in heaven are privy to what's happening here on earth."

Her eyes misted while they shared a glance of what seemed to be a mutual, comfortable understanding. "I don't know. I guess we'll have to wait to find out." She looked at the sky. "There's one thing I'm sure of, though."

"What?"

She pointed. "Somewhere, it's raining. But it's as dry as a bone here."

The *clomp-clomp* of horse's hooves pulled them from their conversation. They glanced at the long drive off the blacktop that led to the Lantz home.

From inside her open buggy, Trini Lantz offered a big wave.

Serenity parked the wheelbarrow as she and Stephen waved back. When Trini tied her horse to a pole at the yard's edge, Stephen followed Serenity to greet his new sister-in-law.

"I brought ham salad." Trini paused, handing the plate of sandwiches to Serenity. She stopped, and a laugh escaped her when she caught sight of Serenity's dirty hands.

"On second thought, I'll take them inside and stick them in your fridge."

Stephen nodded. "Denki."

The front screen door slammed shut, and Trini disappeared. A loud whinny sounded from the blacktop, and Stephen and Serenity turned toward the new sound. Abby offered a large wave from inside her open buggy, while her horse trotted down the Lantz's lane. Wasting no time, Stephen and Serenity stepped to meet her, and Stephen tied her horse to a post while Serenity helped her friend down the steps.

On the ground, Abby hugged Serenity. She reached inside her buggy. "Ta-da!" She extended her arms to Serenity, then to Stephen as he joined the two women. "Is there a place in Margaret's memorial for this?"

Stephen felt a wave of emotion as he took in the beautiful blue-and-cream porcelain angel. He accepted the angel from Abby, taking great care not to drop it.

He glanced at Serenity before turning back to the angel. "I'm sure this deserves a spot in Margaret's memorial." He paused a moment before offering Abby an appreciative nod. "Denki, Abby."

The three headed toward the house when another loud neigh sounded from the blacktop. At the same time, Trini stepped down the front steps and joined them while Jacob and Gabe waved from inside an open buggy that neared the property.

As his brothers approached, emotion filled Stephen's chest. He said a silent prayer of thanks to Gott for the abundance of love his dear aendi had amassed during her lifetime. Today was surely going to be what he'd been unconsciously yearning for since he'd learned that Margaret had passed on to heaven.

At the flower bed, Stephen listened to conversations that ensued while he and Gabe raked the newly cleaned area. After they'd cleared part of the section, Jacob helped Trini and Serenity plant the beautiful bottle flowers in purple and hot pink, as well as gerbera daisies that Serenity had selected. They planned where to eventually place the bulbs in the fall.

Gabe and Abby agreed on a spot for the angel. By the time the sun began to dip in the western sky, all six stood in silence while they took in the incredibly beautiful memorial in honor of Margaret Lantz.

The *clomp-clomp* of hooves prompted them to turn toward the lane. Serenity's parents waved from their open buggy. On the seat behind them, Trini's mamm shouted an enthusiastic hello.

Jacob and Stephen helped guide their horse to a pole, where they tied the standardbred and helped the three parents down the buggy steps. Gabe brought a canteen of water for the horse. Afterward Trini's mamm helped Serenity's parents retrieve a bird feeder from the back of their buggy.

Stephen's heart warmed because Aendi Margaret had loved the numerous bird species in their area. "I'll carry that for you." Extending a hand, he took the feeder and asked where it should go. There was unanimous agreement that it should be placed in the right-hand corner closest to the house.

Gabe, Jacob, Abby, Trini, Serenity, and Stephen finished their work, cleaned the brick border they'd made around the new memorial, and glanced at one another in approval as they stepped away to assess their efforts.

As they turned, loud applause sounded. Stephen took in the sudden, unexpected crowd of Amish and Englisch who'd come to glimpse the memorial, which had obviously garnered quick interest. Afterward, Serenity's mamm raised her hands above her head and clapped to get everyone's attention.

As she announced the start of the outdoor buffet line, Stephen's jaw dropped. Tables loaded with food covered a section of the yard. Serenity stood on one side of him, Trini on the other. He glanced down at Trini before turning to Serenity.

"I have a hunch that you two planned this."

Serenity smiled. As their eyes met, something inside him warmed so much that he knew if his emotions got any warmer, he'd burn up.

"Thank you, Trini. Denki, Serenity."

To Stephen's surprise, a familiar voice grabbed everyone's attention. "Let's bow our heads," said the bishop, "and give thanks to Gott for the late Margaret Lantz and everything she did for this close community."

After saying the prayer in German, he started the buffet line. But an audible intake of breath pulled Stephen's attention away from the food. As he looked in the direction of everyone's focus, he gasped.

Next to him, Serenity smiled. "Would you look at that!"

Jacob and Gabriel joined them. Jacob put one hand on Stephen's shoulder and squeezed it with affection. "It's the most beautiful rainbow I've ever seen," he said, his voice filled with emotion.

Stephen couldn't look away from the eye-catching rainbow. He gasped in gratitude. "There's no way this can be a coincidence."

Gabe rested his palm on Stephen's other shoulder. He wasn't one to display emotion, but his voice waivered when he whispered, "It wouldn't be Aendi Margaret's party without the guest of honor."

Stephen's eyes burned from salty tears as the colored arches of the perfect rainbow slowly evaporated. Stephen couldn't help but think that his aendi had just made her presence known at their gathering. He smiled a little at where the colors had been painted. "I got your message, Aendi Margaret. And it will stay with me forever."

The following afternoon, Abby and Serenity sat opposite Trini in the back of the Quilt Room. The scent of cinnamon candles floated gracefully through the small area. A bird pecked at the window that faced the small area behind the shop. Serenity could glimpse the beautiful flowers behind her own store next door.

As usual, the young women chitchatted from the moment they got together. This time they couldn't stop talking about yesterday's rainbow. It was common knowledge that Margaret Lantz had loved rainbows and had routinely looked for them after every rain.

But ironically, yesterday had been dry. It had rained north of where they'd gathered. So of course the rainbow was explainable. At the same time, it wasn't. A happy chill swept up Serenity's spine as she recalled the expression on Stephen's face when he'd noticed the luminous colors in the sky.

She'd never witnessed such joy. Serenity threaded her needle and glanced up. "I'm still absorbing yesterday. And the finale."

Abby's scissors made a light clipping noise as she cut around a plastic form. "I thought about it all last night." After a slight pause, she went on. "I'm sure that some would consider the rainbow a coincidence." She shook her head. "But for me, it was a message."

Serenity's voice was soft. "A message?"

Abby offered a firm nod while drawing her needle and thread through a corner piece. "Since we lost Margaret, I've been praying for a sign that she knows how much we love and miss her." She lowered her voice to a barely audible whisper. "I don't care what anyone else thinks. I'm convinced that the rainbow was a message from Margaret's angel." She met Serenity's curious expression with a half smile. "We've heard it said at church many times over the years that Gott speaks to us in unusual ways. But if we're not paying attention, we'll miss the signs."

Serenity nodded. "I agree with you, Abby. There's nothing stronger than the power of prayer. And I've been asking for the same thing."

Abby's expression softened so that the look on her face was endearing. "Really?"

Serenity smiled. "Jah."

Trini's voice was edged with a newfound enthusiasm. "Add me to the list!"

They stopped what they were doing and laughed. Serenity glanced at Abby before her gaze landed on Trini. "The three of us. . ."

Trini and Abby looked at her to continue.

Serenity's voice cracked with emotion. "It's funny. You know, we're all very different, but we're very much the same. Does that make sense?"

Serenity was sure it didn't. Yet for some unknown reason, she believed it with her heart and soul.

Trini added in a thoughtful tone, "I think I get what you're saying. I mean, we haven't been raised by the same parents, and we haven't endured the same set of challenges, but. . ."

Serenity lifted a curious brow. *Where are you going with this, Trini?*

"At the same time, our hearts must have, somewhere down the long line of ancestors, originated from the same bloodline."

Abby agreed. "Most importantly, we all want marriage and children."

Serenity pressed her lips together. She'd never voiced that. Of course she understood why Abby would assume that, because almost all Amish women—and men—yearned for large, tight families. But from many years of knowing Abby, Serenity was fully aware that Abby often believed everyone concurred with her opinions. Still, Abby's heart was big. And she wanted the best for them.

Trini stepped in with doubt-filled skepticism. "Abby, for years I didn't want that. And you know why."

Abby bounced back. "Jah! Because you'd planned to leave the faith—and you never even told us!"

A regretful expression emanated from Trini's eyes. Remorse edged her voice as she worked on a handsewn piece. "And when I finally did—"

"Mrs. Bontranger overheard you and shouted your secret to the entire town!" Abby finished the sentence for her.

Serenity and Trini shared a sympathetic smile. But all the while, Serenity fully understood Trini's difficult decision to convey her secret, even to her besties. Because Serenity also held something so sensitive and so full of heartache within her that she'd never disclosed it to either of these women. And she never could.

# CHAPTER EIGHT

Serenity breathed in the fresh scent of tomato vines while she clipped the red fruit with her small, sharp scissors. She bent, adding one at a time to her basket. As she did so, her gaze swept across her generous-sized garden, and her heart warmed while she marveled at the miraculous manner in which Gott had designed such beautiful, delicious food from a mere seed.

Church members often complimented her on her produce, especially the remarkably sweet taste of her tomatoes. *But they're not my tomatoes. And the credit for their color and taste is not mine. The designer of these wonderful vegetables is Gott, and only Him.*

A mosquito buzzed near her ear, and she dropped her scissors to shoo away the insect. She retrieved them and dusted the dirt from the blades. As she glanced up, the sunflowers held her attention. *Who else but Gott could design a plant whose bloom faces the sun from dawn to dusk?* Until later in the year, anyway, when it became too heavy with seeds.

While the warm sun caressed the back of her neck and her plants' different designs inspired her, she contemplated yesterday's conversation with Trini and Abby. She frowned.

Abby's words pertaining to bearing children had, unfortunately, struck a sensitive chord. *It's not her fault.* While Serenity reflected on the story behind how Trini and Jacob had miraculously ended up together, Stephen entered her mind.

She didn't try to stymie the wide smile that tugged the corners of her mouth upward. *Yesterday was just what he'd needed.* She narrowed her brows while she absorbed and appreciated the numerous blessings that had flowed through the Lantz property during that special time.

Of course they'd held a funeral for Margaret immediately after she'd passed on to heaven. But yesterday had been a true celebration of Stephen's late aendi's life.

Serenity released a satisfied breath and continued her tomato picking. After she'd gathered the ripe ones, she migrated to the neighboring rows of peppers. Cautiously, she stepped through the green bushy plants, careful not to bend or break their delicate vines. The last thing she wanted was to accidentally sever a healthy branch.

Using both hands, she separated the leaves and searched for extra-large green peppers. After she found them, she snipped the stems and added them to her large wicker vegetable basket.

As she walked away from the garden, basket in hand, the sun slipped behind a large fluffy cloud. Instinctively, she sensed that she was being watched. She turned, careful not to drop the heavy container. She glimpsed a black truck down the road. She squinted to catch the license, but because the vehicle was some distance away, she couldn't identify the numbers or letters before it turned at a four-way stop.

Her arms tensed. So did her fingers. She glanced at the barn. As she took in the large, old structure, memories of her worst moments stirred restlessly within her until an eerie, uncomfortable chill swept up her spine. When the unwelcome sensation landed between her shoulders, she shivered.

With slow, cautious steps, she continued to her house. Usually while she transported produce to her kitchen, her heart pumped with joy. She dreamed of canning the fresh veggies. And she imagined homemade chili with tomatoes and green peppers and lots of white onions.

But today that joy was missing. She bit her lower lip. For some reason, it was abnormally quiet. To her astonishment, there wasn't even a call for attention from Angel. Serenity felt very alone.

An uncertain sensation prompted a hard lump in her chest. *I've never been afraid. And I never will be, because Gott is with me. He pulled me through Epstein-Barr, and He's gifted me with so much, including this beautiful farm. And my dear family. And Stephen.*

Again, she glanced behind her. Nothing. Only the spacious garden that she considered one of her most cherished blessings. But Serenity usually went with her instincts. The long illness she'd suffered as a young girl had seemingly gifted her with a strong sense of perception.

*I didn't actually see someone watching me.* Yet she believed that was what had just happened. And she wondered who it had been and why.

Having no proof, she still was sure that the barn episode was ongoing. And that moments earlier someone had been checking out her place. Or her.

*Someone wants something from me. The most valuable material thing I own is this property. And that can't be stolen. I own very little else. There's no cash in my house. I have no idea why someone would even think of checking out my farm. Or me. But there must be a reason. And there's still no explanation for why I was attacked in my own barn. At least I don't know it. Someone just watched me from down the road.*

*Who? And what do they want?*

Stephen offered Gabe a brotherly slap on the shoulder as they entered their barn. Gabriel cut open a bag of oat mix and proceeded to the horse stalls while Stephen checked the water hose that originated at a well south of their property.

Stephen nodded in satisfaction and continued to check that the bridles and harnesses hung from their appropriate hooks. Without thinking, he stepped to a wall, lifted a rake from its hook, and made his way to Survivor's stall. He grinned at the wreath that Margaret and some church ladies had made for the horse's benefit. The piece hung where Survivor could glimpse it. Stephen didn't know if the spoiled standardbred actually appreciated the work. Whatever the case, he wouldn't remove it. His late aendi had obviously made the wreath with love.

As Stephen went through his normal routines, Serenity filled his thoughts. A smile tugged at the corners of his lips.

Gabe's voice pulled him from his reverie. "Perfect time to work."

Stephen agreed. The horses were in the pasture, and a nice, cool breeze floated in through the open doors.

Gabriel softened his voice with gentle understanding. "Hey, I just wanted to tell you. . ." He cleared his throat.

Stephen looked up. Gabe wasn't an emotional guy, but by his sentimental tone, Stephen was anxious to hear the rest of his sentence.

Stephen looked at him to continue. "What is it Gabe?"

Gabe breathed in and resumed his typical, firm, emotionless voice. "Well, yesterday"—he offered an appreciative nod while his voice cracked—"that was nice. Real nice."

Stephen's heart warmed. Just the fact that Gabe had bothered to mention the memorial indicated that it held extreme importance to him.

"The crowd was quite a surprise."

Gabe laughed. "Jah. The entire town must have been here. Word has it that your friend and Jake's wife were behind it."

Stephen offered a quick nod and a laugh. "They were." He let out a low whistle. "Boy, oh boy. What those women can pull off without a hitch!"

The two chuckled.

A barn rat scurried across the floor and disappeared into a hole where the sidewall met the floor. A pigeon sat very still on the hayloft's edge. As Stephen raked dirty straw, smelly dust hazed the air. The metal forks meeting the cement floor made a light scratchy sound. Gabe joined him with a wheelbarrow. While Stephen cleaned the floor, Gabe transported the used bedding to a large piece of used cardboard before emptying the waste into the wheelbarrow.

While Stephen worked, his thoughts lingered on the sequence of yesterday's events. From the love that had filled his late aendi's large yard to the delicious chicken and dumplings, sponge cakes, and mouth-watering casseroles that numerous guests had set upon the large center table.

Gabe's voice was low and thoughtful. "Serenity sure is close to Jake's wife."

Stephen's reply was automatic. "Abby too."

From his peripheral vision, Stephen observed Gabe's surprised expression. Stephen grinned.

"Gabe?"

Gabe eyed him with an uncertain expression. "Jah?"

"I kinda noticed that you and Abby talked awhile."

The response was as Stephen had expected. Nothing. Stephen couldn't stop his lips from curving in amusement. *Wonder what's going on between my brother and the alterations lady.* Stephen wasn't blind. And he'd taken special note of what had appeared to be a conversation between an interested single man and an interested single woman.

After a long silence, Stephen cleared a lump from his throat.

"It's okay. Obviously, this is a subject you'd rather not discuss." He lifted a hand in defense. "You don't have to say a word."

Uneasiness edged Gabe's voice. "She's a nice lady. But a bit headstrong."

The comment gave Stephen pause. For some reason, that's not what he'd expected. "There are a lot worse things."

Gabe shrugged before lifting the wooden wheelbarrow handles and pushing away the vessel. He glanced skeptically at Stephen before transporting the dirty bedding to the burn pile outside the open barn doors.

When he stepped back inside, they moved to the next stall. Then Stephen stepped up to the hayloft.

He turned to look down at Gabe. "Jake sure did a nice job with this ladder."

Gabe's low voice carried to the loft. "Sure did."

Stephen lifted several bales over the side, one at a time, and released them from his hold. After they landed, Gabe carried them to the stalls, cut the twine holding them together, and spread the bedding.

Without warning, the horror in Serenity's barn exploded in Stephen's mind, and he stopped what he was doing.

Moments later, Gabe looked up. "Hey, what's wrong?"

A long silence ensued while Gabe quickly stepped up the ladder to join him in the loft. Facing Stephen, he took him by the shoulders so that they looked directly into each other's eyes. "You okay? You haven't heard me trying to get your attention."

Stephen breathed in, considering the question. It wasn't often he discussed personal issues with Gabe. Not because Gabe couldn't offer gut advice. He could. But Gabe dealt with things so differently than Stephen did. Gabe didn't use emotion when solving problems. He used pure logic.

In many ways, Stephen was the antithesis of Gabe. Stephen was the sentimental, affectionate type—perhaps because he was closer to their mamm. Gabe had always been steady but a bit distant in Stephen's opinion. To his oldest brother, little things didn't seem to matter. Gabe had always considered the important things in life: Gott, church, then food on the table. Yet here he was, ready to lend an ear.

Stephen lifted his chin a notch and decided to try him. After all, he had nothing to lose. "Gabe, you know I'm not a worrier."

Gabe moved his head in a long, drawn-out shake. "Never have been."

Stephen took a deep breath before resting a firm hand on his hip and looking directly at his brother. "I'm real uneasy about the thing in Serenity's barn."

Gabe narrowed his brows with obvious interest. He shook his head. "That's understandable. But how exactly are you uneasy?" His tone lightened a notch. "Maybe I can help."

Several seconds passed while both men descended the ladder and Stephen decided where to start. Finally, Gabe put an arm around his shoulders, and they stepped slowly toward the open doors. "Why don't we take a walk and talk this out?"

Stephen sighed relief. They moved out of the barn and eventually onto the path in the woods. The very trail that he and Serenity often hiked.

Before Stephen spilled his thoughts, he relaxed his shoulders and took in the large oaks while enjoying the fragrance of the huge pines.

Stephen told his older brother about the visit to the jail. "Gabe, I don't want to make too much of this, but today there was a vehicle parked in the distance." He motioned in the direction of the blacktop.

Gabe offered a friendly slap on Stephen's shoulder. "Hey, it's okay. I'm here for you. We'll figure this out. Now tell me about what you saw."

Stephen shrugged. "It was black. Unfortunately, the moment I glimpsed it, it disappeared, and I didn't catch the license. It's like the driver must've seen me glance his way." Several seconds later, Stephen softened his tone. "He was gone."

"Okay. So. . .I'm guessing that your protective mind believes that this might have something to do with what happened in Serenity's barn."

Stephen grimaced. "That's just it. I'm not sure. But Gabe?"

Stephen stopped. Gabe joined him. As a squirrel darted in front of them, they shared an inexplicable look. "How often does someone park on the blacktop?"

Gabe looked away. When he looked back into Stephen's eyes, he shrugged. "Rarely." After a slight hesitation, he added, "But maybe someone had to go to the bathroom. Or the driver needed to talk on his cell phone." He lifted his palms and dropped them to his sides. "I don't know why they pulled over, but there could be a bunch of reasons."

Stephen went on to express his inner fear that whoever had attacked Serenity would return.

They started forward again. Gabe caught a pine branch that obstructed the path and held it aside so they could pass. A woodpecker worked on an oak tree. A yellow butterfly landed on a shrub to their right. A red fox appeared in the distance before disappearing into the woods.

"Stephen, sometimes there's nothing you can do but pray and have faith." He chuckled. "It's funny, but I've heard people say that all they can do now is pray about their problem. But the thing is, praying's what you should do before the problem. Not after."

Stephen offered a sigh of agreement. "I know."

A long silence ensued. Stephen glimpsed the thoughtful expression on Gabe's face. His jaw was set. An inch or so taller than Stephen, Gabe was the strongest of the three brothers. Not only in physical strength but in mental strength too.

When Gabe spoke, his words came out slowly, as if he still considered his response. Stephen knew him well. And Gabe didn't waste time with small talk. Whatever he had to say was worth listening to. And he wouldn't repeat it.

"Here's what you can do." He turned to Stephen while they stepped over a large tree root that stuck up from the ground. After that, the path narrowed, and Stephen stopped for his brother to lead the way. Stephen's heart warmed. He loved Gabe. And that his oldest brother, a man of few words, took time to talk to him, meant a lot.

"There was only one witness to what happened. And that was Serenity."

Stephen nodded.

Gabe stopped and seemed to ponder his words while several seconds passed. A few moments later, he cupped his chin with his hand. Inside, Stephen smiled. He and Jake had the same habit whenever they decided something important.

"You said that the police interviewed Serenity right after the attack?"

"Jah."

Gabe offered a slight nod. "Okay. She must've been really shaken up."

"She was." Stephen rolled his shoulders to relax them. *It's okay to discuss what happened. My brother will help me if he can.*

"You know, Stephen, I'm no detective, but here's what I think." They came to the clearing where Stephen and Serenity had talked many times. A misty haze swept across the sky. The brightness dimmed before the sun made a full entrance. Stephen blinked to adjust to the sudden light.

"Since some time has passed—I mean, since the initial shock of what happened—do you think Serenity might be up for reenacting what she did right before she was attacked?"

Stephen absorbed the question. Before he responded, Gabe went on in a more decisive manner. "There's a chance, maybe, that if she focuses on what she did that day, something new will come to her."

Gabe held up a defensive hand. "I'm not promising that it will." He shrugged. "But it's definitely worth a try. You've got everything to gain and nothing to lose. Because the person who hurt her is still at large."

When Stephen didn't respond, Gabe added, "I mean, she's probably in her barn a lot, anyway."

Stephen understood what his brother meant. Gabe turned toward him and gestured with his large hands. "If she really concentrates, you know, without any distractions, maybe, just maybe, something new will come to her. Something she subconsciously chose to forget?"

Stephen responded with a belated nod of approval. "I guess there's nothing to lose by reenacting what she did before two men tied her up."

"And during. And after." Gabe's brotherly slap on Stephen's shoulder meant the end of their talk.

Gabe turned around. Stephen did the same. As they headed back to their barn, Stephen stayed a couple of feet behind his brother. But as Stephen contemplated their conversation, he acknowledged that this walk had changed two things. First, it had bonded him closer to Gabriel, even though they'd always been tight. Second, Stephen believed that the reenactment could spark Serenity to recall something new. If Serenity would agree to it.

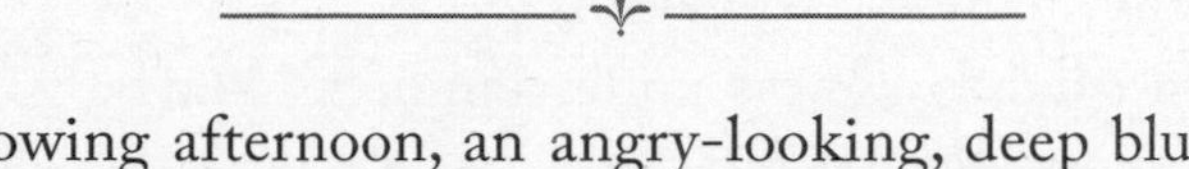

The following afternoon, an angry-looking, deep blue-gray sky reminded Serenity all too much of the "bad day." As she and Stephen traversed the dirt path from her house to her barn, a shiver that was an uncomfortable blend of dread and excitement swept up her arms. She shrugged to rid the unwanted sensation.

A chicken pecked mercilessly at the ground. In the distance, Angel gave a loud neigh and stuck his head over the fence. Stephen arched a curious brow and looked down at her. "Are you okay?"

Serenity slowed her pace and glanced up at him. "Jah. In fact"—she let out a small laugh—"the weather is eerily similar to when it happened. This is a gut time to retrace my steps."

She motioned to the clouds. "Looks like another storm's coming."

"Sure does." While they continued to the old structure, thunder rumbled. The temperature steadily dropped. The garden vegetables swayed with the wind.

Stephen frowned. *She always refers to what happened as the "bad day." I hope what we're about to do won't set her back. Whatever the case, I agree with Gabe, that it needs to be done. And if Serenity remembers anything new, this difficult endeavor will pay off.*

Angel continued to demand attention. Stephen smiled a little. *Don't get too close. He bites.*

He couldn't stop the sudden amusement that curved his lips. "I don't know about your horse. There's certainly a mystique about him. Just like your garage-sale piece. And that one won't bite."

She laughed. He chuckled.

"Daed often remarks that there's not much going on between Angel's large ears." She slowed her pace as her attention lingered on her spoiled standardbred, who intently watched them from the pasture.

Serenity continued in a thoughtful tone. "I don't know. He sure makes clear his likes and dislikes."

Stephen tried to appear understanding. "Maybe you should remove the *s* from *likes*. It's obvious that you're the only one he likes."

Serenity's voice filled with compassion. "I can't help it, Stephen. It might be that he's jealous of anyone who's with me."

Stephen couldn't stop the chuckle that escaped him. "Ya think?"

As they neared the barn, Angel turned and released another loud neigh before disappearing. Stephen guessed that sudden absence meant the horse was entering the barn.

Serenity unbarred the large door, and Stephen slid the entrance open. Inside, they stopped. As Stephen had predicted, Angel was now in his stall. But strangely, he didn't protest Stephen's presence. The standardbred just stared at him as they made their way toward the stall. *I still don't trust him.*

Stephen couldn't help noticing how the ugly weather caused the barn to take on an unsettling ambiance. The building seemed too dark. Serenity stepped to the wall to retrieve her battery lantern. She took it in her hand and flipped on the light. Still, the high ceilings, the lack of sunlight, and the eerie silence made Stephen grimace.

Serenity took a determined breath and met his eyes. She squared her shoulders and firmed her voice. "Okay. I'll do my best to remember everything I did."

"I'm right here with you any time you need to stop."

He took in her tense expression. Her jaw was set. Her lips pressed together. She looked around before placing the lantern directly in front of her.

In silence, he followed her to Angel's stall and watched the affectionate relationship between Serenity and the animal. Serenity's words seemed to soothe her horse as she gently assured him that everything was okay. She planted a kiss on the long nose.

Then she met Stephen's expression with a hopeful look. She

moved toward the doors. She talked in such a soft voice, he could barely hear her. "I heard the noise." She pointed to the numerous bales of straw. She spoke while slow steps moved her toward the back of the building.

She stopped. "Stephen, it was right here."

"What?"

"When someone grabbed my arms and yanked them behind my back. Before I could react, a piece of material blinded me. I could barely hear my cries for help." She breathed in as agony filled her expression. "He pulled it tight. I couldn't scream. I was so focused on escaping, I may have missed some of what they said. But I'll never forget one man's throaty voice."

For long moments they stood in silence. She closed her eyes. Stephen's heart went out to her while she pressed her lips in a straight line. He noted the rapid rising and falling of her chest.

But from what she'd just told him, so far nothing was new.

He narrowed his brows and spoke in a soft, understanding tone. "Think hard. What else can you remember?"

For long moments, she stood with her lips parted, staring at the straw bales as if begging for answers. She set the lantern on the floor and her hands over her chest. Her fingers interlaced. She must have clenched them hard because her knuckles started to whiten.

Finally, she released a helpless breath. Afterward her tone was serious. "I should be able to recall what they said. I mean I was here with them."

"At least you recall the throaty voice."

Stephen paused a moment and cupped his chin with his hand. While he thought, he looked around. He frowned.

"Serenity?"

"Jah?"

"Where did their footsteps originate?"

She thought a moment. "From the next row over. Behind the straw bales. Angel was so nervous. And when he let out an ear-piercing whinny, I turned to make sure everything was okay. What seemed like a million unexpected things happened in a split second."

She lifted her palms to the ceiling and shrugged.

"That's all it took. A second."

Stephen's gaze met Serenity's with understanding. "Follow me."

She picked up the lantern, and slow, cautious steps took them toward the barn's rear wall. Behind him, Serenity aimed the light in front of her. The space between the piles was so tight, Stephen used his hands to protect his face from the ends of the straw. "Be careful."

To his surprise, her voice reflected amusement. "Stephen, don't worry about me. I've been back here many times."

He chuckled. "Of course you have."

At the wall, they stopped to face each other. The area in which they stood left no extra room, with straw poking their hands and clothes. The earthy scent filled Stephen's senses. The familiar smell calmed him. It always had. In fact, the mild aroma invigorated him.

Many years ago, when Stephen's family had dealt with the hardship of having lost their daed, Stephen had passed days in their Lancaster barn thinking and attempting to put things into perspective. And at a very young age, he'd learned that "barn smells" enabled him to do just that.

Thunder crackled. The air smelled like rain. While they seemed to study each other in an understanding silence, a welcomed beam of sunlight floated in from one of the small windows, creating a rosy glow on Serenity's angelic face. As he took in her creamy complexion, a sudden grim reality tugged at his heart and soul until he realized why the ugly incident had changed him on so many levels.

That very realization was so strong and so compelling, he laid a hand on the closest bale for support. The demure expression on Serenity's face was a fierce combination of curiosity and what appeared to be a sort of longing. *This is real.*

As they continued to regard each other, they seemed to connect on a level that Stephen had never experienced with another human being. He swallowed. The lengthy silence between them was not tense or stressful. Or romantic.

*It's comfortable. Like whatever's between us is meant to be. I think she's feeling what I'm feeling, whatever that is. I read it in her eyes.*

The depth of her compelling blue eyes drowned him. It was as if she were an ocean and he a mere fisherman on a small rowboat trying to remain afloat. Something very unfamiliar came over him. It perplexed him. At the same time, it was mesmerizing. He acknowledged he wasn't thinking straight. He parted his lips to talk, but no words came out.

The emotions that passed through him might be unfamiliar, but some things became crystal clear. He knew that he never wanted to spend a day without her the rest of both of their lives. A strong yearning inside him to be her full-time protector tugged at his chest. He needed to be with her not only as an equal but as a strong male figure for her to lean on. At the same time, it was his intent to be gentle and understanding.

*Last year, when I asked Serenity to make a bouquet from her favorite flowers and then bought it for her, little did I know that today I would yearn to marry her more than I ever dreamed possible. I don't want to wait till the harvest. In my heart, I believe what I'm experiencing is true love. She is too. I've never known exactly what being in love is, but right now, I'm sure this is the real thing. The compelling silence between us tells me what words can't possibly begin to say.*

The inexplicable, shocking reality swept through him in a rush that was warm yet uneasy. *I'm going to tell her what I'm feeling. Right now.*

As Stephen started to speak, something pulled her attention away from him. With one swift motion, she lowered her eyes to where one of the bales met the cement floor. He followed her gaze.

She hiked up the bottom of her dress and slowly bent toward a pair of glasses. When he glimpsed the object of her focus, he laid a gentle hand on her arm and stopped her with his voice. "Don't touch them!"

She quickly withdrew her hand and jumped up. "Fingerprints."

"Do you have plastic gloves?"

She thought a moment. "I think so. Let me check."

Quick steps took her back near the entrance, where she opened a drawer. When she left, the area in which he stood darkened several notches. He watched the light go with her. Keeping his place so he wouldn't lose sight of the glasses, he leaned out from the straw to watch her open a drawer and step quickly back to him.

"Ta-da!"

She rejoined him and shined the beam on what appeared to be a silver earpiece that stuck out from between two pieces of straw. He used his gentlest voice and motioned to her hands. "May I?"

"Sure." She handed him the gloves, and he slipped them over his fingers.

With great care not to break the eyeglasses, he accomplished the task he'd set out to do. Then he glanced up from his squatting position to meet Serenity's inquisitive stare.

They focused on their unexpected find. Stephen stood, and they headed toward the front of the barn. For a moment he stopped, and she shined the light on the glasses while they both stared at them in silence.

His voice was edged with intense curiosity. "Do these look familiar?"

She shook her head. They walked side by side to the front wall, where she flipped off her lantern, hung it back on the wall, stepped outside, closed the barn door, and fastened the bar to secure it.

They continued to her house. As the wind tugged at their clothing, he was careful not to drop the could-be evidence. He narrowed his brows and raised his voice to compete with the wind. The house was some distance away.

"Any idea who might wear these?"

Catching her breath, she answered. "It's hard to say. A lot of people wear glasses. But these are different."

"Why do you say that?"

"They just seem kind of. . .sophisticated."

The wind seemed to take their words. "I don't know much about glasses, but you might be right." He chuckled. "Whatever that means."

Serenity continued. "Several men in our church wear eyeglasses, but to be honest, these look more. . ."

"Stylish?"

She caught her breath while she spoke. "Jah. I think the Englisch would call these designer glasses."

At her house, they stopped while she opened the door for him. It sprang shut behind them. The house seemed comfortably warm compared to the cooling outdoor temperatures.

He looked around. "We need something to protect these."

She opened one of her kitchen cabinets and pulled out a plastic container with a lid. "How 'bout this?"

He lifted a curious brow when their glances met. "We'll see."

After she removed the lid, he carefully put the glasses inside the holder. He let out a breath of relief. "Perfect."

"Now what?"

He smiled a little. "We take these to the police."

# CHAPTER NINE

Later that evening, Stephen stood on the opposite side of the new fence that separated the beautiful memorial area from the rest of the yard. *It was created with so much love for you, Aendi Margaret.* The newly discovered eyeglasses found in Serenity's barn were now in police possession. He sighed with relief while glancing at the feeder and smiled with great appreciation. He whispered, "You taught me to be a bird-watcher."

A tear slid down his cheek as he bent to the angel between two plants. With one finger, he touched a wing and considered his aendi and all she'd left him and his brothers. *I wonder if you can see me, Aendi Margaret. I really miss you. And I wish I'd been blessed with just one more moment with you before you died. To tell you how much I love you. I thought you'd be here forever.*

A gentle, brotherly hand on his shoulder made him turn. He smiled slightly. "Jake. Gut to see you. How's everything with you and Trini?"

Automatically, Stephen and Jacob stepped slowly toward the end of the side yard where the grass met their fields. Stephen couldn't stop a grin that gently turned up the corners of his lips. Every time he and Jacob were outside in the yard, their attention gravitated toward the beans.

As they made their way to the field, a combination of curiosity and skepticism edged Jacob's voice. "Hey, is everything okay?"

"Why do you ask?"

Jacob offered him a friendly slap on the shoulder. "I can tell. I'm your bruder."

Stephen sighed before nodding. "I don't know if everything's gut."

Jacob lifted a challenging brow. "Just what does that mean?"

Stephen hesitated.

Jacob nudged his arm in his brotherly fashion. "It's me, Stephen. Go ahead. Spill."

Stephen considered Jake's words that had been stated with a genuine combination of honesty and encouragement. And they'd been spoken with a sense of comfort that only someone very close could offer. Stephen began to talk, starting with the reenactment in Serenity's barn, to the discovery of the eyeglasses, to the buggy trip to the police.

At the line where the beans started, they stopped. Jacob turned to Stephen. "So they'll run fingerprints on the glasses?"

Stephen nodded.

Jacob hesitated before continuing the subject. "If my hunch is right, the owner must be one of the men who harmed Serenity."

Stephen contemplated the thought while he rocked back and forth on his toes. A gentle cool breeze caressed his face. "I can't say for sure, but that's what my logic tells me."

Jacob pressed a finger to his lips and looked at Stephen. "Did the glasses belong to Serenity or anyone she knew?"

"No."

Jacob lowered his voice. "Then jah. It makes sense that one of the intruders owns them."

Stephen nodded. "Maybe." He shrugged. "Of course, we don't know how long they were stuck there. And they could belong to someone who bailed the straw."

A thoughtful silence passed before Jacob resumed the conversation. "But I have a problem with this. I thought the authorities did an extensive search of the barn."

Stephen nodded. "They did. But it's easy to see how the glasses were overlooked. It was simply by chance that Serenity caught sight of the earpiece sticking out from the straw. The color blended in with the bales. The sun happened to come in through the window at just the right angle and at just the right time to land on the earpiece."

"I think it was Gott helping you out." Jacob's warm, reassuring smile matched his tone when he and Stephen looked at each other.

Jacob glanced down at the ground as a squirrel scurried up an oak. He edged his voice with optimism. "The police will find the criminals, Stephen. Hopefully the eyeglasses will lead to a full set of fingerprints. Then we'll be able to wave goodbye to this awful worry hanging over our shoulders."

"So you're worried too?"

Jacob waved a dismissive hand. "Not worried. Wrong choice of words. Remember, one of our church speakers told us that if we worry, we're not trusting Gott to take care of our problems."

Stephen nodded.

Jacob paused to cup his chin with his hand. Then he turned to face Stephen. "*Concerned* is probably a better word. I mean, we have no idea who did it or why." He offered a shrug before squaring his shoulders. "Of course, it could happen again. But hopefully not."

"Thanks for your thoughts, Jake."

When Stephen didn't budge, Jacob cocked his head, and his brows moved closer together until his expression conveyed a frown. After a slight pause, he spoke with a hint of curiosity. "But I have a hunch that there's more to this than just the barn thing. What do you think?"

Stephen smiled with relief. "I'm glad you're persistent, Jake. Jah, there's more. But it's so deep, I'm almost afraid to talk about it."

"Then we'd better have the conversation. Worse case is that I can't offer gut advice. And you know what you tell me won't leave this place." He offered a steady arm and nudged Stephen to move toward the pasture.

Stephen's horse let out a neigh. Stephen thought of Angel and grinned.

Jacob nudged his shoulder. "What?"

Stephen couldn't stop a laugh. "Oh, I was just thinking of Serenity's horse. Have you heard his name is Angel?"

"Jah. I don't think there's a man around who doesn't know about her man-biting standardbred." They chuckled before Stephen pressed his lips together thoughtfully. "I'm not sure how to say this, or even begin to explain this, but. . ." He stretched his arms in front of him before folding them over his chest.

"Just say it."

"Okay."

Several moments later, Jacob nodded. "I'm listening."

"When Serenity was retracing her steps in her barn—just like that awful time she calls the 'bad day'—we ended up in a very tight space at the back of the building."

Jacob faced him, lifted his chin, and seemed to wait for Stephen to continue.

Stephen was fully aware of what he was getting into. *But it will be okay. I can trust Jake with anything, even something he might find amusing.*

"When we looked at each other, something happened."

Jacob stayed silent.

Stephen's breath stuck in his throat, and he coughed to free it. "For some time, I've known that I want to take care of her and protect her forever." He hesitated before softening his voice to a more serious, confidential tone. "But for one long moment, I wanted to marry her more than I've ever dreamed of anything. I want it to be soon."

"Are you sure?"

Stephen smiled relief. "Jah. I want to marry her, Jake. It's the only way I can be with her 24-7."

"Okay. So your protective nature is at work, Stephen. You've always been like that." After a slight hesitation, doubt accompanied Jacob's words. "But why else do you want to marry her?"

Stephen smiled. "I'm deeply in love with her." He sighed with relief and lifted his hands to the sky in a helpless gesture. "I can't believe I admitted it to you."

Jacob offered him a brotherly pat on the shoulder. "I can. And I'm glad you did." Several seconds passed while Jake swatted away a fly that buzzed between them. "Does she feel the same way?"

Stephen looked away while he silently recollected that inexplicable, strong moment in Serenity's barn. "I think so, Jake. I mean she didn't say, but it was that look we shared." Stephen paused. "It's funny. Not long ago when I brought up having a family, she gave me the cold shoulder. I'm not sure why."

Jacob glanced down at the ground before lifting his chin to look Stephen in the eyes. "Does she want the same things you do?" When Stephen started to become defensive, Jacob stuck up a hand to stop him. "I'm just trying to help, Steve. After all, when you propose to her, you want to make sure every possible issue is resolved." He shrugged. "Trust me. I know from experience."

"You're right." Stephen sighed. "We haven't really shared that discussion yet. But do you think we really need to?" Not giving his brother an opportunity to reply, he went on. "I mean, she's Amish.

I'm Amish. We attend the same church, with the same set of people. So of course we'd both want large families."

He held out his hand and lifted a finger. "To be able to count on each other to help with the children and the chores." He extended a second finger. "To raise our family to love one another and love our neighbors as ourselves." He extended another finger and lowered his voice. "And most of all, to follow Christ."

Jacob nodded. "You're right about those things. But brother-to-brother?"

Stephen's stomach dropped while he sensed something was coming that he didn't want to hear.

Jacob laid a firm hand on Stephen's shoulder and looked at him with an expression that was an odd blend of cautiousness and positivity. "After what I went through with Trini, I can say with conviction that I'm qualified to say that things happen that are out of our realm of knowledge."

A few seconds later, Stephen's jaw opened in surprise. His eyes widened. "I get it." He followed with a slow nod of understanding.

Jacob pressed his lips together before offering a wry smile. "Uh, yeah. I assumed the same about Trini. Because we were Amish and went to the same church, I thought I knew what went on inside her head." Jacob shrugged. "Little did I know that she'd planned for a long time to leave our way of life."

That very recollection stopped Stephen's thoughts. "Uh-huh. Now I understand the doubt I detected in your voice."

"I'll tell you, Stephen, I want the same things you yearn for. Only thing is, I wasn't privy to Trini's thoughts. And by the same token, you, dear brother, aren't privy to Serenity's."

As if on cue, they turned and headed toward the house. Suddenly, Stephen realized that his brother was right. Stephen had been thinking only of what he wanted. Without Serenity's input.

As they passed the wishing well, Jacob stepped back to place his hand, with affection, on the beautiful, old brick structure. On the opposite side, Stephen touched the rope with the bucket. He wasn't sure why.

Jacob's voice was firm but held a tinge of uncertainty. "Never underestimate a woman's goals. And as far as Serenity's dreams?" They locked gazes. "You'll never know what they are"—he put his arm around Stephen's shoulders and whispered—"unless you ask her."

Early the following morning, Serenity bent to avoid bumping her head on the chicken house ceiling. As she reached for an egg, a white-feathered bird ruffled its feathers in protest. Dust clouded the space in front of Serenity, and for several moments, she closed her eyes while the dirty haze settled.

The constant clucking and the loose feathers floating in the air before landing on the nest sparked an amusing thought. *At least I don't have to live in this house.*

The corners of her mouth lifted into a thankful grin, but she was careful to keep her lips pressed together for fear of inhaling the filthy dust.

With one careful motion, she balanced the eggs in her basket. Then she finished up her least favorite job. She still found it interesting that a big, strong man like Stephen loved to bird-watch. She wondered if he liked chickens too.

It wasn't as if Serenity disliked the white creatures. Still, she certainly didn't like them. *But they can't help that they're dirty. We're all Gott's creatures.* And they served their purpose in life.

She headed toward the door, holding her heavy basket at the bottom with both hands, and carefully ducked at the entrance to step down without bumping her head.

Outside, she stood up straight and gratefully breathed in the warm, fresh July air. As she made her way to her house, Angel, gave a loud, demanding whinny from behind her. She turned and explained what she was doing. She wasn't sure why. "I'll pamper you after I clean and refrigerate these eggs. Sorry, Angel, but first things first."

Her statement didn't seem to appease him. He let out a series of whinnies and stamped his hooves. This time she didn't acknowledge his protests. *He needs to learn patience.*

Inside, she warmed faucet water, wet a soft washcloth, wrung it out, and began wiping the eggs clean. After she'd carefully placed them in the refrigerator, she proceeded to her washroom and changed into her spare dress. She made a point never to run it through the hand wringer for fear of tearing it. She placed her dirty dress in sudsy water to soak.

Back in the kitchen, she glanced at the wall clock. *I've got to get to the shop. There's a funeral in two days, and by the looks of the number of plant orders, it will be a big one.*

She proceeded to the kitchen, glancing toward the living room shelf to admire her prized garage sale buy. She smiled. *It's inspiration.* She considered its intrigue and parted her lips in awe. The Amish, in general, didn't focus on or covet material things. Neither did she. But to Serenity, this small, hand-carved, painted horse was unique and special simply because of the interesting, sad story behind the particular sale where she'd discovered it.

As she took in the intricate details of her buy, she wondered about the man with Alzheimer's. The horse was a sentimental reminder of him. Since that sale, she'd fervently kept him in her prayers. She yearned to visit him. And she longed to pray at his bedside for Gott to rid his incurable illness. Serenity believed in miracles and that the most powerful strength behind them was prayer.

As she walked back to the barn to get Angel out and hitch

the buggy to him, a chicken darted in front of her. She stopped, nearly tripping over the white-feathered body. In the distance, she glimpsed the edge of the woods—the very timber where she and Stephen had shared wonderful conversations. The thought of him prompted a smile.

Inside the entrance to her barn, she stopped. As she pulled the wooden lock upward, she frowned. *I assure everyone I'm not afraid. Maybe I'm trying to convince myself that I'm not. Because every time I come out here, something inside me tugs me back to that bad day.*

With one swift, forceful motion, she slid open the large heavy door and entered the old structure. She watched as Angel stepped in from the outside. When he joined Serenity at the gate, she ran her hand with great affection across the side of his long nose. The animal closed his large eyes until she stopped. Then his lids flipped open.

"Are you ready to take me into town?"

As usual, he threw back his neck and let out a neigh.

Serenity stepped to the wall closest to her and removed the harness from its large hook. Angel held still while she placed it on him. Then she added the bridle and bit, opened the gate, and led him outside. Hitching Angel to her buggy didn't take long. She'd done it hundreds of times. Besides, her horse loved taking her places. When he did so, it was sort of a bonding time between them.

On the blacktop, Serenity's thoughts migrated from her standardbred to the newly discovered eyeglasses. They were in a lab. *I pray that there's a full fingerprint on them. And that the print's owner is in the database so he can be identified.*

But her mind quickly drifted from the glasses to Stephen and the unexplained feeling she'd experienced when they'd been so close in her barn yesterday. While she pictured his soft, endearing expression, the pulse in her wrist picked up speed. Her heart skipped a beat.

*Stephen. I really enjoy being with him. I'm quite independent, yet when he's with me, I feel a welcome sense of security. With him, I'm comfortable. It's a nice feeling, like when I put on my knit slippers in the winter. He's protective. And he's been open about his longing to protect me permanently. When we locked gazes yesterday, his eyes mesmerized me. The soft brown color of his eyes was so heavenly, I temporarily forgot what we were doing there.*

*But we can't be together. I need to tell him why. And soon.*

It was the right time. At least it seemed like it. Upstairs in his room, Stephen could see Gabe from his window as his brother left their long drive in his open buggy. As Stephen took in what he could see of his eldest sibling, he smiled. He'd never forget how Gabe had tried his best to offer advice about Serenity. Honestly, his heartfelt input had been gut. Jacob had offered pointers too. But Stephen still believed a female's opinion was necessary before he seriously revisited a permanent relationship with Serenity.

The next time he broached the subject of a happily-ever-after with her, he didn't want any surprises. Still, his instincts told him that she was hesitating to commit to him. He needed to know how to respond if she had an unexpected situation like Jacob's wife before they'd married. Stephen stuck his hands deep in his pockets and looped his thumbs over the openings.

Right now, though, he was alone and finally, after over a year, ready to visit his late aendi's room. He didn't intend to clear it out. Or even clean it. What he yearned for was just to be in the private quarters where she'd loved to spend time.

*I've got to do this for closure.* The memorial garden that was positioned directly below him warmed Stephen's heart. He would never reveal to anyone just how lost he'd been without his aendi. His relationship with her was personal and private. Something that he'd never allow anyone close to. Every memory of her was precious. Special. And he never, ever wanted to lose sight of the memories she'd planted in his heart over many years. He yearned for the recollections of those times to grow so he could eventually share them with his own kinder.

He stepped from his room to hers and stopped at her door, which was closed. Before he entered the place she'd considered the heart of her home, he paused. To his knowledge, neither Gabe nor Jacob had been in this very special chamber. Or maybe they had but hadn't mentioned it. Perhaps they too had been moved to feel her presence. He lifted his shoulders in a shrug.

The door handle clicked when he turned it. With slow, deliberate motion, he pushed the entrance open. The hinges let out a light squeak. He stopped and blinked at the sunshine streaming in through her window. When he opened his eyes, the first thing he noticed was her simple blue curtains pulled back and attached to hooks.

This particular window allowed a bird's-eye view of the woods between the Lantz property and Serenity Miller's land. From where he stood on the second story, the vast area looked a bit different than usual. Instead of glimpsing it from the ground up, he now viewed it from the treetops.

He swallowed an emotional knot while taking in the exquisite beauty of the lush green foliage, the gigantic old oaks, and the pines. He'd never actually realized how dense the area was. He imagined that from an airplane, one wouldn't be able to see much besides the thickness of the plants and trees. That is, in the summer.

While he looked around, he thought of Serenity and smiled, recalling how close to his aendi he'd been. His mouth eventually curved in amusement while he acknowledged that his body warmed with great love and affection whenever he thought of the town florist.

But this was his aendi's room. And that he'd entered it was

evidence that he'd taken a big step in addressing his grief. His gaze landed on the simple queen-sized oak bed and two handsewn pillowcases of different shades of blue.

The quilt revealed images of horses. He was certain that the standardbreds she'd taken in over many years had inspired the details. Stephen stood there in silence, quietly imagining his aendi falling asleep every night with the soft covering. She'd loved her horses. In fact, she'd considered them family.

As he remained very still, he breathed in the relaxing scent of lavender. Then he noticed ornate, delicate-looking, purple sachets on her writing area. A beautiful arrangement of dried flowers acted as the centerpiece for the desk. Automatically, he wondered if Serenity had made it.

He then focused on the cream-colored walls. Behind her bed hung a cross-stitch of what looked like the front of her barn. Slow steps took him to the art, where he squinted to see her initials, *ML*, sewn in the lower right-hand corner.

As he glanced around the room's four corners, he sighed with compassion. Compared to his late aendi's room, his own seemed empty. He couldn't speak for every Amish person, but typically the rooms of Plain Faith members—at least those he'd glimpsed—were more austere.

But Aendi Margaret's... He let out a low whistle while noticing numerous cards placed throughout her bedroom. *There must be twenty.* Some were on her desk. Others were taped on her four walls. And a few decorated the small pegboard in front of him.

With one slow, cautious motion, he opened a card that showed a hand-drawn horse. *Obviously, this is from someone who knows her very well.*

He touched the corner and studied the detailed pencil sketch. He opened it to see the words *Happy Birthday*. He narrowed his brows at Serenity's signature.

Then he glanced again at the picture, wondering if she'd been the artist. If she had, she was even more talented than he'd already known. He continued to check out the cards from his sister-in-law, Trini, from Abigail, and from various church members.

Some had merely signed their names. Others had penned heartfelt messages: "Margaret, Happy Birthday! We wish you many more years filled with excellent health! Love, Jesse and Mary Yoder."

He continued reading the handwritten messages. As he did, emotion welled inside him, and he blinked back tears. The second hand of a small battery-operated clock circled all twelve numbers, and he realized he'd lost track of time. He drummed his fingertips against the desk.

It became clearer to him how extremely special his late aendi had been to so many. Numerous messages came from people he'd never heard of. And given their non-Amish names, he acknowledged that Margaret's goodness had obviously extended to many lives.

He turned and made his way toward the west wall, where a pair of teal knitting needles and a purple ball of yarn topped a magazine pile. From the looks of it, she'd started a pair of slippers. He wondered who she'd intended them for.

He touched the semifinished project and closed his eyes a moment in great appreciation of experiencing something so soft and obviously personal of his aendi's. *There's something about being in her room. It's as if she's telling me what she did before her sudden death. Being amid her personal belongings makes me feel close to her in an odd yet wonderful way.*

He moved the project to the comforter and scanned the magazine pile. With one careful motion, he made himself comfortable on the edge of her bed. As he did so, he continued to enjoy the light, comforting scent of lavender. He looked down to his left and glimpsed a purple heart sachet between her pillows. He smiled a little and plucked the top issue of the *Good Samaritan* from the stack.

Immediately, he recognized the title. Mamm was an avid reader of this particular Christian magazine. So were numerous other church members. Then he glanced at the date and pressed his lips together thoughtfully. *It's on top. But why? This issue is nearly two decades old.*

Curious, he skimmed through the pages until he discovered something she'd highlighted in yellow. It was the popular Christian advice column where "Charlotte" answered people who wrote to her for advice. It was common knowledge, at least to Mamm, that "Charlotte" responded with well-thought-out answers, utilizing scripture.

He held the magazine closer and read out loud:

*Dear Reader,*

*I am sorry to hear that your brother has left his wife and children. It must be devastating for the family. I've given this situation much thought, and unfortunately, this is an occasion where I'm not able to offer you something that will bring a happy ending to you or your family.*

*But here's what I can say: Multiple Bible verses speak about forgiveness. Realize that simply forgiving your brother won't bring him back. It won't provide your nephews the role model they need and deserve. But there's a poignant Scripture about forgiveness in the book of Luke, chapter seven. It tells us that forgiveness is a path to love.*

*Ultimately, here on earth, we cannot control many things that happen. But I believe that through our trials and tribulations, God teaches us, and in that process we become closer to Him.*

*My favorite verse about the problems we face rests in the book of John, where we're reminded that there will be problems in this world but not to be discouraged, because God has overcome the world. My ending comment: forgiveness is a beautiful thing, and it's only through forgiveness that you'll truly heal.*

*All my best,*
*Charlotte*

Absorbing the personal letter, Stephen laid the magazine on his lap and parted his lips in awe. As he considered what he'd just read, a bright beam of light soared in through the window opposite him. He didn't look away. Nor did he blink. The revelation in front of him revealed many important elements.

*Aendi Margaret requested advice.* He sat very still for some time. Then it sank in how truly agonized she must have been when her own brother had left their family. Stephen had always believed that Mamm and his brothers had suffered most. Now his eyes had opened to how distraught the betrayal had left his late aendi. For one thing, Margaret's printed message revealed how very distressed she'd been when Stephen's daed had deserted him and his family—that Aendi Margaret had been in such dire need of answers, she'd turned to a well-known advice columnist for help.

While the bright ray of sunshine landed on the typed words, Stephen leaned back on the pillow. Still holding the advice column, a mélange of emotions whirled inside him. There was such chaos in his heart, he finally laid the magazine on the bed, stood, and stepped to the window.

As he took in the beautiful land that seemed to go on forever, homes that dotted the country, and woods that loomed between the Lantz property and the Miller dwelling, he rocked on his toes before shoving his hands into his trouser pockets. He took a deep breath.

*Relax. It's okay. . . But is it?*

He pressed his lips together in a straight line. He focused on what he'd read. That his dear aendi had reached out to a total stranger for consolation prompted a painful knot in his throat. For many years, he'd looked to her for strength. To him, Aendi Margaret had been the solid rock that had remained courageous and strong in faith when everyone else around them had sought answers.

Now he acknowledged that she had been as devastated and helpless as the rest of the family when her brother had left. When she'd stayed in Lancaster, helping them regain composure, inside she'd been as burdened as he and his brothers.

*Aendi Margaret, who did you lean on? Who was your rock?* A dull ache in his stomach tugged fiercely at Stephen as he realized the vulnerable person inside his tough, role model's facade. *She was a human being, just like the rest of us. She bore the same emotions. And what her brother did to us left her searching for answers.*

While his gaze lingered on the barn, he imagined her finding solace in midst of the chaos. He could envision her feeding him and his two brothers every morning while their beloved mamm prayed for strength and guidance.

The very realization that Aendi Margaret had been just like the rest of them struck him with such strong ferocity that the truth suddenly changed him. How he wished that she were here to offer guidance and strength to Serenity as she recovered from the "bad day." It hit him that the woman he yearned to be with the rest of his life was, perhaps in many ways, like his late aendi.

He'd been impressed at Serenity's calmness and logic throughout the days after her barn incident. But now he imagined it was very possible that inside she agonized more than was discernible.

He paced to the bed and back to the window, where he studied the woodsy area. To him, his walks with Serenity on the dirt trail between their homes meant much more than birdwatching. After he'd begun his hikes with her about a year ago, his binoculars had become a mere prop.

Talking with her and sharing things had taken on a life of its own. Because when he conversed with the Pink Petal owner, their discussions and the thoughts behind them had enriched his life to the point where their time together had become as vital to him as drinking water. As important to him as eating breakfast and attending church every week.

Now that he'd been exposed to something that his late aendi had obviously considered very private, he realized that he must care for the florist with the very same nurturing that Aendi Margaret had never had but had desperately needed.

He barely saw the trees and thick foliage that encompassed the beautiful gifts of nature as his mind focused on the woman who'd so lovingly and generously gifted him and his brothers everything she'd owned.

As he reminisced about his precious relationship with her, he could recall time after time when he'd requested her help about something he couldn't understand. He'd sought out her advice on so many things that didn't even matter. He shook his head.

*But did she ever lean on me?* For long, thoughtful moments, he tried to remember one occasion when Margaret had approached him for assistance. *Try harder. You talked to her so many times over your twentysomething years. Surely you helped her. . .*

Then it came to him. She had asked his opinion on what to make for dinner. Or his thoughts regarding a certain church message. Even if he'd predict that the crops would do well. But as far as actually heeding personal advice?

The woods continued to blur while his shoulders tensed. His fingers cupped the hems of his pockets. He continued to think while he returned to her cards, which had obviously held great importance for her—at least enough that she had displayed them in her private room.

He looked at the birthday card Serenity had given to Margaret, and at last, he focused on the beautiful, detailed pencil drawing. His heart warmed but also ached. The woman who'd so graciously and generously offered him, his brothers, and their mamm so much love and comfort hadn't once come to Stephen with a personal issue.

*I never realized it. Aendi Margaret, you continue to teach me. Even though you're not here. I won't tell anyone what I've learned from you today. Never. But know that I feel an even closer bond with you than I imagined possible. And my respect for you is the highest ever. While I've learned about you today, I've also acknowledged something very important about Serenity. She too lives alone. She too makes it a large part of her life to bring joy to others by creating special arrangements for total strangers. But you've made me extremely aware that even those who appear strong need comfort and strength. And because of you, my dear aendi, I'm going to make sure that Serenity knows she can lean on me. I'll take Jacob's advice: I'll learn everything I can about her. But most of all, I need to reach her heart so that very soon, Serenity Miller will be Serenity Lantz.*

Stephen knew that something was keeping Serenity from a man-to-woman relationship with him. He yearned to talk to a woman about how to help Serenity open up to him. His brothers could only offer so much. And he didn't want to talk about his personal feelings with Trini or Abby. Then he thought of Margaret's letter to Charlotte.

He made his way to the stack of magazines, picked up the top copy, and proceeded to Margaret's desk. He pulled an envelope, a pen, and a blank piece of paper from her drawer, sat down, and addressed the envelope to Charlotte's column. Then he wrote a heartfelt letter.

# CHAPTER TEN

The Quilt Room finally cleared out, and Trini heaved a sigh of relief. She had nothing to complain about. Her business was bustling, to say the least, but it had been a long day.

The door chime sounded. Trini looked up from her cash register to see Abby and Serenity. "Gut afternoon," she said, suddenly recalling that it was that very special day of the week when she and her besties met in the back room to quilt and to spill their deepest secrets.

Enthusiasm edged Abby's voice. "I have gut news about Gabe and me!"

Trini and Serenity glanced at her. Trini responded, "He asked to court you!"

Abby sealed her lips and shook her head. Then her mouth lifted at the corners into a happy smile. "You'll have to wait to find out!"

Serenity stepped to the back while Abby and Trini chitchatted. At the same time, Trini compiled some lists into a neat little pile. During their conversation, the gentle, unique scent of herbs began to migrate into the main area.

Trini and Abby shared a glance. "That's our health guru!"

Abby nodded. "And that's one of the many reasons we love her." After Trini agreed, Abby looped her arm around Trini's waist.

Side by side, they entered the small area and claimed their usual chairs.

As they organized their quilting materials, Serenity directed her attention to Trini. "Customers have come in and out of your shop all day."

Abby agreed. "And we're not even approaching a holiday." After a slight pause, she added, "What's up?"

Trini heaved a sigh. "Lots of stuff going on." After a slight hesitation, she softened her voice. "I hate to say this, but I think my business has picked up because of what happened to Serenity."

"What?" Serenity's voice reflected surprise.

Trini nodded. "You know how Margaret said that something gut usually comes out of something bad?"

Two heads nodded.

"I think the enormity of what happened to our Serenity has made our community more appreciative of our loved ones." She smiled. "In my opinion, the awful attack has sparked more love and generosity. Customers have mentioned that because of the unexpected incident, they have become more aware of how they want to show their love to each other. And gifting quilts is a unique way to do that."

Serenity shrugged. "Same thing with my floral business." She paused. "At least, something good came out of it. Showing our love for one another is what Gott wants from us. But I still don't understand why the men were in my barn or why they attacked me."

Abby's voice was filled with emotion. "I've wracked my brain trying to figure out why it happened."

Trini pulled a needle from her blue pin cushion and squinted while she threaded the eye. After she completed her task, she pulled the short end, ran her fingers over the doubled thread, and scooted her chair closer to the frame.

"Not to change the subject, but I've hired a part-time clerk to help with bookwork, so that'll free me up for more time to design."

She stopped a moment and set down her needle. She couldn't stop an appreciative smile from lifting the corners of her lips when she glanced at Abby and Serenity. "How are both of you?" Before either could respond, Trini's voice filled with emotion. "I've missed you."

Serenity released a small sigh while she addressed Trini's heartfelt statement. "Oh, Trini, I've missed you too." Then she turned. "And you too, Abby."

Abby lowered her eyes to the frame before dropping her work to her lap. "A lot has happened since our last meeting—that's for sure."

Trini and Abby both turned to Serenity as Trini spoke. "I don't think our lives will be normal again until those guys are caught. We just have to accept that."

Serenity crossed her legs at the ankles and sipped her tea. Trini took in her calm expression. But she was quick to glimpse the anxiety behind Serenity's baby-blue eyes. Trini empathized with the florist so much that frustration filled her day and night for not being able to do more to help her to carry on from the "bad day."

Abby softened her voice to a sound that was half urgency and half curiosity. "Do they have any new leads?"

Trini chimed in. "How about the fingerprints on the eyeglasses?"

Trini was quick to note the expression of disappointment on Serenity's face as she put down her cup and leaned forward a bit. "Not yet." She crossed her fingers. "Please keep praying that we'll get a match."

Abby looked down at her sturdy black shoes and spoke in a low tone that was barely more than a whisper. "I hope so."

Trini thought a moment before responding. Then she narrowed her brows while she considered what had happened right here in the safe little countryside town of Arthur, Illinois. In her best friend's barn. "The question everyone is still asking is *why*. Do the police have any inkling yet of why those two were on your property?"

Serenity lifted her hands in a helpless gesture and gave a strong shake of her head. "No."

Abby moved toward the edge of her seat and straightened her shoulders. "I feel so helpless! There's got to be a next step."

Trini narrowed her brows. "A next step?"

Abby waved her hands in frustration. "Jah! You know! Something else we can do. There's always a next step."

All three women had ditched the project to focus on this serious subject. Trini was the first to stand. Then Abby. Then Serenity. Quick, urgent steps took them to the window, where they stood in a circle.

They joined hands. Trini looked at Serenity, then Abby. "I know what we can do, ladies." After two curious sets of eyes met hers, she spoke. "Pray."

Serenity nodded. Abby smiled with affection. "Trini, you always know what to do."

At the same time, they bowed their heads, and Trini prayed with a great sense of urgency. "Dear Gott, we're only here to serve You. Thank You for all You do for us. But right now we have a special request. Dear Lord, please catch the men who hurt our friend. Answer our questions. And please. . .guide us to do what needs to be done to catch them. Amen."

Serenity thanked Trini and Abby. Trini smiled slightly. She could feel the blood rushing to her cheeks as she began to get lightheaded. When she reached for a chair for support, Serenity grabbed one arm. Abby caught the other.

Suddenly, the subject of conversation was on Trini as her two besties helped her sit down.

Serenity rushed to the water tank and began filling a glass with water. Abby laid her hand on Trini's forehead. "You're warm.

Honey, I think you're sick."

Trini looked up. "No. I'm pregnant!"

That evening, Serenity enjoyed time with Angel. Inside the barn, she ran her hand with great affection over both sides of her horse's long nose. As she did so, she thought of today's conversation in the Quilt Room with Trini and Abby. Her stomach ached. Her whole body felt tense.

While she considered the recent unusual happenings, she reached for Angel's brush, stepped inside his stall, closed the gate behind her, and made her way to his side to caress his thin hair. "I'm at peace here. Mostly because you're with me." After a few long, drawn-out strokes, she said in what was barely more than a whisper, "But it's time I figure things out."

Angel closed his large eyes while Serenity moved her brush over his strong body. She breathed in the animal smell and the earthy scent of fresh straw and oats. It was funny. In this very barn the worst thing in her life had happened. But it was also inside this old, comforting structure that she found a sort of peace and solitude that she'd never experienced anywhere else.

For many reasons, Angel made a good sounding board. He didn't criticize. He didn't offer bad advice. But here, with Serenity's dear four-legged confidant, she felt at ease enough to convey her thoughts. "I know it's not easy being a horse. It's hard being a human too."

She ran her free hand down the sensitive place between his eyes. He gave a soft whinny. Serenity's movements appeared to calm the standardbred. The motions also slowed the anxious pace of her own heart to a speed that enabled her to relax and finally sigh in relief.

Outside the Plain Faith, there were many means to help alleviate stress. She spoke to the Englisch every day at her shop. There were therapists. Facials. Massages. Spas.

Serenity was fully aware that there were numerous brands of churches, and that most of them shared what was important: belief in Jesus Christ, that He'd died on the cross, and that He'd risen from the dead. She was sure that if she'd been born to Catholic parents, she'd be Catholic. If her parents had raised her Lutheran, she'd most likely be Lutheran. Of course, the truth was that many within her church didn't think as she did, but that was fine. *We all walk our own path. And I'm on my journey alone with Gott.*

The smell of straw, the scent of oats—even the old wooden steps leading up to the hay loft—were Serenity's loves. So it was only fitting that this very structure would be where she voiced what really bothered her.

*It's time to decide how to handle my feelings for Stephen. I learned a lot from my sickness as a youth. It taught me what a strong role the mind plays in emotions.*

*I believe that Gott blessed me with an extraordinary amount of tenacity to recover. And I'm forever grateful. But right now I need to figure out another matter. Stephen has serious romantic feelings for me. And I reciprocate. But I must use my mind to rid them, the way I did when I said goodbye to my virus. The two scenarios are different. But in a way, aren't they the same?*

She stopped to consider the question. When her hand dropped to her side, Angel clomped his hooves and gave such a strong shake of his head that saliva hit Serenity in the face. She laughed as she closed her eyes and ran the back of her hand over her eyes. "Really?"

She considered Trini's unexpected, joyous announcement. Serenity couldn't stop a wide smile. Serenity had already started planning the dried flower arrangements she would create for the baby's room. That way, whenever Trini rocked the little one, she'd breathe in the most calming scents that nature offered.

That thought quickly reminded Serenity to check the eucalyptus that hung from lines in her darkroom. She gently patted her horse on the side and used her most reassuring voice. "Don't worry. I'll be back."

Serenity pulled hairs from the brush, threw the handful in the trash, returned the brush to its place on the oak shelf, and stepped to the corner room near the entrance. Before opening the door, she pulled the lantern from its hook on the wall and flipped the On switch.

At the entrance to the small floral room, she adjusted the lantern in her right hand. Drying flowers and greenery were best accomplished in a dark room since light faded the plants' colors. She turned the handle, stepped inside, and quickly closed the door behind her.

Inside, the fresh scent of her favorite filler made her close her eyes to appreciate the fragrant moment. She opened her lids and carefully checked the lines that traveled from one wall to the other. Dried eucalyptus branches hung upside down so the oils would drip toward the top of the branch, and therefore the leaves would also dry upward. In this room, there was no need to worry about rodents. Mice and rats didn't like the smell.

Because there wasn't much space, Serenity was very careful not to bump the stems, which had been in this dark, dry area for a few weeks. The small light enabled her to check the bundles, held together by rubber bands.

She checked the floor. No twigs had fallen from the line. She smiled with satisfaction, lifted the light to see the handle, turned it, and closed the door behind her. On the opposite side, the vast contrast of scents was hard to ignore. She appreciated both.

She flipped the Off tab on the lantern and hung it next to the spare. For long moments, she stood very still while taking in the piles of straw at the back of the barn.

*I will not be afraid.* But amazingly, her fear didn't stem as much from the intruders as it did from the way she'd warmed inside when Stephen was with her.

*All of this time, I've ignored what I came in here to address. I can't continue to sweep my feelings for him under the rug. Or his obvious love for me.*

Angel let out a demanding neigh. Serenity rolled her eyes. "I promised you I'd come back. But no caresses right now. I've got to replace your straw so you're comfortable."

Serenity stood on her tiptoes to reach the rake handle hanging from a hook near the horse bridle. Rake in hand, she made her way to Angel's stall and began clearing the corner closest to the gate. The moment the metal spears met the concrete with an unpleasant squeaking sound, the horse made an abrupt turn and proceeded out to the pasture.

*I can't say that I blame you. I don't like that sound either.*

She cleared dirty straw and continued to transport it outside until the burn pile was large. Ensuring that the gate to Angel's stall stayed locked, she gripped the wooden handles and pushed the wheelbarrow from and to the stall. As she did so, she contemplated the horse's obvious longing to explore the main area of the barn. Serenity wasn't sure why he longed to go on the prohibited side. She supposed it was just the nature of the animal.

Serenity had taken notice that the bar that separated the stall from the open barn area had been moved. In fact, somehow, Angel had managed to push the latch out of its holder. If he figured out what to do next, he'd have access to the entire barn. *I must have the old latch replaced.*

*It's weird, Before the intruders, Angel never tampered with the latch. My horse tried to warn me, but I assumed that his chaotic behavior was the result of the storm, despite weather never before causing such a reaction in him. How wrong I was. Angel has never feared bad weather. But I never would've suspected strangers were in our barn.*

After she filled the wheelbarrow, she pushed it back outside to the burn pile and emptied it. Then she moved it back into the old barn. She needed to designate thinking time. About Stephen. Now.

Outside Serenity's barn, Stephen shoved his hands into his pocket and heaved a sigh of satisfaction. He had mailed his heartfelt letter to Charlotte. At least, he'd taken a step to hopefully move his relationship with Serenity forward. There was no guarantee that he'd get a response. And if he did, he had no reason to be concerned about his letter being printed in her column. The fine print had made it clear that if the magazine intended to publish a letter, the sender would be required to sign an authorization form.

Stephen's heart pumped with a combination of uncertainty and excitement when he glimpsed Serenity raking Angel's stall. After giving his letter much thought, he realized that he still wanted Serenity to know his feelings and his intentions. And that Charlotte, if she responded, could add important helpful details to assist him to better understand Serenity's stance from a woman's viewpoint.

He stood at the entrance to the barn, lifted his hand, and knocked to announce his arrival. As he did so, his arm froze in midair while he watched her work.

As he took in her slender figure and the long, loose blond hairs that had escaped the confines of her kapp, his heart fluttered. But the excitement that passed through him wasn't so much a physical longing as it was a deep respect and great appreciation for everything gut this woman offered the world. And for what she'd contributed to his life.

As she loaded her wheelbarrow, he noted her agility. Her entire body radiated energy and positivity. An enthusiastic shiver swept up his back and landed between his shoulders.

She hadn't spoken so much as one word to him, yet just watching her had energized him. Since adulthood, Stephen had never encountered anyone who'd ignited something so wonderful and inexplicable.

*Don't get tongue-tied. You can do it.*

He knocked again, louder. She turned and smiled. "Stephen!" She motioned. "Please. Come in."

He stepped toward her. She was inside the stall. When he stood on the opposite side of the gate, she rested her rake against her thigh and let out a breath. "You're just in time to help." Before he could say anything, she went on. "I'm only kidding, you know."

He opened the gate and joined her. "But I'm serious."

She lifted a curious brow. "You can work with me on one condition."

"What's that?"

The ray of sunlight coming in allowed him to glimpse the creamy flecks that danced behind her irises with an odd blend of uncertainty and determination.

She leaned forward slightly and spoke in a soft tone. "You must let me help you clean your barn."

He narrowed his brows. Then he grinned and gripped the wooden handles of the wheelbarrow, which was filled with dirty straw. As he opened the gate, pulled the barrow backward over the metal hump that divided the open barn from the stall, then started to move toward the entrance, he stopped a moment to offer her a conciliatory nod of agreement. "Deal."

Outside, he emptied the used straw into the burn pile and made his way back into the building. *Ask her. Now. There won't be a better time.*

Inside, Serenity was headed toward the back of the old structure. "If you want to bring that over here, I'll stock it with a fresh bale."

They stopped where the straw piles started. He watched as she retrieved an aluminum ladder from the wall and pulled the legs apart. He stopped her with his hand. "Allow me."

She stepped aside while he ascended the steps and shoved the nearest bale off the top of the stack so that it fell into the wheelbarrow. He jumped down, folded the ladder, returned it to its hook on the wall, and pushed the load of straw. She walked behind him.

"Stephen, I'm used to doing this, you know."

At the stall, he stopped, lifted the straw by its twine, and turned to her. "Where do you want it?"

She motioned to the back right corner. "There."

He placed it where she'd pointed.

"I usually start at the back and rake forward."

Their eyes met. Then he pulled his cutting knife from his pocket. "I do it the same way."

With one swift motion, he slit the twine in the middle. The straw immediately fell into a pile. Serenity started spreading the bedding as Angel stepped into the barn.

When the horse entered the area, Stephen held up a hand and moved to the other side of the gate. He clicked the latch into place and chuckled. "I don't intend to be your horse's next victim."

Serenity immediately stroked her standardbred's long nose. It never ceased to amaze Stephen how she and her horse seemed to share a mutual understanding. And when she planted a kiss on him and told him to go back out to the pasture, Angel obeyed.

*It's a relationship I'll never understand. But if I'm going to be part of their family, I'll have to figure out a way to be friends with him. It's ridiculous that I'm even thinking like this.*

Serenity propped her rake in front of her and met Stephen's expression with sudden curiosity. "Are you okay?"

Stephen stepped closer and offered a delayed nod. "I've been doing a lot of thinking."

"About what?"

"That I never want you to go through anything like that 'bad day' again."

She smiled appreciatively.

"Me neither. I don't expect it will happen again. Once was enough—that's for sure. But Stephen, if it does, I'll be strong. Gott will protect me. Just like He did before."

Stephen cleared his throat and tried to think how best to tell her what he'd come here to say. "Uh, Serenity?"

"Jah?"

He was so close to her, he could smell the fresh citrus scent of her hair. He glimpsed the unsure look in her eyes.

He took the rake from her fingers, lifted it over the gate, and propped it against the nearby wall.

His voice came out as barely more than a whisper. "Serenity, we make a gut team, don't you think?"

After a slight pause, she responded. "Stephen, you've become a gut friend to me. You must know that."

Their noses nearly touched. But he took great care not to physically touch her. It wouldn't be appropriate, and he would respect that. He was on one side of the gate; she was on the other.

The breeze came in through the open doors and moved a loose strand of hair on her face. With one very gentle, deliberate motion, he held the strand between his fingers and carefully placed it back behind her ear.

"Serenity, I want us to be more than friends. I've been picturing you as a mamm, chasing our kinder in the yard. I dream of us going to church in a buggy filled with little ones. Serenity, I've never felt so strongly about a woman." He paused, and his voice caught with emotion. "I want to be your protector 24-7."

After a slight pause, he asked, "Will you be my wife?"

# CHAPTER ELEVEN

*He asked me to marry him.* That evening, Serenity's fingers shook as she changed the placement of the eucalyptus in the arrangement she was working on. Inside her kitchen, the gentle smell of herbs filled the area with a scent that was a combination of medicinal and floral.

Her pulse jumped on her wrist. She tried to focus on her work, but all she could hear was Stephen's voice, which had been so gentle, genuine, and filled with love and honesty.

She hadn't answered him. Immediately after his heartfelt question, Angel had reentered the stall. This time her horse had let out a loud whinny and his teeth had clutched Stephen's right suspender.

There was no more putting it off. Serenity had to tell him she couldn't marry him. And why. At least begin the conversation. And it would be tomorrow.

Laughter filled the new home of Jacob and Trini Lantz as silverware clicked against porcelain plates. At the dinner table, Stephen tried to display a normal facade. Inside he was torn. Serenity's horse had reentered the barn as she'd opened her mouth to answer, but even so, her uncertain demeanor had warned him that she'd been hesitant to respond. And this evening as they'd gathered for dinner, she'd avoided him.

The low timbre of Gabe's voice broke his thoughts. "Stephen, would you pass the dumplings?"

Stephen nodded and forced a half smile as he reached for the large casserole dish. Jacob nudged him. "Eat up! You're gonna be an *onkel*!"

Stephen glanced at Jacob and his pregnant wife. He couldn't stop the corners of his lips from lifting into a huge grin. "I can't wait to hold the little guy. Or girl."

Gabriel chuckled while returning his glass to a white napkin.

Trini's eyes sparkled with joy. "If it's a boy, I hope he'll grow up big and strong like his daed." She leaned excitedly against Jacob. "And his onkels!"

Trini's mamm jumped in on the conversation. "And if it's a girl?"

Jacob spoke with pure joy. "If it's a girl, I hope she'll quilt like her mamm. And"—he added, glancing with love at Trini—"I hope she's independent like you."

Trini laid an affectionate hand on her husband's arm. "Careful what you wish for!"

Everyone laughed.

"If you remember, my independence took me away from you."

Jacob met her gaze with the most endearing expression Stephen had ever seen in his elder brother's eyes. "But it also brought you back to me so we could finally get married."

As Trini's mamm reminded everyone of how Trini had migrated from their close-knit community, Stephen recognized something that lifted his spirits a bit. He would never forget how Trini had left Jacob devastated. Inside, Stephen ached as he mentally relived the hard times that Jake had endured before Trini had eventually returned to Arthur and had confessed her love for him.

*She put him through a lot. I'm relieved things worked out, but for several months, I didn't know how to help my brother deal with losing the woman he loved and had planned to marry from a very young age.*

Stephen pressed his lips together in a straight line. *But Gott answers prayers. Only Gott can work miracles. And He did. Hopefully the same result will befall Serenity and me.*

Gabe nudged Stephen, and obvious enthusiasm edged the eldest Lantz's voice. "Did Steve tell you what we're doing?"

Trini and Jacob glanced curiously at each other before returning their attention to Gabe. "No."

"We're working on a walnut crib. Stephen has already arranged to buy the wood from a friend who owns a logging mill out east."

The words of Trini's mamm came out in a soothing tone as she rested her fork next to a piece of fried chicken. "That is a lovely idea." After a slight pause, she continued. "And walnut. . ." She sighed. "It will be beautiful." She eyed Jacob before her attention landed on Gabe. "What a nice idea. Oh"—she drew her arms over her chest and breathed in—"I can already see that our new baby will be nourished with plenty of love and attention."

Trini's eyes misted. When she responded, her voice cracked with emotion. "I can think of no better family to welcome our little one into this world. More important than anything, he or she will be raised with Gott's love."

Trini glanced around the table and got up out of her chair. "With this invigorating conversation, I almost forgot to offer seconds on lemonade."

Stephen held up his glass. "That sounds gut. But I'll get it." He looked at her tenderly. "Conserve your energy."

Stephen got up, and Trini sat back down. "My, I'm already enjoying this special attention!"

Stephen stepped toward the kitchen. "Is the pitcher in the fridge?"

"Jah. Denki, Stephen."

Stephen opened the door, retrieved the pitcher, and carried it to the table, where he filled the glasses that Jake, Gabe, and Serenity held out for him.

After dinner, Jacob helped Trini's mamm into his buggy while Gabe and Stephen helped Serenity into hers. As Stephen sat next to Gabe on their way to the Lantz home, Gabe was unusually talkative. "Stephen, all of this talk about nephews and nieces is getting me in the mood to meet new additions to the family."

Stephen's lips curved in amusement. "Looks like you'd better get busy, Gabe."

"For what?"

Stephen chuckled. "To find a wife. Age doesn't go backward."

To Stephen's surprise, Gabe shook his head. "No children on this end, Steve. I love kids, but long ago I decided not to marry. There was enough drama when Daed left to last a lifetime." After a slight pause, he went on in a more serious tone. "But. . ."

The buggy wheel hit a bump, and Stephen sat up straighter. "But what?"

"I've been taking note of you and the town florist. When are you two gonna start courtin'?"

Stephen pressed his lips together in a straight line. He wasn't sure what to say for two reasons. For one, he hadn't expected the question. And second, Gabe's interest in the subject wasn't without justification. Both brothers were keenly aware of Stephen's interest in Serenity. But in his heart, he was sure that something was off. Little did Gabe know that Stephen had already proposed. That he'd been so enamored with Serenity Miller that he'd skipped the courting step and darted right to the proposal.

But for some reason, Serenity wasn't interested in discussing a future. And going by her apparent avoidance of him this evening, he was certain something stood in the way of the happily-ever-after he longed to have with her.

Maybe the "bad day" had affected her more than she let on. He couldn't imagine that she didn't have feelings for him. Over the past year, they'd shared a closeness that he could only conclude was love.

*But something's off. And I vividly recall Jacob's dilemma with Trini. She'd had plans that Jake hadn't known about. Maybe with Serenity there's something I'm not aware of. How can I read a woman's mind?*

Serenity obviously harbored something she hadn't conveyed to Stephen. *And I have no idea what it is. I wish she trusted me enough to be honest with me.*

Surely she wasn't planning to leave the Amish life.

*I don't think so. But something's causing her to pull back. What is it?*

This afternoon would be special. As the chime above the Quilt Room door sounded, Trini greeted Serenity. Stepping into the main area, Serenity extended a large, fresh floral arrangement.

Trini bent to smell the blooms. When she looked up, she smiled. "Oh! To what do I owe this pleasure?" Before Serenity answered, Trini softened her voice to a serious tone. "They're beautiful!"

Trini's face flushed. Already Serenity noticed that her pregnant friend's glow gave away her excitement at carrying a little one.

As Abby stepped from the quilting area to join them, she echoed her approval of the gorgeous flowers. Serenity commented as they moved to the back, "I wanted to do something to celebrate Trini's great news. At the same time, the two of us"—she pointed to Abby—"will enjoy them while we quilt."

Trini retrieved a vase from a lower cabinet, added water, and arranged the flowers in it. As she took in the arrangement, which she placed on a table, she turned to her friends. "They energize me! Thank you, Serenity!"

"You're welcome. Glad you like them."

Abby claimed her usual seat near one of the corners before addressing Serenity. "I'm not sure I've ever told you this, but you create the most gorgeous combinations of plants and flowers I've ever seen in my entire life. The way you place each stem—they're picture perfect!"

Serenity dipped her head modestly to accept the compliment. "Denki."

Trini claimed her usual chair, but Serenity made her way to the vase and turned to her friends. As she breathed in the sweet floral scent, she spoke with passion and didn't try to hide her excitement. "I've got news for you."

Two sets of eyes lingered on her face.

She smiled a little as she motioned to the flowers. "I'd like you to know that this isn't just an ordinary arrangement.

"No?" Abby countered.

Trini's eyes met Abby's curious expression before looking at Serenity, who offered a firm nod.

"They may look like gorgeous blooms—and they are—but in the floral world, each of these beauties holds a significant meaning."

With tenderness, she touched the stem of a pink tulip. "These, for instance, symbolize love." Her smile widened as her heart warmed. "I want to make sure that you always know I love both of you." She glanced at Abby before turning toward Trini. "I don't really need any other flowers in this arrangement." She paused to breathe in before continuing. "But so many emotions are intertwined with love."

Serenity lightly touched a bluebell. "These are lovely. And fragile-looking. Did you know that they represent kindness?"

Trini's and Abby's mouths opened in surprise.

Serenity moved her finger to a freesia and softened her voice.

"This, my friends, just happens to be connected to trust."

Abby's voice was filled with wonder. "That's so interesting."

Trini sat up a little straighter and pointed. "How about the white roses?" Serenity's brows narrowed a bit as she gently touched one of the delicate blossoms.

"These, my dear, are meant solely for you. They signify a new beginning."

Trini looked down and gently touched her growing belly. Her cheeks flushed with a becoming shade of pink. "And that's so appropriate," she exclaimed with awe, "because I'm newly married. And now Jacob and I are starting a family."

"That's right!" Abby blurted.

Serenity joined her two friends at the quilt frame.

"People underestimate the power of plants. There's so much more to them than their beautiful blooms and sweet scents."

While Serenity made herself comfortable on her straight-backed chair and began organizing her pile, Abby's scissors made a clipping sound as she snipped cream-colored material around a large plastic piece. Trini glanced up at Serenity before inserting sky-blue thread through the eye of her needle.

While Serenity enjoyed the comfortable, easy silence with her two besties, a sense of peace filled her with a much-welcomed sense of satisfaction. A light, sweet floral scent floated through the small quarters. She looked around at the familiar things that had been staples in this quilting area for a long time.

Of course everything was organized. Serenity couldn't stop the grin that pulled at her lips—it was common knowledge the owner of the Quilt Room had once been addicted to list making. But before Trini and Jacob had married, when Trini had returned from living out of state temporarily, she'd decided to cut back on what she wrote on paper.

At first, reducing the size of her lists had seriously challenged the newly married Mrs. Jacob Lantz. But now Serenity's and Abby's best friend seemed to have adjusted to one list a day. Not to mention, her new home was free of the unending lists taped to the kitchen walls of her former home.

While Serenity started to hand sew a corner piece, she considered how fortunate Trini was to finally have everything she'd dreamed of. Of course her life hadn't come without struggles.

Today Serenity would reveal something she needed help with. As she tried for the right words to convey the issue at hand, she sat up a little straighter and pressed her lips together in a thoughtful moment. "Trini? Abby?"

They glanced up at her.

She softened her voice to a level that was both serious and hesitant. "I'm struggling with something."

As two sets of curious eyes looked at her to go on, Serenity glanced in the direction of the front of the store. "I can't risk it being overheard."

Abby was the first to agree with Serenity's concern. "I understand. We can't forget how Trini's big secret got out!"

Trini shook her head in dismay. "Or what resulted because of it. But we learned the hard way that whenever someone enters this shop, if they close the door slowly, the chime may not sound."

Abby's expression was thoughtful. She lifted an uncertain brow. "At the same time, if our Serenity needs to share something important, we've got to listen. And help her."

Trini got up and stepped to the store's customer area. When she returned, she made her way to Serenity. Abby joined her. Trini pressed her finger to her lips. "No one's here. But just in case—"

"Whisper," Abby cut in.

This wasn't exactly how Serenity had planned to tell her besties what tugged at her, but Abby was right. If she whispered it, even if someone entered the shop, they wouldn't hear her.

She looked up at Abby. Then Trini. "I'm afraid I'm in a bad situation. The way Stephen feels about me. . ." She offered a helpless shrug. "It's serious. In fact, he wants to marry me."

Two gasps of joy and surprise followed.

Serenity waved her hand for them to stop. "But it should come as no surprise to you that he wants a home full of children. Kinder from his family bloodline. Little ones to carry on his family's legacy." She nearly lost her voice as she continued. "And the virus that I had years ago. . ." She looked down at the floor and fought back tears. "I'm very lucky to be alive. But unfortunately, I'm unable to have kinder."

That evening, Stephen stepped quickly down his front porch steps and stopped. He turned to admire the beautiful remembrance garden that had been created for his beloved aendi. He closed his eyes and whispered. "Oh, Aendi Margaret. I wish you were here. I wrote Charlotte for help with Serenity. Thanks for the idea. Don't worry. I'll never tell anyone that you wrote to her too."

When he opened his eyes, he breathed in the fresh country air, and his heart warmed while he glimpsed the bird feeder. In the distance, he could see gray smoke from a ditch fire that made him recall wonderful family memories of hot dog and marshmallow roasts. As his attention returned to the bird feeder, he smiled. Margaret had been the ultimate bird-watcher. When he'd been old enough to walk, she'd purchased binoculars for him and had patiently taught him how to use them. The two had shared the special hobby as they'd walked the beautiful hills of Lancaster.

As she'd shared her knowledge about various species, his aendi had convinced him that birds were Gott-made distractions to pull people's minds away from irritating worries and instead focus on the interesting, feathered creatures that could disappear as quickly as they appeared. While the gentle breeze caressed the back of his neck, he took in the plants with great appreciation.

For long moments, he stared down at the leaves and the blooms. They seemed perfectly set in place, as if they'd been born there. Then his gaze traveled to the porcelain angel.

He crossed his arms over his chest and considered the vast similarities between real angels and Aendi Margaret. He swallowed an emotional knot that blocked his throat. A buggy traveled down the east-west blacktop. Behind it came a tractor. Stephen frowned. It was common knowledge that farm equipment driven by the Englisch made loud noises and frightened the horses pulling Amish buggies.

While he studied the angel's delicate wings, he tried to recall scriptures and church sermons and finally admitted that he didn't know a whole lot about angels. What he was sure of was their goodness, and in his mind, they were Gott's faithful helpers. *Aendi Margaret is with them.* That sudden realization prompted his shoulders to relax. He tapped the toe of his boot against the ground.

He stretched his arms and, with a gentle motion, laid his hands on top of the wooden fence. With great affection, he wrapped his fingers around the bar that he and his brothers had set in place after the interior of the bed had been finished.

He looked up to the second story. As he considered the great comfort he'd found while he'd sat on Aendi Margaret's bed and read her cards, something unusual stirred inside him.

*I talked to Margaret numerous times about my sadness when my daed left our family. I was so young when he moved out of the house, it took me a few years to fully understand that he was never coming home. And it was Aendi Margaret who kindly explained to me in terms that*

*I could comprehend that his absence had nothing to do with me, my brothers, or Mamm.*

*She'd gone on to explain as best she could what had happened so the facts had come out logically and were easy to understand. She'd conveyed the sad truth in such a way that I fully understood yet felt no anger.* A shiver swept up his spine, and his entire body shook. He rolled his shoulders to rid the uncomfortable sensation. He strummed his fingers against the fence and leaned forward a bit. *How did she do that?*

Long moments later, the question lingered in his thoughts. He wasn't sure, but later in life, during his teenage years, his outlook on his daed—his selfishness and irresponsibility—had hit Stephen with such a fierce, unyielding reality that his natural inclination had become to be the great protector of Mamm and his brothers. *Almost overly protective.*

That astounding realization turned his thoughts to Serenity. *I long to protect her. Always. Especially after that "bad day." Something's off. And it's understandable that her hesitation causes me to pause. It's not that I don't love her. I do. Very much. And for me, there will be no other woman. Serenity is intuitive. She senses and understands things that most other people don't.*

The sound of a horse trotting up his drive broke his reverie. From her open buggy, Serenity waved. He waved back and stepped to her buggy. When Angel stopped, he tied the horse to the nearest pole. With the bit in Angel's mouth, Stephen didn't need to worry about the horse biting him. As he helped Serenity from the buggy, he narrowed his brows. "To what do I owe this pleasure?"

"Stephen, we need to talk."

As Angel pulled Serenity's buggy down the Lantz drive, Stephen stood very still. He dug his hands deep in his pockets and looped his thumbs over the top edge. His jaw was set. Inside he was numb.

As the buggy turned out of the lane and slowly onto the blacktop, Stephen reflected on their short time together this evening. And especially on Serenity's shocking revelation.

*Now I understand her aloofness. Just now, she confessed something so tender and so delicate that I can only imagine what she's going through.*

As his gaze encompassed the vast area of bean and corn fields that loomed all around him, the narrow blacktop roads, and the two-story homes that dotted the country landscape, he cupped his chin with his hand. *I'm a simple person. Why is my life so complicated?*

He meandered toward the soybeans and crossed his hands over his waist as he took in the beauty of the deep green crops. The even rows. The clean field.

*I love Serenity. But my longtime dream of extending my family's bloodline has been nixed.* He shook his head and looked down. He barely saw his leather boots. Or the grass on which he stood. Or the grasshopper that hopped onto a leaf, blending in with the crop. *Charlotte can't fix this. Is there a way to solve this problem?*

He made his way down the border of the Lantz yard and the field. From where he stood, he could easily glimpse the beautiful woods where he and Serenity had shared numerous walks over the past year. So many conversations.

"We can always adopt," he thought out loud. A few moments later, he stopped and pressed his lips together thoughtfully. *That's fine, but I'd still like to continue my heritage. It would be like recreating Mamm and Aendi Margaret. My kinder will keep alive my favorite family members. I don't know if I can let go of that dream. And I can't pretend it's not important.*

Stephen loved Serenity. He couldn't imagine life with anyone else. Slow, uncertain steps took him back into the old home and up the stairs to Margaret's room. As usual, the door handle clicked when he turned it. His fingers lingered on the brass knob before he dropped his arm to his side. He let out a sigh of relief and stepped inside. Immediately, a sense of warmth and reassurance swept through him.

He turned to the magazine pile next to her bed, where his gaze lingered. He considered the letter he'd sent to Charlotte. More than ever, he hoped for a response. But now that he understood Serenity's inability to bear children, he doubted whatever the magazine lady told him (if she even responded) could help him with this situation.

*But Aendi Margaret, you could.* Stephen's late aendi had always been the epitome of strength and faith. Still, even she'd needed guidance.

He looked around. The floorboards creaked lightly as he stepped to the window that overlooked the barn and the crops. He glimpsed Gabe. Stephen went back and closed the door. It clicked into place. Then he narrowed his brows, sat on Margaret's bed, and retrieved a magazine. He thumbed through the pages. Finally, he laid down the issue and continued exploring the rest of the pile. Each time, he turned to Charlotte's column.

Heaving a frustrated sigh, he got up and stepped to Margaret's desk. As he pulled out her chair, he dropped his pen, which rolled underneath the desk to the baseboard. When he bent down to pick it up, his fingers touched the baseboard. It moved.

He forgot about the pen as he gently put his thumb on top of the baseboard to carefully press it back into place. Instead the board flipped open. His jaw dropped in shock. His pulse began to beat in double time. Hidden inside a hollow place in the wall was a small hope chest. He barely noticed the light cedar scent as he removed the chest.

Chest in hand, Stephen moved out from underneath the desk. He stood up and laid the unexpected find on the desk. As he looked down in awe, he slid his finger underneath the latch and opened the lid.

# CHAPTER TWELVE

That evening, inside her small, comfortable living room, Serenity breathed in the relaxing scent of lavender as she sewed the corners of a handmade sachet.

She'd deliberately chosen this particular project tonight because she was familiar with lavender's aroma and its calming effects on the brain and nervous system. It was the best natural remedy for stress. Anxiously, she pulled the sachet to her face and breathed in slowly before releasing the air.

Immediately, her anxiety eased. Her heart didn't pound as quickly or as hard. She relaxed her shoulders and laid the bundle of purple on her lap while leaning back on the soft cushion of her navy, cloth couch. She parted her lips.

A few seconds later, she crossed her hands over the soft, scented cushion while reflecting on her difficult admission to Stephen. She frowned and stayed very still while vividly recalling his obvious disappointment. The abrupt silence that had followed her revelation was deafening.

She tried to remember an indication in his expression or in his words that could lead her to believe everything would be okay. Serenity gave a sad shake of her head. Tears welled in the corners of her eyes. He'd not expressed one sign that what she'd conveyed to him was by any means acceptable.

A morose combination of dismay and disappointment swirled inside her. Still, she forced herself to stay composed. Serenity was no stranger to conflict. While suffering from the virus that had robbed her of her ability to conceive, she'd had plenty of time to accept her fate. And because of it, she'd vowed never to fall in love. She'd been fully aware of how important children were in an Amish marriage. In most marriages, she guessed. And during her long hours in bed, she'd convinced herself that if she did indeed fall in love, there was a wonderful alternative to not producing children. She and her husband could adopt.

But some time ago, Stephen had openly expressed how much he longed not only to have children but to pass down his family's bloodline. Heritage.

She swallowed and sat up straighter. Then she forced herself to practice the positive thinking that she'd applied for years. She'd exercised it so much over so many years that she'd talked herself into believing that infertility wasn't a disadvantage.

She sat up a little straighter and pressed her lips together in a straight line. *I'm a child of Gott. He's given me much to be thankful for. He created me with a gift to make people smile. I'm me. That's enough. It's always been enough.*

Of course she'd had years to accept the truth. And she'd garnered plenty of opportunity to, in her mind, make it okay. But today Stephen had heard it for the first time. Given his dream to continue the Lantz heritage, no matter how she worked out the situation in her mind, there was no way she could help him have biological children.

*I'm not going to let this upset me. What I did took great courage. At least I was honest with him. I started the dialogue about my secret. And now I won't feel as if I'm leading him on.*

Her gaze drifted to the front window, where a large oak branch made a light sound as the wind moved it against the glass. She glanced down at her lavender. The scent was a godsend as it continued to help ease her anxiety.

He'd reacted. *Why did I dare to hope it wouldn't matter?*

The following day inside Trini's new kitchen, Abby washed a tray of glass jars while Serenity dried them. An evening sunbeam floated in through the small kitchen window and lightened the oversized, black-speckled granite countertop a notch.

Serenity blinked to adjust to the sudden brightness before she rested a dry quart jar on the towel to her right. "This worked out well!"

Behind them, Trini agreed. "And it just so happens that Jacob will be home later than usual." She let out a satisfied sigh. "Having you here with me feels gut. You know—" She stopped.

Serenity looked behind her to see why Trini had abruptly stopped speaking midsentence. But the moment she glimpsed Trini's blanched face and painful expression, she nudged Abby. "Trini, are you okay?"

Serenity rushed to her pregnant friend. Abby followed. At he table, Trini closed her eyes and let out a painful moan while she clutched her abdomen. Serenity knelt beside her. On the opposite side, Abby bent to take Trini's hand in hers.

Serenity pressed her ill friend to respond. "Trini, honey, please tell us how we can help."

Trini cried out, still clutching her belly. "Something's wrong with my baby." Her voice suddenly became breathless. "Please, Gott. . ."

Serenity looked down at the blood on Trini's apron and knew they needed an ambulance right away. All that mattered was saving Trini and her baby.

She glanced up. "Abby, go to the barn and call an ambulance."

"Jacob. . .please get Jacob. He's still in the field."

Serenity hollered to Abby to notify the Lantz brothers. It would be impossible to reach Jacob. But hopefully Gabe or Stephen would pick up the message soon enough.

Abby rushed out of the house. The screen door banged shut behind her. As Serenity took in the enormous amount of blood on her friend, she knew she had to act right away. She squeezed Trini's hand. "Honey, please tell me what I need to relay to the paramedics when they get here." She gave Trini's cold hands a tight, extra-reassuring squeeze. "You'll be okay. The baby will be fine. Help will be here soon." After a slight hesitation, Serenity spoke with a firm voice. "Would it help to lie down?"

Trini winced. "The cramps are unbearable. Serenity, I can't lose this baby." As they looked at each other, Serenity couldn't ignore the desperation in Trini's eyes or that her lips were losing color and her face was filled with fear and pain.

Trini moaned. "Serenity, would you rub my back?"

"Of course." Serenity positioned herself behind her friend and moved her hand gently up and down Trini's back. Her navy dress was wet. Serenity took in Trini's blanched face. Her closed lids.

Automatically, Serenity moved her hands to Trini's shoulders and began massaging them. Her heart ached for her friend's obvious agony as well as what appeared to be the risk of losing her precious baby that she and Jacob yearned for.

Trying for something encouraging, she whispered, "Just hang in there. It's going to be fine." As she took in Trini's distressed expression, Serenity doubted her last statement. *Gott, please. Let this be okay.* When Trini's eyes opened and widened in fear, Serenity moved her massage to the back of her head. Her caresses deepened on her neck, which was slick with perspiration.

Over the years, Serenity had read plenty of books on homeopathic relief. Unfortunately, she was short on information for miscarriages and childbearing techniques. But she vividly recalled what she'd learned about the power of the human mind.

*Continue to encourage. She can't lose hope.*

Serenity forced her voice to remain calm. Even so, her words weren't all that steady. "Just take a deep breath and think of the times we made sponge cakes in Margaret's kitchen."

That statement sparked an unexpected grin on Trini's mouth as she appeared to study Serenity with welcome amusement. Serenity continued her line of encouragement. She offered a firm nod. "Slow, deep breaths." As she listened to Trini breathing in and out, Serenity spoke in her gentlest voice. "There you go."

All the while, she wondered when the paramedics would arrive. And how long the drive to the hospital would take. *Please, Gott. Get them here.*

Suddenly, the screen door sprang open, prompting both women to see who was entering. Abby bounded inside. Her face was flushed. Numerous hairs had broken free from her kapp. Serenity noticed tiny creases around Abby's eyes that she'd never observed before.

"Good news! Help is on the way!" The words came out in a rushed, desperate breath. "And I called Margaret's house and left a message."

"Denki." The word came out of Trini's lips in a barely audible whisper.

Abby bent closer to Trini's face. "Do you have a heat bag I can fill with hot water?"

This time Trini didn't respond. Her face had lost more color. Her eyes were closed. Her lips were parted. Serenity's heart pumped so hard, she thought it would jump out of her chest. For a tense moment, she and Abby looked at each other before focusing on their friend.

After what seemed an eternity later, Serenity heard an emergency siren. She'd never been so impatient for anything in her entire life. The back porch window and the kitchen window offered a view of bright flashing lights. The door flew open and hit the wall with a bang. As three men rushed inside, Serenity stood from her kneeling position and rushed to them. As succinctly as she could, she updated them on what had happened.

Without wasting time, one man knelt next to Trini and began taking her pulse. Two others stepped quickly back outside where they retrieved a stretcher layered with a white sheet. They carried it inside.

Trini was not responding, visibly or verbally, but Serenity continued reassuring and encouraging her as the paramedics positioned her onto the narrow, flat bed. With one simultaneous, swift motion, a medical worker on each side lifted Trini and transported her out of the house where they hoisted her into the ambulance's large rear opening. From inside, the third man pulled the stretcher until it was fully inside the vehicle. Serenity's voice was firm as she spoke to the first responders. "I'll ride with her."

Abby cupped her mouth with her hands and shouted from several yards away. "You go! I'll find Jacob and meet you at the hospital."

Once Trini was in, one tech jumped up into the emergency vehicle. The last one outside slammed the rear doors closed and rushed to the front passenger side, where he jumped in and shut the side door.

In a firm tone, Trini called Serenity by name and reached out her hand. Serenity took it and squeezed it with a hopeful reassurance. One of the techs spoke to both women. "Which hospital do you prefer?"

When Trini moaned and closed her eyes, Serenity was quick to answer the question. "Decatur Memorial."

Some within their Amish community had been patients there, and the hospital's reputation was good. While a tech continued monitoring Trini's pulse, Serenity continued her softest, most encouraging tone. From experience, she was fully aware that a person's determination—or lack thereof—could make a difference between life or death with medical issues. It was vital that Trini didn't give up.

As the siren blared, all Serenity wanted was for Trini not to lose her child. "Please, Gott. Protect my friend and her baby. Please let them be okay."

Trini's face was extremely pale, and she'd lost a lot of blood. Her eyes were closed, but Serenity was sure her friend had heard every word of the prayer.

"Her pulse is weak," one of the techs reported.

The ride to the hospital went quickly. All of a sudden, the emergency vehicle stopped, the back doors opened, and a hospital crew worked in unison to lift the stretcher out of the ambulance and transport it through the sliding doors of the emergency room. Serenity followed in a rush.

"Room 2," someone said. They slowed to get the stretcher in through the hospital room's doorway. They maneuvered the stretcher beside the hospital bed and together moved a semiconscious Trini onto it.

Serenity watched Trini's eyes open and saw the combination of fear and agony on her face. As a worker typed on an electronic device, Trini's labored voice made all heads turn her way. "I'm losing my baby."

Inside the spacious waiting lounge, Stephen, Gabe, Abby, and Trini's mamm joined Serenity. Jacob was with Trini. Stephen sat next to Serenity, staring straight ahead. Neither spoke. She glimpsed the tense expression on his face. His jaw was set. With a sudden movement, he leaned forward. He propped his elbows on his thighs and eventually pressed his palms over his face. Despite her sympathy for Stephen, his callous response to her painful, honest revelation the evening before still stung.

A sober-faced Gabriel paced from wall to wall. When he stopped in front of Abby, they spoke in low tones. Serenity couldn't hear the conversation, but she guessed that it was speculation about Trini and her baby. The nurse had promised to come out and update them as soon as there was news.

Trini's mamm was on Serenity's other side. She didn't say a word but took Serenity's hand in hers and squeezed it. Mrs. Sutter's fingers trembled. Serenity cupped her other hand with great affection.

Time seemed to stand still. In front of them, a small television hung from where the cream-colored wall almost met the ceiling. As a news commentator predicted the weather for the coming days, Serenity barely heard him. Her mind was on Trini, how much blood she'd lost, and Serenity's desperate prayers that this nightmare would produce a happy ending.

Besides the voice of the television reporter and a few low-pitched conversations, there wasn't much noise. Abby followed Gabe to the information booth, and he said a few words to the woman on the other side of the plastic window. While Gabe and Abby stood very still, the clerk turned and proceeded back into the secured area.

When she returned, she reclaimed her post opposite Gabe and shook her head as she muttered a few words. Serenity squeezed her eyes shut and said another silent, urgent prayer. When she opened her eyes, she began to pay more attention to the dismal surroundings and quickly ascertained that the place was in dire need of inspirational touches. Serenity imagined colorful quilts hanging from the walls. While she checked out the entrance, she envisioned a table boasting a huge, bright floral arrangement and a cross-stitched scripture inside a beautiful oak frame.

The room was large but austere. Perhaps this waiting area's designer had purposely made it bleak. But why? *People are sick here. This is the very place where inspiration is truly needed. Something to encourage their spirits. To reassure the family and friends of the ill patient that Gott prevails.*

*Oh, Gott, please prevail tonight.*

Serenity's voice pulled Stephen from his reverie, and he turned to her.

Her words came out softly and with reassurance. "Stephen, Gott will protect Trini and the baby."

He swallowed an emotional knot and smiled slightly. It suddenly occurred to him that they hadn't said anything to each other during what seemed like an eternity that they'd been next to each other.

When he leaned closer to her, his sleeve touched hers on the black armrest. The heat from her body seared through his sleeve to his arm. *It's reassuring. Like when mamm made me sponge cakes. This comforting sensation reminds me of what went on inside me the moment I rescued Serenity. Right now she needs me. We need each other. But I don't deserve her. My poor reaction to her deep-seated issue must have hurt her terribly. I need to keep my mouth shut until I hear from Charlotte. I might not get a reply. And if I do, it might not give me direction in this dire situation that isn't Serenity's fault. Or mine.*

He swallowed. As much as he loved her, right now things between them were stressed. And the trouble Trini and her baby faced only made things worse.

Serenity's eyes glistened with moisture. They reminded him of dew on the crops. His low voice broke the silence. "Serenity, this will be okay. Don't you think?"

Serenity stood and glanced down at him. She offered a small nod. "Stephen, I hope so. But what we can do is ask Gott to protect them. All of us. Because there's tremendous strength in the power of prayer. And at the end of the day, it's all in Gott's hands."

He watched in awe as she gathered the group. Serenity extended her hands, and without words, they formed a circle. Stephen took her left hand. Abby held her right one. Serenity closed her eyes and pleaded for protection for her friend and the unborn baby. When she lifted her head and opened her eyes, there was a unanimous *Amen*.

At that moment, the sliding double doors opened. A man with a long white coat appeared and looked around.

"Gabriel Lantz?"

Serenity stood extremely still. So did Stephen. Gabe stepped forward and introduced himself.

While the doctor spoke in a low, serious tone, Stephen took in the physician's expression as well as Gabe's. The oldest Lantz brother listened with his lips pressed together in a straight line.

Neither man smiled. At what appeared to be the end of the conversation, the doctor offered Gabe a pat on the shoulder before Gabriel lowered his gaze to the floor. A few seconds passed before he turned to the group. The sad expression in his eyes told Stephen everything.

"Trini's going to be okay. But the baby didn't make it."

Stephen and Gabe hugged. Abby and Serenity did the same. Trini's mamm walked away from the group. Serenity's breath caught in her throat as she absorbed the devastating news. She watched Gabriel head to the parking-lot window and stop. He shoved his hands deep into his pockets and stood very still while staring into the distance. Serenity's heart ached for Trini. For Gabe and Stephen. For Jacob and for Trini's mamm. For everyone.

As a couple entered the lounge area, the sound of the sliding glass doors parting and closing made a soft noise. The man and woman proceeded to the information booth.

Serenity's attention shifted to Stephen. His devastated expression left no doubt in Serenity's mind how he was taking the news. *I need to help him. Even though he's causing me so much pain, he has always been there for me. But what can I say to ease his agony? Maybe it's better to just stay quiet and support him by being present.*

While a nurse came out to talk to an elderly couple, slow steps took Serenity to Stephen. Her voice cracked with emotion. "Stephen, I'm so sorry."

He motioned to the sliding doors that separated the lobby from the large parking lot. "Let's get some fresh air."

Without saying a word, she stepped with him through the exit. Outside, reality began to sink in. Serenity shuddered.

Stephen stopped, turned to her, and softened his voice to a tone that was a combination of comfort and reassurance. "I'm sorry for you, as well." His voice cracked with emotion as he attempted a smile. "We'll get through this together. Serenity, right now I'm so thankful you're with me."

The statement was offered so genuinely and so honestly, she should have been appreciative of his admission. Instead she stiffened. The endearing expression on his face and the affectionate sound of his voice conveyed a man-to-woman connection. Serenity looked away and forced herself to stay calm. *He shouldn't behave in this manner. He knows I'm not able to provide him what he dreams of having. And his reaction to that news was hurtful to me.*

But Stephen was persistent. Very gently, he pressed the small of her back, nudging her toward the sidewalk. As they walked in silence, she absorbed the chaotic background. Ironically, the parking lot took on another life as an emergency vehicle's loud piercing sound pulled into the hospital's emergency unloading. Paramedics worked quickly, jumping from the back of the ambulance and transporting a person strapped to a stretcher into the hospital while other medical staff took information from them.

On a nearby road, a horn blared, and Serenity turned in the direction of the ear-piercing noise. She winced as one car nearly hit another head on. Serenity released a shaky breath and drew her hands to her chest in dismay.

The brevity of human life sank in. For a very long time, Serenity had been aware that every second was precious, but tonight the reality of it shouted at her until her ears rang.

They continued the walk downhill as different makes of vehicles pulled in and out of parking spaces. *So many are in dire need of medical care*, Serenity observed. *Once upon a time, I was one of them. Tonight it's my dear friend.*

As they turned to go up the concrete steps, a car alarm sounded with a steady, irritating beeping that blocked out everything else.

Neither she nor Stephen spoke until the deafening noise finally stopped. The alarm's echo rang in Serenity's ears. She took in Stephen's expression. Tiny creases showed around his eyes. Small lines etched themselves near his mouth.

Stephen sighed. But Serenity was keenly aware that it wasn't an expression of relief. Not by any means.

"I guess all I can do is lend my support to Jake and my sister-in-law." He formed a weak smile. "And I'll test your theory of positive thinking. I was really looking forward to becoming an onkel." His voice drifted off to a dreamlike tone. "I imagined helping the little one to walk. Teaching him or her how to bale hay. In my mind, I saw us taking buggy rides together. Fishing."

Serenity relaxed a little, and the corners of her lips pulled upward a notch. His words were said with such love and honesty, she felt badly that she wasn't the woman to offer him his dream. "Give it time, Stephen. There's no doubt in my mind that when Gott makes the decision to provide you nieces and nephews, you'll be a wonderful onkel."

He hesitated and an unexpected expression crossed his face. "Thank you for reminding me of that, Serenity. I had forgotten that Gott already knows our future. He's even aware of the number of hairs on our head. Jah, I trust Him. And that very faith will get me through this." Sounding more hopeful, he added with a half smile, "It's how we'll all survive this night."

Serenity agreed with a nod. She softened her voice to an emotional level. "Life is all about overcoming our trials."

Her heart sank. What energy she'd had seemed to evaporate. She was feeling not only Trini's deep pain but her own.

*I'm a valuable person just the way I am*, she reminded herself. *It's just that Gott gave me a purpose other than bearing children. I trust Him. He's never made a mistake. He never will.*

# CHAPTER THIRTEEN

The following afternoon, Trini tried to display a brave face as voices filled her new home. In her downstairs bed, she smiled a little while taking in the chorus of chitchatting that emanated from the kitchen. After all, not many women were blessed with so many close friends and family members. From where she lay, she could hear Mamm directing everyone on where to place the food they'd brought to Trini and Jacob. Her numerous sisters talked at the same time, and it was difficult to make out what each was saying.

Mouthwatering aromas gleefully morphed into one solid wonderful scent and floated deliciously into Trini's room. Her stomach growled. With a gentle, slow movement of her hand, she touched her now childless abdomen. As she rested her fingers on what had been her baby's home, warm, salty tears slid down her cheeks. A sob escaped her.

*Do not be sad. Trust in Gott.* She wiped away the moisture on her cheeks and forced the corners of her lips upward. She sniffled and realized that dealing with loss was a common necessity of life. Twenty days from now, her situation wouldn't change. Twenty years from now, it would be the same. *So I have to accept it and move on.*

All her life, she'd been taught to look at the glass half full rather than half empty. Margaret Lantz had insisted this was the way to go. And that's how the late aendi of Jacob, Stephen, and Gabriel had lived her life. Perhaps that's why Trini had never heard her complain or seen her sad.

Trini sighed. *I can't recall one time when Margaret complained.* And despite the great loss that she and Jacob—and their entire family and friends—had suffered, there was still much to be thankful for. *Gott has been so gut to us. Even when Jesus died on the cross, He didn't complain.* The enormity of that realization nearly stole her breath.

She tried to dismiss the trip to the ER and the awful moment her doctor had told her that their baby boy hadn't made it. For a powerful moment, she closed her eyes, added a pillow underneath her head, and imagined an angel holding her baby and carrying him through heaven's gates. *What about a blanket? Does the angel have a blanket to keep him warm? I won't get to see his first smile. Hear his first word.* Her heart sank again. But she wouldn't allow sadness to overcome her. She thought of Margaret Lantz and tried to do as she would have done in Trini's position.

Trini drew in a determined breath and then released it as she enjoyed the comfort of the beautiful quilt that she pulled up to her chin. She parted her lips in awe as she imagined holding her little one in heaven. As the emotional picture tugged at her heart, she wondered if the child she'd carried in her womb yearned to be with his mamm. *What do babies do in heaven? Do they cry? Do they crawl? Does Gott give them puppies to play with?*

*I'll have to wait to get there to find out. But I'm sure my baby is happy. In heaven we want for nothing.*

For some reason, Margaret just wouldn't leave Trini's thoughts. Jacob's late aendi had always stressed to her, Abby, and Serenity that there were no guarantees in life. *That's for sure.* But Margaret also insisted that a person becomes strong by overcoming obstacles with logic and prayer. In the end, everything working against us in this life teaches us. And these barriers must be regarded as training in order for us to become wise and more patient.

The corners of Trini's lips curved upward. Eerily, it seemed as though Margaret was in the room with her, advising her and explaining everything the way she'd seen it. She certainly had relied on humor.

*But she's right, even now.* The theory sounded simple when emotion was taken out of the situation. In Trini's opinion, the mind was easier to deal with than the heart. *The mind has no emotion. The heart does. But that's the way Gott made us. Be positive. You'll get through this. Be strong for Jacob.*

The clinking of pots and pans carried into her room. Familiar voices continued to travel there as well. She turned onto her side, and her gaze landed on a small corner nightstand where homemade baby bibs had been stacked in a neat little pile.

Another hot tear slid down her cheek. Again, she forced a smile. *So much to be grateful for. Don't overlook your blessings because of one painful loss.*

But in her heart, she knew she'd never be able to shove this miscarriage out of her memory. Till the day she died, she'd always wonder what kind of personality her lost one would have had. If he would have looked like her or Jacob. If he would have fished with his daed and onkels. If he would have eventually been a daed himself. If he would have loved sponge cakes.

She wished she had answers. But she didn't. And she wouldn't until she got to heaven. In the hospital, she'd overheard a nurse comment that she was still young and that there were plenty of years to produce offspring. Trini was sure that nurse had never lost a baby. And even if Gott blessed her and Jacob with twenty kinder, Trini was fully aware that at every dinner, there'd be an imaginary empty seat.

A light knock on her door made her look toward the sound. "Come in." She sat up straighter and tried to act normal when Abby appeared with a bowl on a small tray.

Abby's voice was soft and concerned. Trini was quick to note her friend's red eyes and the tiny crinkles around them. But she knew Abby would try to disguise her sadness for Trini's benefit. "I thought some homemade chicken noodle soup might help you feel better." After a slight pause, she added with what appeared to be a forced smile, "Compliments of your mamm."

Abby patiently held the tray in front of Trini while she adjusted the pillows and her hips to sit in a position that would allow her to eat. With great care, Abby placed the tray on her lap. Trini glanced at the unexpected rose.

"Let me guess. The flower is from Serenity."

Abby laughed. Suddenly, Trini's heavy load seemed a lot lighter. Abby shoved back a lone tendril of hair that had escaped her kapp. "And trust me, it took her forever to pick it out." Abby's voice cracked. "She wanted the most beautiful bloom for you."

Trini's heart warmed. "Tell her I love it."

As Trini sat with the tray on her lap, she handed the rose to Abby. "I'd hate to waste this beautiful flower."

Abby offered an understanding nod. "I'll find a vase and put this beauty in water." Gently, she took the flower from Trini's fingers.

"Denki."

Trini noticed a cross-stitched napkin. Her jaw dropped as she looked up at her alterations friend. "Did you. . ."

Abby offered a nod. "My bestie can't have just any old napkin."

The two laughed. Trini placed the beautiful work to her side. "It's too nice to use." She winked at Abby. "It will give me something to admire while I recover."

Abby responded quickly. "Oh, it's washable." After a concerned pause, she asked, "How are you feeling?"

"My heart is heavy, but physically I'm ready to go about my business."

Abby shook her head. "Not yet. The doctor insisted on forty-eight hours of bed rest." Then Abby glanced at the soup. She spoke in a motherly fashion. "You'd better eat that soup before it gets cold."

Trini's voice was edged in delight. "Mamm always did make the best chicken noodle soup."

As Abby walked away, she nodded agreement. She turned back to Trini. "And she worries enough for all of us."

Before Trini ate, she bowed her head and prayed. "Dear Gott, thank You for all You've given me."

At the Pink Petal, Serenity silently prayed for Trini and Jacob's emotional recovery as well as Trini's physical rebound while she relished the fragrant aroma of newly delivered gardenias. She gently touched a dark green leaf and admired the beautiful, fragile-looking flower.

Gardenias were her all-time favorite bloom for scent. Unfortunately, she rarely carried them. Although she loved the beautiful petals, two main drawbacks kept customers from purchasing these delicate flowers and kept her from buying them from vendors. For one thing, they were high maintenance, and their white blooms easily and quickly yellowed. Still, a large funeral would take place tomorrow, and it just so happened that the Englisch deceased had, while living, requested gardenias for his casket.

She opened the glass door to her refrigerated room, stepped inside, and carefully positioned her new arrivals into an empty holder. For a moment, she enjoyed the coolness. Outside the temperature was unusually hot for early August, and she ran her store's solar power conservatively.

After placing two sweet-scented beauties in her refrigerated room, she automatically ran her palms over her apron to smooth the wrinkles before closing the heavy door behind her and stepping toward her worktable behind the shopping area.

She regarded today's long list of orders and tapped the toe of her sturdy black shoe against the tiled floor while pressing her lips together in a straight line and trying to form a logical order in which to create her arrangements.

She glanced at the wall clock and carefully considered the most sensible order for projects. As the second hand made a circle around the numbers, she pressed her finger to her lips and thought hard. *The birthday arrangements come first because the delivery person will be here to get them within the next two hours. Then I'll arrange the funeral plants and bouquets since that pickup will be midafternoon.*

While serenity organized the different sizes of holders, the strong gardenia aroma lingered in her shop area. She smiled a little and began adding soil to the pots on her table. Her attention quickly returned to the gardenias and what a pleasure it was to work while enjoying their delightful fragrance. Without a doubt, she sensed a connection to them because they were most appropriate for the current stage of her life.

*Gardenias represent hope and renewal.* She used her right-hand scooper to transfer potting soil to the plant holders. *They also carry a special message of self-reflection. That's exactly why I'm focusing on them.*

Today, however, Serenity couldn't help but mourn Trini's loss and wonder how she and Jacob would move forward. She also considered her very difficult admission to Stephen, his devastated reaction, and how she could use these challenges to garner positive energy to enable her to grow as a person.

As she removed the first *spathiphyllum*, commonly known as a peace lily, she admired its deep green leaves and the three large, white, heavenly looking blooms. They often appeared at funerals, but there were many reasons to use them as houseplants. Their leaves absorbed airborne toxins. And they were among the hardiest genuses of plants. They could survive many days without water, and when they drooped and appeared to be near death, they could easily be revived. They didn't need much sun either.

*Think of this as a brand-new start. You can't control what the virus did to you. You do not have control over Stephen's need for a large family—or your inability to offer that to him.*

She sighed while sticking a eucalyptus stem into a vase. *There's no way to change his obvious disappointment at your predicament. But look at the positive side of this! Stay grateful. At least you survived the virus and are able to carry out your life's passion, which is to create beautiful arrangements that make lives happier. Something gut comes from something bad.*

At this moment, however, her heart ached at the vivid recollection of the devastated expression in Stephen's eyes when she'd told him of her infertility. Suddenly, the turbulent green shade of the eucalyptus turned into a beautiful, calm blue. A strange sense of peace overcame her, and she smiled.

*At least I told him about my inability to bear children before his feelings for me grew stronger. I will no longer carry the heavy truth that has weighed me down since we met. Stephen is free to choose a wife who's able to bear kinder.*

Serenity dropped her scissors while cutting another stem. The noise of metal meeting tile pulled her back to her arrangements. Margaret Lantz had been at her side when she'd suffered the long bout of Epstein-Barr. During Serenity's illness, life hadn't been easy. But just as Margaret had predicted, gut had come from something bad. The bedside talks with Stephen's late aendi had offered Serenity useful and practical insights on what Margaret had referred to as the other side of the coin.

Margaret had always stressed how setbacks often help us move forward with more zest and positivity. Serenity's mouth curved in amusement.

She admitted that Stephen's late aendi had harbored some unusual thoughts. But her opinions seemed to have come from within. Rarely from anyone else.

*So there are two categories of people: the strong and the weak. I choose to be strong, which means I will not let this situation impede my life. How can I use my inability to bear children along with Stephen's need to have kinder to my advantage?*

As she fished for answers, Serenity moved some stems and studied her creation with a critical eye, deciding how to make it even more beautiful than it already was.

She continued seeking the "something gut" that should result from this most difficult situation. Finally, she laid her palms flat against the table in front of her, leaned forward a bit, and laughed. As hard as she tried, she couldn't come up with one thing. Tears slid down her cheeks.

*Stop. You're at work. Maybe you need to absorb the pain before you try to turn it into something positive.*

She sniffled, dabbed a soft tissue on her cheeks and under her eyes, and forced a positive outlook. She lifted her chin in determination. The last thing she intended was to focus on negative thoughts, but she couldn't help wondering when she and Stephen would talk again.

Her focus moved back to Trini. *I am strong. So is she. But I can only begin to imagine the heartache that she and Jacob are experiencing.*

Serenity stepped to the countertop to select a birthday greeting to attach to the nearly finished arrangement. She smiled satisfaction, reached for a black ink pen, and signed the sender's name on the card.

With one quick motion, she stuck it between the two clamps on the green stick, shoved the holder into the dirt base, carefully placed the arrangement into an appropriate box, and closed the sides. Her heart smiled. *This gorgeous gift will make someone very happy. I'm blessed to have played this role in creating joy.*

Suddenly, the heavy weight of defeat lifted from her shoulders, and she felt much lighter. Again, she faced hard reality. But now she was determined to survive and grow stronger. There was much to be grateful for, and her life was still full, despite loving an Amish man. A man she couldn't marry.

*Serenity, it's time for a new start.*

# CHAPTER FOURTEEN

At the Glick home on Sunday, Stephen missed much of the church service, distracted by other thoughts. The myriad of information inside his late aendi's hope chest continued to consume his attention. Her birth certificate was the first thing he'd seen. He'd also been contemplating his relationship with Serenity—his guilt at how he'd dealt with her. And sadness filled his heart for Jake and Trini.

After the service, he sat quietly between his two brothers as they readied for the dinner prayer. The breeze pulled a hair loose from Trini's kapp when she sat down next to her husband. She glanced down at Stephen's plate and narrowed her brows in skepticism. "That's all you're eating?"

She laid her hand on his forehead and grimaced. "It doesn't feel like you have a fever." She softened her voice. "I've heard there's a bug going around."

Stephen made light of the attention by teasing that he needed to diet. Jacob turned to his wife. "Let's give him a break. I think each of us is going through a rough patch." Jacob gently nudged Stephen's shoulder. "Our family has always rebounded from crises. We'll get through this too."

Stephen gave an appreciative nod. However unintentionally, Jacob had deflected attention from the actual root of Stephen's loss of appetite. He hadn't discussed Serenity's admission with anyone. But now, her inability to bear children wasn't even the crux of his thoughts.

Trini grinned, and her brown eyes sparkled when the sunlight met her face. "Don't worry, Stephen. Jacob and Gabe will make up for you."

The brothers joined in the laughter.

Trini's voice took on a more serious note as she forked her dumpling. "Guys, I don't think I've thanked you for your support. So denki. I don't know how we'd have gotten through this without you."

Jacob added, "Double thanks."

Affection accompanied Gabe's gruff voice. "That's what family's for. And we didn't do much, really. Your barn was already in good shape. All we did was feed and water the horses."

Firmness edged Trini's voice. "You did much more than chores. You provided us emotional support at the hospital and when we got home. I think your encouragement was what helped us more than anything."

Jacob shook his head. "It's a tough thing to go through."

No one responded.

After lunch, Stephen joined his bruders for a walk to the fishing pond in the far backyard while Trini stayed to talk with the women. Stephen listened to Jake explain how he and his wife had prayed more than ever and had begun to accept their loss. After a long silence had passed, he went on to explain that they would try again after Trini recovered.

As Stephen listened, his mind drifted to Serenity's disappointing disclosure to him. He decided right then and there that he'd never reveal what she'd told him. Not to anyone. It wasn't his place to discuss her burden. Not only that, but it was no one else's business.

He'd never forget the regretful expression in her eyes, the slight shaking of her hands, or the way her bottom lip had quivered as she'd shared her secret with him.

In disgust, he shook his head. Not because of her admission but for his callous reaction. He realized his ignorance. And his insensitivity.

As Jake and Gabe discussed the bean crop and the weather, Stephen's mind stayed on Serenity, whom he still loved. The woman he'd disappointed. By now he'd somewhat absorbed the actual reality as well as the shock of her admission. *Do I still love her?* He smiled a little. *Do I deserve her?* He shook his head.

From a very young age, he'd dreamed of a large family and caring for a wife and kinder. He acknowledged he still had a strong need to right his daed's wrong by being a good, dependable father. Of course, he could never change what had happened. But raising a family and being a role model for his children was vital to him.

Although he loved Serenity in every way, dreaming of a brood of little Lantz boys and girls following him around the farm wasn't something he could forfeit with a snap of his fingers. Not after it had been etched in his mind for so many years.

A knot in his throat became uncomfortable as he recalled his cold reaction to what must have been the most difficult thing Serenity had ever done. How he wished he'd comforted her. He should have reassured her that even if she wasn't able to have kinder, no one could ever replace her. That his heart had chosen her, and that his strong feelings for her had nothing to do with having children. That it was his duty to accept what she'd told him.

He stiffened. He realized his destiny. *I'm not good enough for her. I don't deserve her. I'm ashamed of myself for my own selfishness and not supporting her the way I should have. I need to let her go so she can find someone worthy of all she has to offer.*

Stephen's thoughts drifted to his late aendi's hope chest. Her obvious hiding place. The hope chest was now inside his closet. He swallowed as he considered the questions some of its papers had raised. And what had been made crystal clear.

Early the following morning, Serenity stepped toward her barn. She enjoyed the feel of the summer breeze. Something told her that it was going to be a gut day. As she walked, an oak leaf fell from a tall tree and onto her dress sleeve. She plucked the leaf with her fingers and took in what she considered to be a miracle that people seemed to overlook.

For a moment, she stopped to study the leaf. Thanks to the immense amount of reading she'd done during her illness, Serenity had learned a lot about plants. She enjoyed looking at them and breathing in their different aromas for inspiration. They had captivated her interest at a time in her life when joy had been a rarity.

It was amazing how Gott had designed plants. The leaves, for instance, were similar to solar panels. They captured sunlight. The different variations intrigued her as well. Their unique designs and purposes often were taken for granted. *Miracles are all around us. But often they go unnoticed.*

At the barn, she slid open the heavy door and stepped inside the tall, open structure. The lack of sunlight inside the building reminded her that Angel must need brightness too. Surely the sun was gut for horses.

As she approached Angel's stall, her standardbred trotted in from the outside. At the gate that separated the animal from the main barn area, Serenity leaned forward a bit to caress his long nose as she spoke to the beautiful creature with affection. "I'm sorry I haven't given you the attention you deserve the last few days. But you see, my best friend suffered a misfortune." After a slight pause, she added in a lowered voice, "This isn't something I can fix or make okay. All I can do is pray for her and her husband."

As if sympathizing, Angel gave a soft neigh and lifted his head for Serenity to rub his neck. As she did so, she laughed. "I know what will make you happy." She stepped to the nearby shelf and reached for a gunny sack. After she plopped the bag on the cement floor, she used the metal scoop to retrieve oat mix. She used both hands to transport it to the wooden feeder that was at the horse's mouth level. Without wasting time, Angel began to indulge.

While Serenity watched the standardbred, her thoughts automatically migrated to Stephen and his huge disappointment. *I promised myself not to think about this. It's a situation that's out of my control. And if he truly loves me, he should understand. At the same time, I can't expect him to give up his long-held dream with a snap of my fingers.*

She continued to review her revelation and how his insensitive reaction had injured her heart. *It was extremely difficult to have confessed to him that I'm not able to bear children. But given his obvious strong feelings for me, I was obligated to do so. What I never anticipated was how hurtful his response, or rather, lack of response, would be.*

She drifted back in thought to the many days when his late aendi had stood by her during her long bout of Epstein-Barr virus. Margaret had stuck with her through thick and thin, regardless of Serenity's prognosis. Stephen's aendi had always stressed Serenity's great worth as a human being. Of course, Margaret had obviously understood all too well what Serenity's life would be like as a childless Amish woman.

Serenity acknowledged that much of Margaret's wise advice had most likely been born from her own personal experience. It wasn't that Stephen's late aendi wasn't insightful—she certainly had been. But she had learned from years and years of being a single, childless Amish woman how to value her own self-worth.

*Because of my heartfelt confession to Stephen, I have acknowledged something very important. I now fully understand that Gott has my journey decided for me. What I can contribute to others might be even more important than producing offspring. And if I ever find true love, it will be with a man who wants me exactly as I am.*

Serenity and her mamm shared a skeptical glance while her daed removed the old gate latch to Angel's stall. Then they smiled as if they shared a secret. And they did. Serenity's daed was not good at fixing things. But they'd never tell. Fortunately, he was well known around the area for his expertise at making furniture.

From inside the stall, he extended his hand. "Hammer, please."

Serenity handed it to him. As she did, she noticed beads of sweat dripping down his face. "Daed, I'm getting you a glass of iced water. It's awfully hot this afternoon."

In the barn's main area, a bicycle horn beeped. Serenity and her mamm glanced in the direction of the sound. Serenity grinned. Her four-year-old nephew, Amos, enjoyed the large area to play.

He joined the three and stopped his bike with his feet. "Aendi Serenity, could I please have a lemonade?"

She stood and joined him while tousling his wavy blond hair. "Jah. We're headed to the house to get your dawdy a water."

Serenity glanced at her daed. "We'll be back in ten minutes or so with your drink." She edged her voice with doubt. "Why don't you come inside and sit under the fan for a bit?"

He waved a dismissive hand. "This won't take much longer." He added with a grin, "Thanks for locking your Angel out of the barn."

Serenity gave her daed a thumbs-up. Then she and Mamm took the dirt path leading to the house. Amos passed them on the grass before guiding his bike back onto the trail.

Serenity's mamm motioned to the flourishing garden. "Your plants look gut." She glanced at one side of the path, then the other, and spoke with approval. "And your flowers are gorgeous."

Serenity delighted in her plants. As she took in what she considered Gott's art on both sides of the path, she parted her lips in awe.

"This place is special to me." Her voice cracked with emotion. "Huge thanks to you and daed for helping me buy it."

Her mother's voice was hoarse. "All your daed and I have ever wanted is your happiness. Ever since you were ill. . ." She cleared her throat. "We've given thanks to Gott that you're still with us."

Serenity contemplated the loving comment, and an unexpected appreciation swept through her veins. She thought of what she'd told Stephen—and his less-than-excited reaction to it—and a new gratefulness overcame her.

Serenity edged her voice with positivity. "Everything's gut." After a slight hesitation, she added, "Better than gut!" Several seconds of silence passed. Serenity's voice filled with emotion. "You just reminded me how very blessed I am to be here." Serenity threw up her hands in joy. "Even if I had to live on the street. . .I'm alive and productive!" After a pause, she raised her voice with excitement. "And I've got the best parents in the world!"

They stopped while her teary-eyed Mamm wrapped her arm around Serenity. She planted a firm kiss on Serenity's forehead before they continued to the house.

Ahead of them, Amos stopped at the step. He turned around and waved. "Hey, come on! We've got to get something to drink for dawdy!"

Trini remembered this walk's original purpose, and she and her mother quickened their pace.

Inside the kitchen, Mamm adjusted the battery-powered fan's speed to high. Serenity washed her hands. She opened the freezer and removed a green tray. Ice cubes popped out as she squeezed them from their holder. They clinked against the sides of the glasses she placed them in.

She proceeded to refill the empty trays and place them in the freezer while Amos talked to his grandma about the "new" bike he'd inherited from his older brother.

She glanced at Mamm, who'd claimed one of the dining room chairs that faced the fan. "That air feels gut."

Serenity poured her daed's water. Then Amos's lemonade. Then a water for herself.

"What can I get you?" she asked her mother.

Mamm lifted a curious brow. "An explanation."

Amos gulped his fresh lemonade and politely carried his empty glass to the sink. While Serenity held her own beverage and her daed's, Mamm walked with her, drink in hand. In front of them, Amos led the way on his wheels.

Mamm turned to Serenity with an expression that implied she needed an answer. When Serenity didn't respond, Mamm used her motherly tone. "Honey, you can fool the others, but you can't fool the one who gave birth to you and raised you. What in the world is going on?" Before Serenity could say anything, Mamm went on. "In the barn, you didn't hear half of what I said."

As the warm breeze moved the oak branches, Serenity decided what to say. Whatever she revealed to her own mother would be conveyed to Serenity's daed. That's just the way it was. Serenity's parents had always stressed that being married meant no secrets.

Of course, her parents were aware of her inability to bear kinder. What they didn't know was that she'd told Stephen. Serenity offered a conciliatory nod. "Okay. I'm dealing with something that's out of my realm."

Her mother waited for her to go on.

"I told Stephen I couldn't offer him the children he's always dreamed of having."

Mamm gasped and put a hand over her mouth.

Serenity lowered her voice to a more serious tone. "I'm not sure if you realize how close Stephen and I have become over the past year."

Mamm darted her a half smile. "I had an inkling."

"Stephen told me he loved me."

Another gasp followed.

Serenity continued. "He even asked me to marry him. You and daed used to often tell me there should be no secrets between a man and his wife." Serenity shrugged.

Mamm's eyes were wide. "How did he react?"

Disappointment edged Serenity's voice while she related what had happened.

They were near the barn. Holding the glasses in front of her, Serenity stopped. So did Mamm. They looked at each other.

Mamm pressed her lips together in a straight line. Then the corners of her lips turned down. But after sighing, Mamm softened her voice. "You know what?"

"What?"

"Remember what I used to tell you when you were growing up? That you can't always read a person's mind?"

Serenity lifted her shoulders in a shrug. "I didn't have to. His expression said it all. You should have seen his look of despair. I felt awful."

They stepped inside the barn, and Mamm said in a firm tone, "Gott will never let you go through something you can't overcome."

Serenity nodded.

"You know what I think, honey?"

Serenity lifted a brow with curiosity.

"That this is a test. In your short time here on earth, you've already experienced a big test." She smiled lovingly at Serenity. "One that you passed with flying colors. Surviving Epstein-Barr." Mamm nodded her head. "Now you're going through another difficult trial."

Serenity offered a weak smile. "That I am."

As a beam of sun lightened Mamm's face, warmth filled Serenity's heart. How fortunate she was to have two wonderful parents.

Seriousness accompanied Mamm's voice. "Never think that this problem weighs more than all the blessings Gott's given you." After a slight pause, she continued thoughtfully, "Honey, if Stephen truly loves you, he'll accept what you've told him and deal with it." She smiled a little. "I'm not an expert on psychology. But I do have plenty of experience with men." She laughed. "I mean your daed. And in this world, we can't always have everything we want. But there's one very important thing I can tell you with full confidence."

"What?"

"Life is full of battles, but at the end of the day, love always wins out."

He had a plan. As he glanced out the window that overlooked Route 51 in Decatur, Illinois, he mentally walked himself through the newly decided steps to take back the wooden horse his grandpa had made just for him. No one except the two of them was privy to what was hidden inside.

Unfortunately, his dear grandpa couldn't help him now. Alzheimer's had progressed so quickly that the old man had been admitted to a nursing home. Nothing was good about the disease or its complications. So it was vital to reclaim the hand-carved wooden horse. At any cost.

Thanks to his clueless sister-in-law, the horse had been sold with his grandpa's other belongings at a garage sale. *Imagine that!* Of course Ellen hadn't been aware of the key inside. Or what the key belonged to. There was no spare. And although other family members were listed on the bank box, they had no means to access it. Grandpa had planned it that way to avoid a family rift.

*Now I'm faced—again—with the burden of getting it back.* Slow steps took him to his weapons cabinet, where he studied his gun collection through the glass. Thoughtfully, he tried to consider other ways to retrieve the horse.

*The easiest means, of course, would be to buy it back from the Amish woman who now owns it.* He grasped his hands together to make a fist. He gritted his teeth. While that idea entertained him, he took in his run-down house and acknowledged that the funds he'd soon have would allow him to sell this dump and move into a nice place. In a respectable neighborhood.

He continued the thought of approaching her, explaining what had happened, and humbly asking to buy it back. It was possible that she would surrender it to him. *On the other hand, what if she refuses?*

He wasn't extremely knowledgeable about the Plain Faith. What he did know was that they lived very simply, and because of that, they didn't own much that didn't play a necessary role in their lives. *They don't even take pictures.*

So logic told him that the extras they had they considered special enough to own. The problem with trying to buy the horse back was that if she said no, he'd have to force her to give it to him, and this time he'd have to kill her so she couldn't identify him. He considered himself a decent human being, and of course he didn't want to do anything so extreme. If he killed her and got caught, the consequences would be dire. Prison wasn't an option—money wouldn't help him there.

The best way to retrieve the key his grandfather had gifted him was to simply steal the horse. The last time he'd planned to break into the Amish house to get it, the storm had surprised him and his buddy, and then the Amish woman entered the barn where they were hiding. After they'd subdued her, they'd panicked and quickly cut back through the woods to the truck. Word had it that a neighbor had found the Amish woman and untied her.

In the process of protecting their identities, he'd lost his glasses. Even if they'd been discovered, he doubted the police would be able to trace his glasses back to him. Even so, he'd learned his lesson. Next time, he'd be more careful. His buddy would drop him off in front of the woods behind her home. If he parked in front of her house, his black truck would easily be noticed by someone in the primarily Amish area. If he parked where he had last time, the truck might also be noticed.

Unfortunately, the only option was the long walk through the woods that separated her home from another Amish house. Next time would be different. He lit a cigarette, took a puff, and relaxed. *Everything's okay.*

He'd received word from his contact in Sullivan that Amish church members had a large church cookout planned in the country between Arthur and Sullivan.

*That's ideal. First of all, the Amish woman will more than likely be gone for a few hours, which will offer me ample time to find my horse. Second, it's not plausible that anyone will drop by her home if the gathering is as large as anticipated.*

This time he'd go solo. He gave his cigarette another puff. After he got dropped off, he'd quickly move through the woods, past the barn to the house, where he would find his horse. Finally, the key would be in his hands—where it rightfully belonged. And if anyone surprised him, he'd have his gun. He coughed after he expelled another puff of smoke. *Tomorrow I'll have what's mine.*

# CHAPTER FIFTEEN

Early the following morning, Serenity stopped behind her barn to drink from her water bottle. As she swallowed, raw emotions filled her heart until it ached.

*No. This walk is all about positivity. Relaxation. Remember Gott's wonderful blessings. There are so many.*

For a moment, she took a deep breath and looked around to refocus. She proceeded down the narrow dirt path. As she made her way to the spot where she and Stephen had sat and talked many times, she smiled. As she continued, she passed the very place where he'd allowed her to look through his binoculars at the brown-headed cowbird.

*Dear Gott, to add salt to my wounds, Stephen is avoiding me. For many years, I've known not to fall for a man. But now I have. And his obvious rejection of me is painful. Even though I cannot have him as my husband, please bring back the joy I once had in my heart. I know Your true purpose for me. Help that realization to make me stronger. Amen.*

She took in Gott's beautiful art. The different species of trees and the unique leaves they bore. The butterflies. The birds. The smell of the pine that floated lightly through the air. An appreciative shiver darted up her back.

Of course, she knew she wasn't the only person in pain. Trini was fighting to recover from her big loss. While she would most likely bear other children, she'd never have the one she'd lost.

Today she'd see Stephen at the potluck. She loved church gatherings. She enjoyed her friends and family, along with the delicious food that always brought a smile to her heart. Today would differ from other get-togethers, however, because of what Stephen now knew about her. She hadn't asked him to keep her burden to himself. But she truly hoped he wouldn't share it. Her dilemma was no one else's business.

She walked up an incline, and her endorphins went to work. *It feels gut to exercise. Today will be what I make it. And I will make it gut.*

---

Something bugged Stephen. It had to do with the contents of Margaret's hope chest. *Something doesn't add up.*

He glanced up at the wall clock and straightened. *I'm going to be late for the potluck.* As the front screen door sprang shut behind him, he took quick steps forward, acknowledging that he would see Serenity today. It was inevitable. Of course there would be roughly two hundred other people there, so he could hopefully avoid her. If they did cross paths, he'd simply greet her and ask how she was.

Outside he stopped by the memorial garden and gazed across the way at Serenity's home. From where he stood, he had a bird's-eye view of her place. In a sense, it was comforting because despite the news she'd told him, he still had an innate need to care for her and protect her. He loved her. He just didn't deserve her.

As he glanced with affection at the beautiful floral garden that had been created in memory of his late aendi, he wished he could talk to Margaret. Automatically, his gaze landed on the angel.

Serenity swept into his thoughts. He frowned. He felt like a hypocrite. Revealing something so painful and personal to him must have been difficult. His cold reaction hadn't been deliberate. It's just that shock had overtaken him. After all, he'd imagined the two of them living in a large two-story house with kinder running all over. Perhaps she'd hoped for some type of reassurance that it really didn't matter. That he loved her for who she was, not merely as a woman to produce Lantz heirs.

*I love Serenity. For so many years, I dreamed of extending my family line. Gott, You have opened my eyes. And I see the larger picture of my life.*

He spoke with emotion as he gazed at the angel. "Aendi Margaret, I didn't think it was possible to love you more than I did. But I do. You were far more complex than people knew."

He turned and stepped toward the field. He took in the beautiful bean crop and lifted his chin appreciatively. He glanced at Serenity's yard. Her buggy wasn't parked outside. Of course most of the time she kept it in the shed. As he continued to look around at the beautiful country panorama, his eyes landed on the woods. He smiled a little as he recalled the great talks they'd shared during their walks.

From where he stood, he could barely glimpse the road that met the back of the timber. The only reason he could see it through the trees was because the road was a bit higher than the ground he now stood on. He squinted. A black vehicle stopped. After it continued forward, he tried for a better view. Had someone stepped out of that truck? Had he imagined that a figure had slipped into the woods?

Afternoon came and Serenity had returned from her walk in the woods.

Something was wrong with Angel. He hadn't eaten his oat mix. He wasn't sticking his nose over the gate for Serenity to caress it.

He hadn't clomped his hooves. *What's the matter, Angel?*

*I'll be late to the potluck.* While she caressed her standardbred, she heard a car engine in her drive. She planted a quick kiss of reassurance on Angel's nose. *Gut. The vet will know what to do. He'll get you fixed up again.*

Serenity pressed her lips together in a straight line and rushed toward the car. The vet met her halfway between his vehicle and the barn.

"Dr. Peterson, thanks so much for coming on such short notice."

He nodded. "What seems to be the problem?"

Side by side, they stepped quickly to the barn. She briefed him on Angel's lack of zest. Lack of appetite. As she conveyed the details, she tried to stay calm. Still, her voice shook even though she was fully aware that being stressed would offer no help at all. But her bond with her horse was so strong. And in the back of her mind, she couldn't bear the thought of losing him.

At the barn, she stopped and threw up her hands in a frustrated gesture. "I don't know what's up with him." They stepped inside. "But something's very wrong if he won't touch his oat mix."

While the afternoon August sunlight floated into the building, the doctor asked several questions. He unlatched his large bag and pressed the sides open. "Is he drinking water?"

"Jah." When he reached inside his bag, she added, "At least that's good."

He looked up at her as he pulled out a pair of plastic gloves. "It is."

The vet approached Angel and talked to him. Serenity warned him about Angel's habit of biting men. To her surprise, Angel allowed Dr. Peterson to examine him without protest. When she sensed the doctor could work magic with her horse, she said, "I'm going to make a call. I'm expected at a potluck, and I need to tell someone I'll be late."

His attention didn't leave the horse as he shined a light in Angel's eyes. He spoke while he examined. "Do what you need to do. I'm going to have a heart-to-heart with your Angel and find out what's wrong."

Serenity stepped to the wall phone and dialed Trini. Of course Trini didn't answer. She was never late to anything. Serenity clenched her free hand into a fist while she listened to three beeps. "Trini, it's Serenity. Doc Peterson is here. Angel is under the weather. If by chance you're still home, know that I'll be at the potluck. Just later than expected."

She hung up. Next she dialed Abby. Same thing. After the beeps, she left the same message.

She placed the phone back into its holder and rejoined Angel and Doc Peterson. He looked at her with a reassuring smile. "At first glance, I don't think there's anything seriously wrong. His vitals check out like they should."

Serenity pressed her hands against her hips while she considered his assessment. The doctor's voice reassured her. "Let's give it a couple of days. See if he starts eating again. There's a livestock virus going around. If he still doesn't have an appetite in the next two days, I'll run more tests on him. But. . ." The vet's eyes seemed to peer right through her.

She leaned closer and stood very still. "Jah?"

He pressed his finger on his chin, and his lips curved in an odd blend of amusement and hesitancy. "Would you like my humble opinion?"

She regarded him with interest and nodded. "Of course."

He chuckled and began returning his medical paraphernalia to his bag. "A lot of people don't realize that horses are a lot like us."

Serenity parted her lips in surprise. She had thought that she was the only one around who believed they were. But obviously, this kind doctor had seen enough horses to know what he was talking about.

"When their routine changes, sometimes they suffer anxiety. Or depression. In this case, I think it might be the latter."

Serenity narrowed her brows as she looked at him to go on.

"Has his routine changed?"

Serenity finally offered a firm nod. "Now that you mention it, yes. My friend—she had a miscarriage, and I've been helping her."

"And your Angel. . ."

She offered a shrug and spoke in a serious tone. "I guess I've neglected him. Not really neglected," she quickly corrected, "but I haven't been spending the amount of time with him that he's used to."

The vet smiled. Serenity suspected this doctor's hunch was right. If her horse was depressed due to lack of attention, she could—and would—change that right away.

At Doc Peterson's car, she thanked him. She watched as he left her drive and turned north on the blacktop. When he was out of sight, she heaved a sigh of relief and made her way to her house.

The screen door banged shut behind her. Inside her kitchen, she glanced up at the wall clock and thought. *I'll be an hour late. But Angel is more important. Besides, potluck dinners usually don't start on time, anyway.*

She had an idea. She knew that others, if they were aware of what she was about to do, would think she was crazy. But from her illness, she knew all too well that inspiration had played a huge role in her recovery.

*Would inspiration help Angel recover too?* She wasn't sure, but it was worth a try. Quick steps took her across the dining room and into the living room, where she stood on her tiptoes to retrieve her beautiful carved wooden horse from the shelf.

Taking great care not to drop the unique piece, she took it in both hands and offered it a quick glance of admiration before returning to the back porch, where she proceeded outside and down the dirt path that led to the barn.

Apparently there wasn't much at this point that could be done for her horse. If anything, placing this beautiful piece where Angel could glimpse it might help her standardbred. But Serenity would be spending a lot of time with Angel to help him rebound from whatever was wrong, and glimpsing her favorite garage-sale buy would inspire her too. At least she was doing something to expedite the healing process. *If it doesn't help*—she shrugged—*I'm not out a thing.*

As she approached the open barn door, the sun slipped under a mass of fluffy clouds. She missed the bright light. Sunlight had always lifted her spirits. Inside the building, she searched for a spot for the wooden horse where Angel could see it. She decided to place it next to his box of sugar cubes. Most definitely, her standardbred would eye the treats. And when he did, he would glimpse the horse too. She smiled with satisfaction as she reached to position the horse.

As she did so, she smelled something unusual. She froze while ordering her lungs to relax. She recognized the odor. The corners of her lips dropped. Her heart nearly stopped. Because she remembered she'd once breathed in this same unpleasant smell. On the "bad day." She'd forgotten. Until now.

The horse fell from her stiff fingers and landed on the cement floor. Just that quickly, her happy demeanor was replaced with great fear. She looked down to find that the horse had broken in thirds. But it wasn't the ruined work of art that claimed her attention. It was something small and gold that lay between the pieces. A sunbeam streamed in through the side window and landed on the key.

Serenity swallowed when she heard a man's raspy voice. She

turned and gasped as he stepped close and pointed a gun at her chest. He wore glasses, just like the ones she'd found and had turned in to the police with Stephen. Her adrenaline kicked in. She had to protect herself. But how? As his throaty voice ordered her to turn around, she eyed the phone on the wall. It was many steps away. Focused on surviving, she took in the rakes and hoes and other tools that hung from wall hooks.

His voice was firm. Cold. Determined. "Just do as I say."

The raspy, unpleasant voice burned her ears until her head felt like it was on fire. The strong smell of cigarette smoke stung her eyes. For some reason, she'd forgotten the odor. A strong combination of irritation and fear swept through her until her entire body shook. "Just take what you want."

Slow steps moved her forward as the gun remained locked onto her chest.

Everything became clear to her. She yearned to scream. But what good would it do? No one was close enough to hear her. "You wanted the horse all along, didn't you? Because of the key."

He laughed. Then he coughed. All the while, she tried to decide a plan of action. *I'll converse with him to distract him while I move closer to the hoe.*

His wicked voice pulled her from her thoughts. "I'll make this as simple as I can. I'm surprised to see you. I was told you'd be gone this afternoon."

Behind her, Angel gave the loudest whinny Serenity had ever heard. The gun's barrel briefly strayed from its target as the man whirled around in surpise. At that moment, she reached for the hoe on the wall, turned, and swung it at her opponent.

The metal end hit his torso and knocked him to the ground. She screamed for help as loud as she could, hoping against hope that someone would hear. The gun fell from his hand, and she dropped the hoe and went for the weapon. For the first time, she got a good look at him, even though his face was to the floor. He was medium height. Thin. He reeked of smoke. His hair was an ugly shade of gray.

In the background, Angel continued a string of neighs. Whinnies. The clomping of hooves stirred straw dust in the air. When Serenity's fingers touched the cold metal of the weapon, she tripped on her dress hem. Determination swept through her veins as he lunged for the gun. They battled for the weapon. Serenity screamed. "You'll have to fight me!"

She didn't let go of the gun. He was barely taller than she was. In a silent, desperate prayer, she begged Gott to come to her rescue. She'd never laid eyes on a gun, let alone touched one.

Her long dress worked against her. It was in her way as she tried to move her legs. As her dress stuck between her thighs, he shoved her to the floor. He pushed her so hard, the back of her head hit the cement floor. He straddled her and bent to point the gun at her. With every ounce of energy she could muster, she swung at his face.

His temper flared. His face was red, and his eyes conveyed hatred as she continued to battle him. She shouted, "Dear Gott, please help me!"

He was so close to her, she could smell cigarette smoke on his breath as he pointed the barrel of the gun on the sensitive spot above her nose and between her eyes. She screamed, "Stop! Please stop!"

"I'm going to kill you!"

"No!"

She heard a click and instinctively closed her eyes.

*Dear Gott, please forgive me of my sins. I'm going to die.*

Something in the background captured her attention.

Loud screams came from Serenity's barn. Stephen's lungs gulped for air as he moved toward the old building. At the entrance, his jaw dropped as Angel bit into a man's hind end.

The man screamed in pain while Angel let out a loud whinny. At the same time, on the floor, Serenity screamed and pointed to the weapon. "Stephen! The gun!"

Immediately, Stephen followed her finger with his eyes before rushing to the black object to retrieve it. He clutched it. Taking great care not to pull the trigger, he made his way to Serenity, placed the weapon under a bale of straw, and gently helped her to sit up. "Serenity! You're okay!" He planted an affectionate kiss on her cheek.

The close, loud stomping of hooves made him freeze. He glanced up at Angel. The horse appeared enormous from where Stephen was. The standardbred's large teeth showed.

Stephen held up a hand in defense. "Whoa. I'm on your side, buddy."

The horse shoved his nose into Stephen's chest. Stephen closed his eyes, preparing for the worst. But a few seconds later, Angel's wet nose moved across Stephen's face, and he chuckled. It was an expression of pure relief that the horse had spared him the bite that Stephen had suspected was coming.

He focused on Serenity. "Are you okay?"

Serenity smiled. "I'm better than ever."

With one quick motion, Stephen stood and looked down at her. She was disheveled. But the relieved expression on her face reassured him that she was fine. "We'll call the police. But first"—he winked—"there's business to take care of."

He headed to the man on the floor who continued to scream in pain. From his obvious inability to stand, Stephen knew the intruder was no longer a threat.

As the thin-haired man looked up at Stephen, the youngest Lantz brother put his hands on his hips, looked down, and said, "Her horse outsmarted you."

Angel's newest victim went quiet. Stephen eyed the roll of twine on the nearest shelf. He unrolled a generous amount and cut it with his pocket knife. With swift certainty, he pulled a dirty rag from a pile and stuffed it into his pocket. Twine in one hand and knife in the other, he stepped to the criminal.

The man struggled to move. He lifted his head enough to meet Stephen's eyes. "I need a doctor."

Stephen chuckled and knelt next to him. With a rough motion, he rolled the man so that he was flat against the floor, face down, yanked his hands behind his back, and tied them together. As the man pleaded for help, Stephen said in a firm, unforgiving voice. "This is for hurting her."

The man pleaded. "Please. Get me to the hospital. I just wanted the key."

Stephen ignored the request. He gritted his teeth while reaching into his pocket. With one swift motion, he pulled out the rag and yanked it around the man's face. As he did so, the pleas stopped. Stephen tied a tight knot at the back of his head. "This is for being a coward."

Wasting no time, he cut another piece of twine and bound the man's ankles together. Afterward Serenity knelt beside Stephen and laid her hand on his shoulder as he glanced at her before returning his focus to the man who'd turned their lives upside down. Stephen stood. Serenity did too. After glancing at Serenity, Stephen raised his voice. "And this one's for me."

He took Serenity's hand and led her to the closest bale of straw. He helped her to sit down. He gently pressed his finger under her chin and tilted it up so that their eyes met. "I want you to sit here while I call the police and the paramedics."

She teared up and started to speak. He shook his head. "Shhh. Everything's going to be okay."

Stephen watched in the distance as Angel returned to his stall. To Stephen's surprise, an emotion so strong overcame him he made his way to the horse and studied the wondrous animal with a newfound curiosity and appreciation. "You saved her life. And I'll never forget it."

The next evening at Margaret's house, Trini served Jacob and his brothers fresh sponge cakes while Stephen answered question after question. The screens allowed a nice breeze into the house. On one of the walls hung the last quilt that Margaret had made. Abby had gifted it to the brothers as a welcome present.

The day's newspaper had been moved from the table to the top of a nearby chair. Next to the sink were a couple of unwashed mugs.

As chitchat floated through the Lantz dining room, Stephen took a drink of coffee, and his thoughts drifted to yesterday's incident in Serenity's barn. At the same time, something in Margaret's secret chest continued to tug at his curiosity. Something in the back of his mind tried for his attention. *What is it?*

Stephen dismissed the nagging sensation and returned his thoughts to Serenity. He was slowly absorbing the shock of what had happened yesterday. And the reality that the nightmare one man had created for Serenity, her friends, and the entire community was finally over. Serenity was staying at her parents' home. As his shoulders relaxed a notch, he sighed with relief. At the table, his brothers and Trini talked a mile a minute about Serenity, what had happened, and most significantly, what would have occurred had Stephen not showed up when he had. But Stephen knew the truth.

Angel had been the true hero.

A chuckle escaped him as three sets of eyes focused on him. Gabe edged his voice with an odd blend of amusement and irritation. "How can you find what happened funny?" Before Stephen could respond, Jacob added, "Do you realize what would have happened had you not shown up when you did?"

Trini exclaimed, "I can't bear to imagine the what-ifs! And to think that we were concerned about having enough plates and silverware at the potluck!"

Stephen cleared his throat. He glanced at Gabe before looking at Jacob, then Trini. "An explanation is in order. And I need to give the real hero his credit."

Jacob moved in his chair while Stephen talked. Next to Jacob, Trini laid an affectionate hand on his shoulder.

Stephen smiled. "I have a new love and respect for Angel."

Around the table, jaws dropped while the three looked at him to go on.

Stephen knew that no matter how long he lived, he'd never forget the sight of Angel biting the man, Dillan, in Serenity's barn. The image would forever be etched into his mind.

Jacob broke the silence. "Stephen?"

Another chuckle escaped Stephen before he explained what he'd witnessed.

"That horse!" Gabe exclaimed.

Jacob spoke in his usual logical tone. "Over the past year or so, I've taken in Serenity's unique relationship with Angel. For a long time, I didn't really understand the depth of their bond. But after yesterday. . ." He looked down at the table and shook his head before lifting his chin. "It might be something that most don't experience, but there's no doubt in my mind that something very deep exists between those two. Serenity once told me that love is love. It doesn't matter who it's between. Now I finally get what she means."

Gabe grinned and popped his knuckles on his lap. "I believe you, Steve. If I were hearing this from anyone else, I'd be skeptical. But you?"

There was a slight pause as Gabe's expression turned serious. "You never exaggerate. Since you've been a toddler, you've always told it straight on." He added with a spark of amusement in his eyes, "Trust me"—he chuckled and rolled his shoulders—"I would have given my new buggy wheels to have witnessed that horse bite that miserable man's rear end."

Everyone laughed. Jacob stood and held his mug in front of him. "This calls for another cup." His gaze traveled around the table. "Anyone else?"

Gabe stood. "Sounds gut." Jake turned and stepped toward the pot. Gabe followed. While they poured refills, Stephen dared to imagine Gabe witnessing Angel showing Serenity's attacker who owned that barn.

While Jacob poured refills, Trini watched her husband. Stephen's heart melted when he glimpsed the angelic expression on her face, the love and admiration in her gaze. She couldn't take her eyes off Jake. While Stephen acknowledged what the two had just gone through, he choked back tears. What had happened to Serenity only yesterday certainly hadn't been anything to smile about. But Stephen sensed that the horrendous, shocking distraction had temporarily diverted Jake and Trini's attention from their great loss.

When his brothers returned to the table, the steam from the coffee floated through the air between them. After a brief silence, the interrogations restarted. Although Stephen had already related the sequence of events that had led to the capture of Serenity's attacker, he responded to the same questions, over and over.

After caressing Jacob's shoulder, Trini scooted her chair forward a bit and turned her attention to Stephen. "Just to make sure I have this right, all of this time, the grandson Dillan wanted the key to his grandpa's bank box? The key inside the horse?"

Stephen nodded. "Serenity had no idea that something was in that horse. Who would?"

Trini shrugged.

Stephen could tell from the way she looked at him that she still struggled to believe what Stephen had told them. So he tried to help her understand. "Apparently, the grandpa had designed his wooden horse with the key tucked tightly inside so that it would go unnoticed. In other words, when the horse was moved around, the key wouldn't be heard."

Jacob stepped in. "It must've really been important to the grandpa to secretly pass on his money to Dillan. Serenity's usually quite observant, but she never had a clue."

Trini cut in. "Until the moment the horse slipped out of her hands and broke into pieces and the key caught her eye.

Stephen nodded. It was so quiet, he could have heard a pin drop. He recalled a detail he'd not mentioned. He broke the stifling silence. "The time of the theft had been carefully planned."

Jake lifted his chin a notch. "Oh?"

Stephen nodded. "Dillan chose yesterday because of the big potluck that had been scheduled."

Simultaneous sighs rose from the others. Trini finally spoke. "Of course. Smart. Because no one in our church would have been home. Including Serenity."

Gabe stepped in. "Which meant that not only would the thief have free and full access to her house but, most likely, there wasn't reason to be concerned about anyone stopping by."

Stephen nodded.

Trini frowned. She fidgeted with her hands in her lap. "I wonder how he found out about the potluck? He doesn't live here."

Stephen offered a firm nod. "Correct. And I'm not sure how he learned about it. But it wouldn't have been difficult. He could've asked anyone, maybe at one of the stores. Or, if he'd been in the vicinity, he might've heard it in everyday conversation." He lifted his palms. "I mean, it's not like the potluck was top secret."

Trini spoke in a soft, thoughtful voice. "Just think. If the grandpa had given the horse to Dillan before the sale, Serenity would have been spared all this drama." She looked down at the table and gave a disapproving shake of her head.

"Yeah." Stephen nodded. "From what I got from the cops, the dawdy's Alzheimer's took an unexpected turn for the worse. And when it did, Dillan's grandpa rushed to get his affairs in order."

Gabe cut in. "I guess this is a lesson to make sure everything's in order while you're healthy."

Jacob added, "So Dillan knew about the horse because his dawdy had told him?"

Stephen nodded. "Exactly. But Dillan's a salesman, and he was out of town and unaware of the last-minute garage sale that particular Saturday."

Trini nudged Jacob before addressing Stephen. "It seems like Dillan would have made a point of getting that horse in his hands the moment he knew about the key."

Stephen shrugged. "You know what they say about life not being perfect?"

The others nodded.

After a slight pause, Gabe frowned. "But here's where I'm confused. So the guy's dawdy wanted him to inherit his cash?"

Stephen nodded.

Gabe went on. "Why didn't he just leave a will?"

Stephen hesitated, giving the question some thought. "I'm guessing that he didn't want to cause a big rift."

Jacob leaned forward. "But eventually, the other family members would've figured out that Dillan got all the money."

Stephen shrugged. "You would think. But people do crazy things. Especially when money's involved." After a slight hesitation, he went on. "The police told Serenity and me that he'd confessed that his grandpa had crafted the horse to hide the key when he was first diagnosed with Alzheimer's, but then it took a turn for the worse. And he hadn't seen the grandson in time to give it to him. Then Dillan was out of state when his sisters held the sale." He shrugged. "The rest is history."

Jacob clarified. "And Serenity spotted the horse, loved it, and bought it."

Gabe lowered his gaze and scooted back in his chair before crossing his legs at the ankles. He took a drink of coffee and returned the mug to the table before resting his hands on his lap. "Remember how Aendi Margaret used to tell us that it's always better to take time to prepare than to be surprised?"

Stephen and Jake nodded.

"Obviously, our aendi got her plans in order when she was healthy. Otherwise, we wouldn't have this wonderful house and land she left us with so much love."

Jacob glanced at Trini before focusing on Stephen. "I still don't understand."

Stephen lifted his hands in a helpless gesture. "What don't you get?"

"If Dillan was aware that the key was in the horse, why didn't he go and claim it right away?"

Gabe nodded. "Good question."

Trini cut in. "Of course, it would have taken some time to learn who bought the horse and where Serenity lived."

Gabe countered. "But Dillan's sisters wouldn't know Serenity, right? I mean, she's Amish."

Stephen shook his head. "But apparently, they'd talked to her at the sale and had remembered her and that she was from Arthur." He blew out a breath and paused. Then he turned to Gabe. "Turns out that later Dillan talked to an Amish woman at one of the furniture stores here to garner information. And don't ask me how he found Serenity, but eventually he did."

Trini drummed her fingers against the table before frowning. "But the first time, why were they in her barn and not in her house?"

Jacob was the next to speak. "Wait a minute. That was the day of the storm."

Gabe turned so that he half faced Stephen. "They must've parked in front of the Miller home."

Stephen shook his head. "No. They came in through the woods behind our house, where it would be less noticeable."

Jacob cut in. "But the storm surprised them."

Stephen offered a slow nod.

Trini added, "And that's what they were doing in the barn." After a slight hesitation, she sighed. "Where Serenity was checking that Angel had what he needed before the weather got worse."

"That's it," Gabe concluded.

Stephen added, "And when she made her way to the back of the barn to find the source of the unusual noise, they attacked her to stop her from seeing who they were."

While Stephen studied the thoughtful expressions of the other three, he could tell that he'd satisfied them. But something still nagged at him. *Something's not right.* He rubbed his forehead while he tried to figure out what wasn't right.

Gabe looked down at the table and fidgeted with his hands.

When he looked up, curiosity edged his voice. "Why didn't the grandson just contact Serenity, say something like the horse held sentimental value, and ask her if he could buy it back?"

Jacob nodded. "Jah. I'm sure she would have given it to him."

Stephen shrugged. "Maybe he didn't want to risk it. I know to us there's no doubt that Serenity would have returned it. But remember, we know her. He wasn't aware of how wonderful and generous she is. And I believe that when people are desperate, greed takes over. The authorities said that if he'd approached her to buy back the horse and she'd said no, then he would've had to get it back at whatever cost—including killing Serenity so she couldn't identify him. He didn't want it to go that far."

A comfortable silence swept through the room. Stephen hoped that, maybe now, things would return to normal. The Amish church members as well as other people in the area would return to the comfortable way they'd always lived. But in Stephen's life, there was still something that needed to be addressed.

He sat up straighter when he finally realized what had been tugging at his mind. The criminal had been dealt with and the danger from him was a thing of the past. But there was still unfinished business.

# CHAPTER SIXTEEN

The following day, a bright ray of sun beamed in through Serenity's shop window. As she arranged eucalyptus stems, she smiled. The Pink Petal was busier than usual. But it didn't have anything to do with Serenity's beautiful arrangements. Today her shop bustled with customers because of what had happened inside her barn. And because her horse had escaped his stall to save her.

As Serenity answered customer's questions, she let out a yawn. Between the ugly, horrifying incident she'd just experienced and the hours she'd spent at the police station answering questions, she yearned to be in her barn with Angel.

People couldn't get enough of her story. Somehow, through the entire ordeal, she, Stephen, and Angel had achieved a sort of celebrity status. The rumors had taken what had happened to an entirely new level. Serenity couldn't stop a grin that tugged up the corners of her lips.

A newspaper reporter had even heard that Angel had used his teeth to steal the gun from Dillan's hand. Serenity's heart warmed as she recalled Angel coming through for her. It didn't matter if her parents or anyone else understood her relationship with her horse. She knew their bond. No one else's opinion would ever change that.

The interest in her story would eventually die down—and

hopefully soon. She tapped the toe of her sturdy black shoe against the floor and pressed her lips in a straight, thoughtful line. Whatever the case, she was grateful that the man who'd caused her and the entire town so much worry and grief had been caught. And Angel had been her first line of defense!

Despite the chaos since the first incident, Gott had made sure that a resolution had been achieved. *And I'm most grateful. Thank You, Gott.*

The phone rang. She answered. "No thank you. I'm not interested." She hung up. Her hand lingered on the receiver while she blew out an uncertain sigh. Another newspaper reporter had wanted to interview her.

*I just want my safe, quiet life back. I'm too low profile for this level of attention. At the same time, the attacks in my barn do make pretty good stories. And I fully understand why everyone appears to be absorbed with what went down.*

She looked around and smiled as she breathed in fragrant floral scents. A new shipment of fresh flowers had arrived this morning. But they wouldn't be in her shop long because of another large funeral two days from now. She was barely keeping up with the orders. Dillan and his try for her wooden horse had set her back on her work schedule.

*But everything's resolved now. Almost, anyway.*

Inside his buggy, Stephen was ready to leave the post office. He glanced at his mail. At the top envelope. Immediately, he breathed in. Because the postmark was from a Chicago suburb. The same town he'd printed on the envelope of his letter to Charlotte.

Wasting no time, he opened the letter and He read her response. And frowned. Folding the letter and sticking it in his trousers pocket, he used the reins to tell his horse to move.

As the clomping hooves and a whinny sounded, he struggled with Charlotte's response. Her words advised Stephen that love is a two-way street. That one person can't make a marriage. *I won't be discouraged.* Then he considered the last two words and grinned. "Exactly."

While he breathed in the familiar odor of manure, he reflected on Charlotte's response in its entirety. He lifted his chin a notch higher. He could almost hear Margaret's firm yet sweet voice telling him that life is short and that sometimes compromises are necessary in order to live our dreams.

*Now everything will hopefully fall into place. Charlotte, you gave me what I needed to know. In one short sentence. If I truly want Serenity as my wife—and I do—we need to have a sit-down. Forfeiting the opportunity to pass on my heritage to another generation no longer holds the importance that it once did. How my life has changed since visiting Aendi Margaret's room. I'm sure my aendi would have told me that extending my bloodline is secondary to spending the rest of my life with the woman I love. I'm as sure of that as I am that she was present the day we saw the rainbow.* "Dear Aendi, just to be clear, I will convince Serenity to be my wife. And we'll adopt as many kinder as she wants, and we will raise them as you, Mamm, and Serenity's parents have raised us." *I'll leave it to Jacob and Trini to extend the Lantz bloodline.*

As he took in the white homes scattered throughout the countryside and the fields of healthy beans and corn, he heaved a deep sigh of relief. He'd come a long way to accept that his role in life was something other than to produce heirs.

He grinned as his horse picked up speed on the country road. *The warm breeze is good for the soul. Margaret used to say that too.*

He waited to cross the street until the Glick family buggy passed.

He waved a hand in greeting. Samuel waved back.

The August sun appeared from under a white, hazy cloud. He lifted his hand to the brim of his hat and adjusted it. He proceeded north. On the east-west blacktop, he glimpsed a tractor. Since it was traveling away from him and his horse, he wouldn't be concerned about the loud noise scaring his horse.

While the uneven sound of hooves on pavement beat out its familiar rhythm, Stephen focused on his pending relationship with Serenity. He didn't frown. This time, he smiled.

Serenity raked used straw in the Lantz barn. As she did so, gut memories of Margaret floated in and out of her thoughts. She'd never forget the time Margaret had taught her how to harness her standardbred. Or the day that Margaret had shown her the basket of treats she kept near the stall.

As Serenity raked the bedding into a pile, she smiled a little. *I guess Angel can thank Margaret for the treat basket I keep near his stall.* She'd shared so many creative ideas with Serenity. The two Lantz horses were in the pasture this cool August morning. The open door allowed a nice cool breeze to come into the barn.

In the neighboring stall, Stephen piled bedding into a wheelbarrow. They glanced at each other. Stephen's lips curved in amusement. While Serenity worked, she occasionally glanced at him. She raised a curious brow while assessing him. The sting of his hurtful reaction to her childbearing revelation was starting to lessen. *I'm not close enough to him to read his eyes, but he's not acting normally. I've never seen this side of him. The tone of his voice is usually calm. And it is, but a hint of something I can't identify accompanies it. And he seems a bit distracted. As if his mind is on something totally different from cleaning the horse stalls.*

His voice pulled her from her daydreaming. "You look contented."

She sighed and stopped her work to prop the rake with her right hand. "I am." She paused a moment to consider his statement. And its veracity. "You know what your aendi used to say about something gut coming out of something bad?"

He offered a firm nod. "Sure do." After a slight hesitation, he lowered his voice and put a hand on his hip while offering an expression that was a blend of disbelief and curiosity. "You surely don't believe that something gut resulted from the attempt on your life?"

After she carefully considered his question, she shrugged. "Jah. That's exactly what I'm saying."

He looked down at his boots before sending her a frown. "Please. Do explain."

She laughed. Not at his request. But because he obviously hadn't contemplated the gut that Serenity's two bad experiences had brought to the table.

"Oh, Stephen. Just think about it."

He arched a doubtful brow and stepped closer so that they were now only a few feet away from each other, separated by the boards that divided the two stalls.

She motioned to the door. "Let's go sit outside and I'll explain."

He pointed. "Ladies first."

Outside, she made herself comfortable on the wooden bench behind the barn that offered a pristine view of the woods. Stephen sat next to her. As he took in the beauty in front of them, he nodded approval. "Do you know that this is the first time I've actually enjoyed this bench?"

She considered his question. "Did you know that I used to sit here with Margaret?"

His voice softened. "Really?"

Serenity nodded. "She taught me so much. And not only about the beauty of nature but about the beauty of learning from mistakes." He looked at her to continue.

She turned, bending her left leg at the knee to better face him. "Stephen, I know that Dillan's actions affected us in a negative way." She spread her hands in front of her for emphasis. "Our families, our church, and the entire community."

He offered a slow nod of his head. "Exactly. And there is absolutely nothing positive about what happened, Serenity." Then he offered a wry smile and lifted his finger as if to make a point. "Oh, I take that back."

She waited for him to continue.

"My opinion of your horse has done an about-face. I can honestly say with a straight face that I'm grateful for your Angel and that I hope we can be friends."

She nodded appreciation. "That's really nice, Stephen."

For several moments, she took in the woods in front of them. Different songs rang out from numerous species of birds. Tall trees swayed in the breeze, and twigs and leaves that cluttered the ground created their own beauty.

She couldn't stop the happiness that accompanied her words as she looked into Stephen's eyes. She parted her lips in awe. His eyes reminded her of the brown shade of leaves after they'd turned.

He cleared his throat. "So what is the gut that came out of the bad?"

She breathed in and ran her palms over her apron to smooth the wrinkles before resting her palms on her thighs. "Where do I begin?"

His eyes reflected amusement.

"For starters, I think that we all have a much deeper appreciation for the safety we're blessed with here in Central Illinois."

"True."

"Before this happened, we didn't realize how different our lives would be if we had to lock our doors and look both ways every time we walked into our barns." She paused before lifting her palms. "Now that Dillan is behind bars and we're aware of why he tied and bound me, we can feel relief. At the same time, this has taught us to be more careful."

He looked at her.

"But when we're in our buggies, we no longer have to fear that anyone's watching us." She smiled a little. "It's wonderful to have the freedoms that we have always enjoyed."

"We are quite fortunate. I agree."

A laugh escaped her throat. "And your relationship with Angel certainly has taken a turn for the better."

He grinned and nodded. "I never dreamed that I could have such admiration for a horse." He let out a low whistle. "The moment I saw him bite Dillan's hind end..."

They both laughed. Then Stephen's voice took on a more serious tone. "It was nothing less than impressive." After a slight pause, he continued. "Angel obviously knew you were in danger, and he impressed me with flying colors."

They enjoyed a comfortable silence as quiet sounds from the woods floated through the air. Serenity reflected on Dillan and his dawdy. "You know, Stephen, I truly hope that Dillan's dawdy doesn't learn what happened. I don't know him, but I'm guessing that he would be terribly disappointed that Dillan went to such lengths to retrieve that key—that is, if he is well enough to understand what happened."

Stephen nodded. "Greed has never been a good thing."

"Yes, look what it did to him. Now he'll never have that money. The other grandkids are listed on the bank box. Even worse, his family knows what he was up to. And that his grandpa basically tried to exclude them from owning a large part of the inheritance."

Stephen shook his head. "This story has another important element."

Serenity waited for him to go on.

"Secrets have a way of getting out."

Serenity stiffened.

"I recall when Jacob's wife kept a secret from him. I know she believed that being honest with him would've ruined her plan, but when the cat got out of the bag, it did much worse. Because it hurt my brother."

Serenity couldn't speak. Suddenly, her throat was dry. Her lungs struggled much harder than usual for air. *Relax. It's okay.*

With one swift motion, she stood and offered Stephen a half smile. "I'd better be going."

Her stood and looked down at her. "I'll walk you to your buggy." He smiled a little. "I have to admit that I kind of look forward to spending time with Angel." He winked. "I mean, now that we're friends."

The admission brought a grin. In silence they stepped toward Angel. As they did so, Stephen stopped a moment to take in the crops. Serenity stood next to him. "Gott has been gut to the farmers."

He nodded before they continued. He gave the infamous standardbred a friendly pat on the head before helping Serenity up the steps. He untied the horse. And she waved goodbye.

Before Angel pulled her open buggy, Stephen stepped so close to Serenity that she could smell his woodsy scent. But she also noticed something else: an unusual sparkle in his eyes that appeared to be a blend of amusement and disappointment. Their faces were so close that their noses nearly touched. But the words he whispered before she began to move were crystal clear. "Bye, Charlotte."

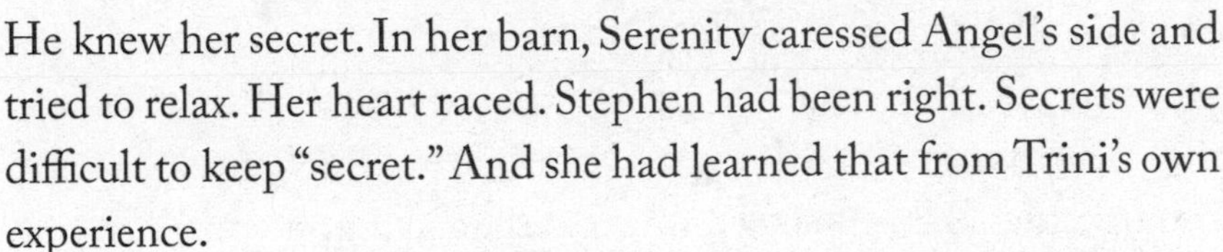

He knew her secret. In her barn, Serenity caressed Angel's side and tried to relax. Her heart raced. Stephen had been right. Secrets were difficult to keep "secret." And she had learned that from Trini's own experience.

But Trini's story didn't matter right now. Serenity's did. She'd deceived Stephen. Unintentionally, of course. Still, could he ever trust her again?

The following evening, Serenity watered the vibrant flowers alongside the path that led to the barn. She bent to pull a butter print and placed it on the trail where she would collect it and other weeds on her way back to the house.

A combination of relief and regret fought inside her until she finally stopped, closed her eyes, and breathed in. As she expelled the breath, she opened her lids. *Be positive. It's not the end of the world.*

She began to review her blessings. *Things are back to normal. At least, as far as the "bad day." I didn't get hurt in the process. Or worse. My parents are relieved.* The talk within their tight-knit church was returning to everyday things instead of focusing on how to enhance security around homes and farms.

*I was placed in a most unusual situation, and sometimes things like this happen. I kept my promise to Margaret. Little did I know that her handsome nephew would enter my life and that I'd fall in love with him.*

Inside the barn, Serenity looked into Angel's large eyes and thought of the eyes of the wooden horse and how they'd always hinted there was a secret. Little had she known that the secret had been right inside the horse all along—and that it had been much stronger and deadlier than she'd ever suspected.

Stephen glanced at his elder brother as they sat side by side in Jake's buggy. As it bounced lightly up and down on the blacktop that led from town back to the Lantz farm, Stephen took in the countryside. The sequence of events that had gone on since he'd met Serenity over a year ago had led to the shocking revelation he'd uncovered.

Jacob's voice pulled him from his reverie. "Okay, Steve, what's up?"

Stephen considered the question. A chuckle escaped him.

"What's so funny?"

Stephen decided to spill. "Jacob, I remember the day in our kitchen when you heard about Trini's plan to leave the Plain Faith."

Jacob nodded before darting an uneasy expression toward Stephen. "And do you recall what Gabe said?"

Stephen thought a moment. "Jah. He said that we'd been raised not to believe everything we hear."

Jacob nodded as he steered the buggy to the left to avoid a pothole. "I remember."

"But Jake, let me ask you something."

"Go ahead."

"What we heard about Trini turned out to be true."

"Steve, I'm not sure where this is headed, but I will tell you this: Life isn't perfect. Neither are people. But Trini and I were able to talk things out. And remember that she'd planned her life long before I stepped back into it."

"But the two of you were so close. Why wasn't she upfront with you? It would've spared you a lot of pain."

A long silence ensued. "Like I said, people aren't perfect. We're fallible. And when Trini didn't disclose her secret to me, it wasn't because she was dishonest. It had to do with her own fears."

As the horse pulled them forward, Stephen contemplated his brother's comment.

"So what did Serenity hide from you?" Jacob asked.

Stephen didn't answer.

Jacob offered a small shrug. "It's okay. You don't have to talk about it. But before you rush to judgment, run your concerns by her. Tell her you're trying to understand why she didn't tell you whatever she chose not to. I don't know Serenity Miller like you do. But over the past year or so, I've spoken plenty with her. I've watched how she treats others. And I've listened to Trini mention her."

He stopped to swallow before he looked at Stephen with a serious expression. "I've seen how she treats you. And. . ."

For long moments, Stephen and Jacob sat in silence while Stephen awaited the rest of the sentence.

When there was no further explanation, curiosity prompted Stephen to probe. "And?"

Jacob breathed in before offering a small shrug of his shoulders. "There's absolutely nothing deceptive or secretive about her, Steve. I believe with no doubt in my mind that if she withheld something from you, she had a good reason. And sometimes. . ."

He softened his voice. "That reason might be something we'd never suspect."

Trini looked up as Abby went on in an excited tone about Gabe's unexpected offer to take her to church next week. In the back of the Quilt Room, the pleasant scent from the cinnamon candle floated through their workspace.

As Trini took in Serenity's somber demeanor and how she'd barely said two words since they'd started working on the quilt, she pressed her lips together in a thoughtful line. Jacob had briefly mentioned something to her yesterday about an unexplained issue between Stephen and Serenity.

Trini wasn't sure what was up, but she knew how difficult it had been for his friend to confess to Stephen her inability to produce Lantz heirs. And she could only imagine the struggle Stephen had accepting this. Through Jacob, Trini was fully aware of Stephen's lifelong dream to leave behind his family's legacy.

But Trini wondered if perhaps something else nagged at Serenity. Because today she hadn't even bothered to bring her herbal tea. This was a first.

The volume of Abby's voice got louder. "I'm shocked that our bishop told us to drive cars instead of traveling by horse and buggy."

Serenity stopped what she was doing and glanced at Abby with a confused expression. "What did you say?"

Abby rolled her eyes. "Finally." Abby threw her up hands in frustration. "You haven't heard a word I've said. What in the world is going on with you?"

Trini motioned to Abby to stop. Then she spoke to Serenity. "Whatever it is, Serenity, we're here if you need a sounding board."

Serenity gave a small smile. "Thank you. Both of you. I know that you only want to help. But sometimes. . ." She stopped to take a deep breath. "Right now, I'm dealing with something that I'd like to keep private."

Abby's eyes widened. Trini's jaw dropped. Serenity had just confessed she was carrying a burden. And that it wasn't something she was going to share with them. At least not now.

They worked in silence. The only noise was the clipping sound of Abby cutting around a plastic form. Out of the blue, Abby changed the subject.

"I have gut news!"

She paused as Serenity and Trini looked at her to continue. "It's about next Saturday. In Sullivan. I've heard there are going to be different kinds of fabrics and lots of art pieces. Even refreshments. A man is going into a nursing home, and his family's selling his things." Abby jumped up in her seat. "Will the two of you go with me?"

In silence, Abby looked at Trini before her gaze landed on Serenity. "To the garage sale?"

Early the following morning, Serenity dumped oats into Angel's feeder. As he ate breakfast, she spoke while returning the scoop to the bag of grain. "I may not have told you this, but I credit you with saving my life." She ran her hand over his nose with affection. "Another storm's coming, but this time, we'll both be safe."

Oak branches made a light noise as the wind brushed them against the side of the barn. Cool air coming in through the open door loosened some hairs from Serenity's kapp, and when they caressed her cheeks, she didn't bother to tuck them back underneath. *Time is of the essence.*

She hoisted a fresh bale of straw into the stall, cut the twine, and watched the bedding fall into a neat little pile. She used her rake to spread it.

Thunder rumbled. She closed Angel's gate, closed the new latch that her daed had installed for her, and proceeded to the wall to return the rake to its hook.

She heard a noise. She stopped. From where she stood, she could see the rain. She listened to it hit the roof. And to her surprise, she saw a figure walking toward her barn.

*It's Stephen.*

He watched as Serenity crossed her arms over her chest. "Stephen!

What are you doing here?"

He stepped inside the barn. For long moments, they faced each other. His wet shirt was rolled up at the sleeves and stuck to his arms. He smiled and spoke in a soft voice. "Can we talk?"

She nodded. "Of course."

He motioned toward a bale of straw. *But first things, first.* He stepped to the horse stall and ran his hand over Angel's nose. "Hey, old friend. How are you doing?"

He turned to Serenity. Her eyes reflected amusement and deep appreciation. He joined her on the straw, where they turned to face each other.

In silence, they studied each other. This time he had questions.

"Uh, Serenity?"

"Jah?"

"I want you to know that I'm okay with you not telling me your secret. I mean, that you're Charlotte."

He noted the fast rising and falling of her chest.

"You are?"

He offered a slow nod of understanding.

"How—how did you know?"

"My aendi hid a hope chest full of paperwork. And notes. And letters. When I discovered it by sheer chance, I had already gone through her pile of *Good Samaritan* magazines. At first I thought that Margaret was merely a reader because I found the letter she'd written to Charlotte after Daed left us. I was heartbroken when I realized that she'd been so devastated, just like us. At the time, she had comforted me and my brothers. But there hadn't been anyone for her to turn to with her pain. So she wrote to Charlotte for advice."

He took in Serenity's face. She didn't smile. She didn't frown. He couldn't read her.

"Jah, she wrote to Charlotte. And she also wrote her own

response."

Stephen parted his lips in surprise.

"Your aendi founded the column after your daed left you. She realized that she had no one to turn to and that thousands of others also had nowhere to garner gut scripture-based advice." Serenity flung up her hands and sighed. "When you think about it, she was a natural at offering advice. And doing so became her most important role in life."

Stephen let out a low whistle. "I found letters from readers in her hope chest. She'd hidden it well."

He explained how the baseboard had opened when he'd reached for his pen. "She'd stapled each response to its original letter." After a slight hesitation, he softened his voice. "What I don't understand is why you didn't tell me that she'd trained you to take on the role of Charlotte should something happen to her."

"How did you figure that out?"

Stephen let out a breath. "In her hope chest, I found numerous notes she'd written. Your name was on some of them. So I thought that you were the new Charlotte. But I couldn't be sure. Then. . ."

He smiled widely. "I received my response from her—I mean, you." After a slight pause, he continued in a low tone. "You mentioned the Calla lily. And that in a world of gerbera daisies, true love is like a Calla lily."

Serenity couldn't stop a smile. "Your aendi once said that no joy is complete unless it is shared."

He nodded.

"I wanted you to know. And I was sure those two words would give my secret away." She shook her head. "I couldn't take the stress of keeping it from you any longer."

She lowered her chin before turning to look him in the eyes. "Stephen, for the longest time, I wanted with all my heart to tell you." She looked down at her shoes before inching closer to him.

As lightning crackled, the bright flash lit up her face. His heart melted. She was so beautiful—inside and out.

"Why didn't you tell me? I would have understood."

"How I wanted to. But I promised your aendi to never tell anyone. And I've never broken a promise. Before this."

"Did she ask you to promise? Surely she wouldn't put something like that on you."

"Margaret knew how important it was for people of all faiths to make the decisions that Gott intended them to make. And she was convinced that it was vital to keep her role as Charlotte confidential to encourage people to write to her, even people within our community. Also, she wanted to help everyone she could reach. In some cases, Stephen, members of our own church have sought her advice over the years. You see, if they'd known who she was, they most likely wouldn't have written to her for help."

"Okay." A long, thoughtful silence ensued before he nodded. "But did she ask you to take on this role, knowing that you could never disclose the secret?" Before she could respond, he went on. "It seems like an awful lot to ask of someone."

"When I was down because of the virus, we talked often, in private, about my inability to produce kinder. It was such a sensitive topic."

He nodded.

"Because she knew what was most vulnerable about me, she must've felt comfortable sharing how she'd started the Charlotte column. The more we talked about it, the more interested I became in the huge role she'd taken on to be there for others. Then, a few years ago, the subject came up again. I shared with her that because of my infertility, I never planned to marry. And from there, she confessed how important Charlotte was to her.

That she never wanted Charlotte to die, even if she herself did. And I was honored that she trusted me to continue her legacy." Several heartbeats later, she went on. "It was an honor to take on such an important role. But Stephen. . ."

He didn't say anything.

"What I didn't know is that you would come into my life."

"You still could have told me."

"I did." She grinned. "I told you the first part of the secret. That I couldn't bear children. I mean, if not for that, your aendi would've never asked me to take on the role of Charlotte. But when I wrote you back, I knew you'd figure it out after you read my letter."

"But if I hadn't sent the letter?"

"That question is so difficult for me. Keeping my promise to your aendi certainly came with a heavy burden. And keeping my word, my commitment to her, was of utmost importance to me."

"We could've still married."

She shook her head. "No, Stephen. I would never keep a secret from my husband. In all the years my parents have been married, they've never hidden anything from each other. They taught me what an important role honesty plays in a marriage."

"So when you committed to my aendi, you were absolutely certain that you'd never marry?"

Serenity offered a slow nod.

She softened her voice. "I'm glad you found your aendi's notes." She lifted her palms. "I'm relieved. You see, now I feel I can talk about it with you."

Angel let out a loud neigh.

Serenity and Stephen shared an understanding glance.

"There was so much interest in her column, Stephen. And Margaret had an unusual talent—blessing really—for using scripture to answer problems. When she started her service many years ago, she never dreamed what a giant resource her column would become to others in need of answers. And the letters she received. . ." Serenity shook her head. "Over the years, thousands, Stephen. It was her life's mission to help others. After she passed on to heaven, it became my mission."

"But the address was in the Chicago area. How did you manage that?"

Serenity adjusted her position. "One of my delivery services brings the mail from a post office box in Naperville when she comes to the Pink Petal. And I give her my Charlotte correspondence to mail so the stamp will reflect a town far from here. That way no one would be able to guess that the real Charlotte is an Amish woman living in Arthur, Illinois. She believes that the mail is related to my floral shop."

"Are you sure?"

"I think so." Serenity shrugged. "If she figured out the truth, I trust she would never tell. I've known her a long time. But whatever the case, it was the only way to protect the anonymity. The last two years of Margaret's life, I'd been sending her correspondence this way."

After a long pause, she added in a soft voice. "I'm sorry, Stephen. I hope you can forgive me."

"I do." He cleared his throat. "If you can forgive me."

Her lips parted as she looked at him.

"I'm ashamed of how I responded when you shared that you couldn't have kinder." He looked away a moment before locking gazes with her again. "I wasn't the understanding, compassionate man that you deserve. And I'm truly sorry."

"I know how important extending your bloodline is to you." She smiled a little. "I'm just sorry I'm not the woman who can give you your dream."

"I've loved you, Serenity, from the moment I met you at Margaret's home. And to me, spending the rest of my life with you is more important than producing a dozen Lantzes. Serenity Miller, you are my dream. Remember what Charlotte said in her letter to me about sharing? Believe me, nothing in this life matters if I can't share it with you."

"What about seeing your mamm and your aendi in your kinder?"

He chuckled. "I'll leave that to my brothers. For the rest of my life, my greatest role is to protect you. And those I love. There are children in this world who have no one. And as I've looked every day at the memorial we made in honor of Aendi Margaret, I've come to believe that my purpose in life is to offer love and a gut home to kinder who truly need me. I'll teach them what I've learned from my aendi and my loving mother. And I'll rejoice as I see them growing with those traits." He softened his voice. "Most of all, I'll love them because we'll raise them with our strong love."

They looked at each other with a new sense of awareness.

"Stephen, I've loved you since I met you, but I never felt about you the way I do at this moment."

"Serenity. . ."

She parted her lips to speak, but no words came out.

"I love you. And as for the Calla lily," he whispered, "Serenity, you are my one and only Calla lily."

A long, emotional silence ensued.

He leaned closer and cleared his throat. "Please tell me you'll be my wife and help me to raise a family. I can't promise that life will be perfect, but I can say that you will have my love for the rest of my life."

He gently took her hands in his and moved so close to her that their lips nearly touched.

"Stephen, you've saved my life. And now you're offering me a new life filled with my dream of true love. I love you."

"Will you be my wife?"

"I will be your wife. And I promise never to keep anything from you again."

"Know that I understand why you didn't tell me. You'd promised my aendi. And I respect you even more for that. Besides, it makes our story that we'll tell our children quite interesting. And it will be a story to be passed down through generations. It has all the elements of a great book: action, mystery, and—most of all—love."

"Our story?"

He nodded.

"What will we call it? Let me see. . . How about *The Life of Stephen and Serenity*?"

"I have a better idea."

"Jah?"

"How about *Serenity's Secret*?"

# AUTHOR'S NOTE

Not all medical professionals agree that Epstein-Barr can in rare cases lead to infertility. However, some do. I experienced firsthand what this ugly, misunderstood virus can do. Twenty-four years ago, the EB virus wreaked havoc with my autonomic nervous system, my blood pressure plummeted and my heart reacted. I was thumped in the chest until I revived and paramedics arrived. Four years of seeking medical help followed with no avail until a brilliant doctor at Johns Hopkins correctly diagnosed me. To my benefit, he was conducting studies on EB and the numerous ways it can harm the human body. My lead character, Serenity Miller, knows all too well what it's like to be seriously ill and to be told that her sickness is in her head. Because of the long timeline she suffered before finally being correctly diagnosed, she's extremely health conscious for fear of EB's possible reoccurrence. Now more people are aware of EB. Unfortunately, however, much more research needs to be done.

**Lisa Jones Baker** writes Amish inspirational fiction. She grew up near Arthur, Illinois, and became acquainted with the Plain Faith at an early age when Amish craftsman custom-made and installed her family's kitchen cabinets. On weekends she and her parents frequented the quaint Amish town, often the setting of her stories, where they purchased meat, cheese, and baking spices. Now, decades later, she still loves visiting; the town and the people yet intrigue her, and she appreciates the talent of quilt-making almost as much as she loves horse and buggy rides. But there is much more to the Amish than meets the eye; they are extremely disciplined, hardworking, and honest. . .and they don't all think alike. For these reasons, writing about them is her passion.

Lisa was fortunate to have been raised in a loving Christian home by two wonderful parents: a reading specialist mother who plays the piano, and a retired junior high principal father who's also an avid fox hunter. She has a BA in French Education and is a former school teacher who loves gardening, cooking, reading, positive thinkers, and every dog she meets. Although a homebody, travel has played a large part of her life. Over three decades of working with the airline industry has landed her on five out of seven continents.